Aristotle

The Poetics of Aristotle

Second Edition

Aristotle

The Poetics of Aristotle
Second Edition

ISBN/EAN: 9783337021849

Printed in Europe, USA, Canada, Australia, Japan

Cover: Foto ©Andreas Hilbeck / pixelio.de

More available books at **www.hansebooks.com**

THE

POETICS OF ARISTOTLE

EDITED

WITH CRITICAL NOTES AND A TRANSLATION

BY

S. H. BUTCHER

PROFESSOR OF GREEK IN THE UNIVERSITY OF EDINBURGH ; FORMERLY FELLOW OF
TRINITY COLLEGE, CAMBRIDGE, AND OF UNIVERSITY COLLEGE, OXFORD ;
HON. LL.D. GLASGOW ; HON. LITT.D. DUBLIN

SECOND EDITION REVISED

London
MACMILLAN AND CO., Limited
NEW YORK: THE MACMILLAN COMPANY
1898

PREFACE

THE following Text and Translation of the *Poetics* form part of the volume entitled *Aristotle's Theory of Poetry and Fine Art*, second edition (Macmillan and Co., 1898). In this edition the Critical Notes are enlarged, and the Translation has been carefully revised. The improvements in the Translation are largely due to the invaluable aid I have received from my friend and colleague, Professor W. R. Hardie. To him I would express my warmest thanks, and also to another friend, Professor Tyrrell, who has most kindly read through the proof‑sheets, and talked over and elucidated various questions of interpretation and criticism.

In making use of the mass of critical material which has appeared in recent years, especially in Germany, I have found it necessary to observe a strict principle of selection, my aim still being to keep the notes within limited compass. They are not intended to form a complete *Apparatus Criticus*, still less to do duty for a commentary, I trust, however, that no variant or conjectural

emendation of much importance has been over-
looked.

In the first edition I admitted into the text
conjectural emendations of my own in the following
passages :—iii. 3 : xix. 3 : xxiii. 1 : xxiv. 10 : xxv.
4 : xxv. 14 : xxv. 16. Of these, one or two appear
to have carried general conviction (in particular,
xxiii. 1); two are now withdrawn,—iii. 3 and
xxv. 14, the latter in favour of <οἰονοῦν> (Tucker).

In the first edition, moreover, I bracketed, in
a certain number of passages, words which I
regarded as glosses that had crept into the text,
viz. :—iii. 1 : vi. 18 : xvii. 1 : xvii. 5. In vi. 18
I now give Gomperz's correction τῶν λεγομένων, for
the bracketed words τῶν μὲν λόγων of the MSS.,
and in xvii. 5 Bywater's conjecture τίς αὐτὸς for
[τινὰς αὐτὸς].

There remains a conjecture which I previously
relegated to the notes, but which I now
take into the text with some confidence. It
has had the good fortune to win the approval of
many scholars, including the distinguished names
of Professor Susemihl and Professor Tyrrell. I
refer to οὐ (οὕτω MSS.) τὰ τυχόντα ὀνόματα in
ix. 5. 1451 b 14 (= b 13 Bekk.), where the
Arabic has 'names not given at random.' For
the copyist's error cf. ix. 2. 1451 a 38 (= a 36
Bekk.), where Aᶜ has οὕτω, though οὐ τὸ rightly
appears in the 'apographa': and for a similar

omission of οὐ in A^c cf. vi. 12. 1450 a 32 (= a 30
Bekk.), οὐ ποιήσει ὃ ἦν τῆς τραγῳδίας ἔργον, the
indispensable negative being added in 'apogr.' and
found in the Arabic. The emendation not only
gives a natural instead of a strained sense to the
words τὰ τυχόντα ὀνόματα, but also fits in better
with the general context, as I have argued at
some length in *Aristotle's Theory of Poetry and
Fine Art* (ed. 2) pp. 367–9 (note).

Another conjecture of my own I have ventured
to admit into the text. In the much disputed
passage, vi. 8. 1450 a 14 (= a 12 Bekk.), I read
<πάντες> ὡς εἰπεῖν for οὐκ ὀλίγοι αὐτῶν ὡς εἰπεῖν
of the MSS., following the guidance of Diels and
of the Arabic. I regard οὐκ ὀλίγοι αὐτῶν as a gloss
which displaced part of the original phrase (see
Crit. Notes). As a parallel case I have adduced
Rhet. i. 1. 1354 a 12, where οὐδὲν ὡς εἰπεῖν, the
reading in the margin of A^c, ought, I think, to be
substituted in the text for the accepted reading
ὀλίγον. The word ὀλίγον is a natural gloss on
οὐδὲν ὡς εἰπεῖν, but not so οὐδὲν ὡς εἰπεῖν on
ὀλίγον.

In two other difficult passages the *Rhetoric*
may again be summoned to our aid. In xvii. 1.
1455 a 30 (= a 27 Bekk.) I have (as in the first
edition) bracketed τὸν θεατὴν, the object to be
supplied with ἐλάνθανεν being, as I take it, the
poet, not the audience. This I have now illus-

trated by another gloss of a precisely similar kind in *Rhet.* i. 2. 1358 a 8, where λανθάνουσίν τε [τοὺς ἀκροατὰς] has long been recognised as the true reading, the suppressed object being not the audience but the rhetoricians. Once more, in xxiv. 9. 1460 a 26 (=a 23 Bekk.), where Aᶜ gives the meaningless ἄλλου δὲ, I read (as in the first edition) ἀλλ' οὐδὲ, following the reviser of Aᶜ. This reading, which was accepted long ago by Vettori, has been strangely set aside by the chief modern editors, who either adopt a variant ἄλλο δὲ or resort to conjecture, with the result that προσθεῖναι at the end of the sentence is forced into impossible meanings. A passage in the *Rhetoric*, i. 2. 1357 a 17 ff., appears to me to determine the question conclusively in favour of ἀλλ' οὐδὲ . . . ἀνάγκη . . . προσθεῖναι. The passage runs thus : ἐὰν γὰρ ᾖ τι τούτων γνώριμον, οὐδὲ δεῖ λέγειν· αὐτὸς γὰρ τοῦτο προστίθησιν ὁ ἀκροατής, οἷον ὅτι Δωριεὺς στεφανίτην ἀγῶνα νενίκηκεν, ἱκανὸν εἰπεῖν ὅτι 'Ολύμπια γὰρ νενίκηκεν, τὸ δ' ὅτι στεφανίτης τὰ 'Ολύμπια, οὐδὲ δεῖ προσθεῖναι· γιγνώσκουσι γὰρ πάντες. The general idea is closely parallel to our passage of the *Poetics*, and the expression of it similar even to the word οὐδὲ (where the bare οὐ might have been expected) in the duplicated phrase οὐδὲ δεῖ λέγειν, οὐδὲ δεῖ προσθεῖναι. One difficulty still remains. The subject to εἶναι ἢ γενέσθαι is omitted. To supply it in

thought is not, perhaps, impossible, but it is
exceedingly harsh, and I have accordingly in this
edition accepted Professor Tucker's conjecture,
ἀνάγκη <κἀκεῖνο> εἶναι ἢ γενέσθαι.

The two conjectures of my own above mentioned
are based on or corroborated by the Arabic. I
ought to add, that in the Text and Critical Notes
generally I have made a freer use than before of
the Arabic version (concerning which see p. 4).
But it must be remembered that only detached
passages, literally rendered into Latin in Professor
Margoliouth's *Analecta Orientalia* (D. Nutt, 1887),
are as yet accessible to those like myself who are
not Arabic scholars; and that even if the whole
were before us in a literal translation, it could not
safely be used by any one unfamiliar with Syriac
and Arabic, save with the utmost caution and
subject to the advice of experts. Of the precise
value of this version for the criticism of the
text, no final estimate can yet be made. But it
seems clear that in several passages it carries us
back to a Greek original earlier than any of our
existing MSS. Two striking instances may here
be noted :—

(1) i. 6–7. 1447 a 29 ff., where the Arabic
confirms Ueberweg's excision of ἐποποιία and the
insertion of ἀνώνυμος before τυγχάνουσα, according to the brilliant conjecture of Bernays (see
Margoliouth, *Analecta Orientalia*, p. 47).

(2) xxi. 1. 1457 a 41 (= a 35 Bekk.), where for μεγαλιωτῶν of the MSS. Diels has, by the aid of the Arabic, restored the word Μασσαλιωτῶν, and added a most ingenious and convincing explanation of Ἑρμοκαϊκόξανθος (see Crit. Notes). This emendation is introduced for the first time into the present edition. Professor Margoliouth tells me that Diels' restoration of ἐπευξάμενος in this passage is confirmed by the fact that the same word is employed in the Arabic of Aristotle's *Rhetoric* to render εὔχεσθαι.

Another result of great importance has been established. In some fifty instances where the Arabic points to a Greek original diverging from the text of Aᶜ, it confirms the reading found in one or other of the ' apographa,' or conjectures made either at the time of the Renaissance, or in a more recent period. It would be too long to enumerate the passages here ; they will be found noted as they occur. In most of these examples the reading attested by the Arabic commands our undoubting assent. It is, therefore, no longer possible to concede to Aᶜ the unique authority claimed for it by Vahlen.

I have consulted by the side of Professor Margoliouth's book various criticisms of it, e.g. by Susemihl in *Berl. Phil. Wochenschr.* 1891, p. 1546, and by Diels in *Sitzungsber. der Berl. Akad.* 1888, p. 49. But I have also enjoyed the special

benefit of private communication with Professor
Margoliouth himself upon a number of difficulties
not dealt with in his *Analecta Orientalia*. He has
most generously put his learning at my disposal,
and furnished me, where it was possible to do so,
with a literal translation. In some instances the
Arabic is itself obscure, and throws no light on
the difficulty; frequently, however, I have been
enabled to indicate in the notes whether the existing text is supported by the Arabic or not.

In the following passages I have in this edition
adopted emendations which are suggested or confirmed by the Arabic, but which did not find a
place in the first edition :—

> ii. 3. 1448 a 15, ὥσπερ οἱ τοὺς
>
> vi. 7. 1450 a 18 (= a 17 Bekk.), <ὁ δὲ βίος>, omitting
> καὶ εὐδαιμονίας καὶ ἡ εὐδαιμονία of the MSS.
>
> xi. 6. 1452 b 10, [τούτων δὲ . . . εἴρηται]
>
> xviii. 6. 1456 a 26 (= a 24 Bekk.), <καὶ> εἰκὸς
>
> xx. 5. 1456 b 39 (= b 36 Bekk.), <οὐκ> ἄνευ
>
> xxi. 1. 1457 a 38, [καὶ ἀσήμου]. The literal trans-
> lation of the Arabic is 'and of this some is
> compounded of significant and insignificant,
> only not in so far as it is significant in the
> noun '
>
> xxi. 1. 1457 a 41 (= a 36 Bekk.), Μασσαλιωτῶν (see
> above, p. xv.)
>
> xxv. 17. 1461 b 14, <καὶ ἴσως ἀδύνατον>

I hesitate to add to this list of corroborated
conjectures that of Dacier, now admitted into the
text of xxiii. 1. 1459 a 24 (= a 21 Bekk.), καὶ μὴ

ὁμοίας ἱστορίαις τὰς συνθέσεις, for καὶ μὴ ὁμοίας ἱστορίας τὰς συνήθεις of the MSS. (In defence of the correction see note, p. 165 of *Aristotle's Theory of Poetry and Fine Art.*) The Arabic, as I learn from Professor Margoliouth, is literally 'and in so far as he does not introduce (or, there do not enter) into these compositions stories which resemble.' This version appears to deviate both from our text and from Dacier's conjecture. There is nothing here to correspond to συνήθεις of the MSS. ; on the other hand, though συνθέσεις may in some form have appeared in the Greek original, it is not easy to reconstruct the text which the translation implies. Another conjecture, communicated privately to me by Mr. T. M'Vey, well deserves mention. It involves the simpler change of ὁμοίας to οἴας. The sense then is, 'and must not be like the ordinary histories'; the demonstr. τοιούτους being sunk in οἴας, and, by attraction, οἶαι ἱστορίαι αἱ συνήθεις becoming οἴας ἱστορίας τὰς συνήθεις.

I subjoin a few other notes derived from correspondence with Professor Margoliouth :—

(a) Passages where the Arabic confirms the reading of the MSS. as against proposed emendation :—

> iv. 14. 1449 a 27, ἐκβαίνοντες τῆς λεκτικῆς ἁρμονίας :
> Arabic, 'when we depart from dialectic composition.' (The meaning, however, is obviously misunderstood.)
> vi. 18. 1450 b 14 (= b 12 Bekk.), τῶν μὲν λόγων :

Arabic, 'of the speech.' The μὲν is not represented, but, owing to the Syriac form of that particle being identical with the Syriac for the preposition ' of,' it was likely to be omitted here by the translator or copyist.

xviii. 1. 1455 b 28 (= b 25 Bekk.). The Arabic agrees with the MSS. as to the position of πολλάκις, 'as for things which are from without and certain things from within sometimes.'

xviii. 5. 1456 a 21 (= a 19 Bekk.), καὶ ἐν τοῖς ἁπλοῖς πράγμασι : Arabic, 'and in the simple matters.'

xix. 2. 1456 a 41 (= a 38 Bekk.), τὰ πάθη παρασκευάζειν : Arabic, ' to prepare the sufferings.'

More doubtful is xvii. 2. 1455 a 33 (= a 30 Bekk.), ἀπὸ τῆς αὐτῆς φύσεως : Arabic, 'in one and the same nature.' The Arabic mode of translation is not decisive as between the MSS. reading and the conjecture ἀπ' αὐτῆς τῆς φύσεως, but rather favours the former.

(b) Passages where the conjectural omission of words is apparently supported by the Arabic :—

ix. 9. 1451 b 34 (= b 31 Bekk.), οἷα ἂν εἰκὸς γενέσθαι καὶ δυνατὰ γενέσθαι : Arabic, 'there is nothing to prevent the condition of some things being therein like those which are supposed to be.' But we can hardly say with certainty which of the two phrases the Arabic represents.

xvi. 4. 1454 b 34 (= b 31 Bekk.), οἷον Ὀρέστης ἐν τῇ Ἰφιγενείᾳ ἀνεγνώρισεν ὅτι Ὀρέστης: Arabic, 'as in that which is called Iphigeneia, and that is whereby Iphigeneia argued that it was Orestes.' This seems to point to the omission of the first Ὀρέστης.

In neither of these passages, however, have I altered the MSS. reading.

(c) Passages on which the Arabic throws no light :—

> i. 9. 1447 b 22. The only point of interest that emerges is that in the Arabic rendering ('of all the metres we ought to call him poet') there is no trace of καὶ, which is found alike in Aᶜ and the 'apographa.'
>
> x. 3. 1452 a 22 (= a 20 Bekk.). The words γίγνεσθαι ταῦτα are simply omitted in the Arabic.
>
> xxv. 18. 1461 b 20 (=b 17 Bekk.), ὥστε καὶ αὐτὸν MSS. The line containing these words is not represented in the Arabic.
>
> xxv. 19. 1461 b 22 (=b 19 Bekk.), ὅταν μὴ ἀνάγκης οὔσης μηδὲν . . . The words in the Arabic are partly obliterated, partly corrupt.

In conclusion, I desire to acknowledge my obligations to friends, such as Mr. B. Bosanquet (whose *History of Aesthetic* ought to be in the hands of all students of the subject), Dr. A. W. Verrall, Mr. W. J. Courthope, Mr. A. O. Prickard, and Rev. W. Lock, who have written me notes on particular points, and to many reviewers by whose criticism I have profited. In a special sense I am indebted to Professor Susemihl for his review of my first edition in the *Berl. Phil. Wochenschr.*, 28th September 1895, as well as for the instruction derived from his numerous articles on the *Poetics*, extending over many years in Bursian's *Jahresbericht* and elsewhere. Among other reviewers to whom I feel

grateful, I would mention Mr. Herbert Richards
in the *Classical Review*, May 1895; Mr. R. P.
Hardie in *Mind*, vol. iv. No. 15; and the authors
of the unsigned articles in the *Saturday Review*,
2nd March 1895, and the *Oxford Magazine*, 12th
June 1895.

To Messrs. R. & R. Clark's Reader I would once
again express no merely formal thanks.

EDINBURGH, *November* 1897.

CONTENTS

EDITIONS, TRANSLATIONS, ETC.

THE following is a list of the chief editions and translations of the *Poetics*, and of other writings relating to this treatise, arranged in chronological order :—

Valla (G.), Latin translation. Venice, 1498.

Aldine text, in *Rhetores Graeci*. Venice, Aldus, 1508.

Latin translation, with the summary of Averroes (*ob.* 1198). Venice, Arrivabene, 1515.

Pazzi (A.) [Paccius], *Aristotelis Poetica, per Alexandrum Paccium, patritium Florentinum, in Latinum conversa.* Venice, Aldus, 1536.

Trincaveli, Greek text. Venice, 1536.

Robortelli (Fr.), *In librum Aristotelis de Arte Poetica explicationes.* Florence, 1548.

Segni (B.), *Rettorica e Poetica d' Aristotele tradotte di Greco in lingua vulgare.* Florence, 1549.

Maggi (V.) [Madius], *In Aristotelis librum de Poetica explanationes.* Venice, 1550.

Vettori (P.) [Victorius], *Commentationes in primum librum Aristotelis de Arte Poetarum.* Florence, 1560.

Castelvetro (L.), *Poetica d' Aristotele vulgarizzata.* Vienna, 1570 ; Basle, 1576.

Piccolomini (A.), *Annotationi nel libro della Poetica d' Aristotele, con la traduttione del medesimo libro in lingua volgare.* Venice, 1575.

Casaubon (I.), edition of Aristotle. Leyden, 1590.

Heinsius (D.) recensuit. Leyden, 1610.

Goulston (T.), Latin translation. London, 1623, and Cambridge, 1696.

Dacier, *La Poétique traduite en Français, avec des remarques critiques.* Paris, 1692.

Batteux, *Les quatres Poétiques d'Aristote, d'Horace, de Vida, de Despréaux, avec les traductions et des remarques par l'Abbé Batteux.* Paris, 1771.

Winstanley (T.), commentary on *Poetics*.   Oxford, 1780.

Reiz, *De Poetica Liber*.   Leipzig, 1786.

Metastasio (P.), *Estratto dell' Arte Poetica d' Aristotele e considerazioni su la medesima*.   Paris, 1782.

Twining (T.), *Aristotle's Treatise on Poetry, translated with notes on the translation and on the original, and two dissertations on poetical and musical imitation*.   London, 1789.

Pye (H. J.), *A Commentary illustrating the Poetic of Aristotle by examples taken chiefly from the modern poets.   To which is prefixed a new and corrected edition of the translation of the Poetic*.   London, 1792.

Tyrwhitt (T.), *De Poetica Liber.   Textum recensuit, versionem refluxit, et animadversionibus illustravit Thomas Tyrwhitt*.   Oxford, 1794.

Buhle (J. T.) recensuit.   Göttingen, 1794.

Hermann (Godfrey), *Ars Poetica cum commentariis*.   Leipzig, 1802.

Gräfenham (E. A. W.), *De Arte Poetica librum denuo recensuit, commentariis illustravit, etc*.   Leipzig, 1821.

Raumer (Fr. v.), *Ueber die Poetik des Aristoteles und sein Verhältniss zu den neuern Dramatikern*.   Berlin, 1829.

Spengel (L.), *Ueber Aristoteles' Poetik* in *Abhandlungen der Münchener Akad. philos.-philol. Cl. II*.   Munich, 1837.

Ritter (Fr.), *Ad codices antiquos recognitam, latine conversam, commentario illustratam edidit Franciscus Ritter*.   Cologne, 1839.

Egger (M. E.), *Essai sur l'histoire de la Critique chez les Grecs, suivi de la Poétique d'Aristote et d'extraits de ses Problèmes, avec traduction française et commentaire*.   Paris, 1849.

Bernays (Jacob), *Grundzüge der verlorenen Abhandlung des Aristoteles über Wirkung der Tragödie*.   Breslau, 1857.

Saint-Hilaire (J. B.), *Poétique traduite en français et accompagnée de notes perpétuelles*.   Paris, 1858.

Stahr (Adolf), *Aristoteles und die Wirkung der Tragödie*.   Berlin, 1859.

Stahr (Adolf), German translation, with Introduction and notes.   Stuttgart, 1860.

Liepert (J.), *Aristoteles über den Zweck der Kunst*.   Passau, 1862.

Susemihl (F.), German translation, with Introduction and notes.   Leipzig, 1865 and 1874.

Vahlen (J.), *Beiträge zu Aristoteles' Poetik*.   Vienna, 1865.

Spengel (L.), *Aristotelische Studien IV*.   Munich, 1866.

Vahlen (J.) recensuit.   Berlin, 1867.

Teichmüller (G.), *Aristotelische Forschungen.   I. Beiträge zur Erklärung der Poetik des Aristoteles.   II. Aristoteles' Philosophie der Kunst*.   Halle, 1869.

Ueberweg (F.), German translation and notes.   Berlin, 1869.

Reinkens (J. H.), *Aristoteles über Kunst, besonders über Tragödie.* Vienna, 1870.

Döring (A.), *Die Kunstlehre des Aristoteles.* Jena, 1870.

Ueberweg (F.), *Ars Poetica ad fidem potissimum codicis antiquissimi A^c (Parisiensis 1741).* Berlin, 1870.

Bywater (I.), *Aristotelia* in *Journal of Philology,* v. 117 ff. and xiv. 40 ff. London and Cambridge, 1873 and 1885.

Vahlen (J.) iterum recensuit et adnotatione critica auxit. Berlin, 1874.

Moore (E.), Vahlen's text with notes. Oxford, 1875.

Christ (W.) recensuit. Leipzig, 1878 and 1893.

Bernays (Jacob), *Zwei Abhandlungen über die Aristotelische Theorie des Drama.* Berlin, 1880.

Brandscheid (F.), Text, German translation, critical notes and commentary. Wiesbaden, 1882.

Wharton (E. R.), Vahlen's text with English translation. Oxford, 1883.

Margoliouth (D.), *Analecta Orientalia ad Poeticam Aristoteleam.* London, 1887.

Bénard (C.), *L'Esthétique d'Aristote.* Paris, 1887.

Gomperz (T.), *Zu Aristoteles' Poetik,* I. (c. i.-vi.). Vienna, 1888.

Heidenhain (F.), *Averrois Paraphrasis in librum Poeticae Aristotelis Jacob Mantino interprete.* Leipzig, 1889.

Prickard (A. O.), *Aristotle on the Art of Poetry. A Lecture with two Appendices.* London, 1891.

La Poétique d'Aristote, Manuscrit 1741 Fonds Grec de la Bibliothèque Nationale. Préface de M. Henri Omont. Photolithographie de MM. Lumière. Paris, 1891.

Carroll (M.), *Aristotle's Poetics in the Light of the Homeric Scholia.* Baltimore, 1895.

Gomperz (T.), *Aristoteles' Poetik. Uebersetzt und eingeleitet.* Leipzig, 1895.

Gomperz (T.), *Zu Aristoteles' Poetik,* II., III. Vienna, 1896.

ARISTOTLE'S POETICS

ANALYSIS OF CONTENTS

I. 'Imitation' (μίμησις) the common principle of the Arts of Poetry, Music, Dancing, Painting, and Sculpture. These Arts distinguished according to the Medium or material Vehicle, the Objects, and the Manner of Imitation. The Medium of Imitation is Rhythm, Language, and 'Harmony' (or Melody), taken singly or combined.

II. The Objects of Imitation.

Higher or lower types are represented in all the Imitative Arts. In Poetry this is the basis of the distinction between Tragedy and Comedy.

III. The Manner of Imitation.

Poetry may be in form either dramatic narrative, pure narrative (including lyric poetry), or pure drama. A digression follows on the name and original home of the Drama.

IV. The Origin and Development of Poetry.

Psychologically, Poetry may be traced to two causes, the instinct of Imitation, and the instinct of Harmony and Rhythm.

Historically viewed, Poetry diverged early in two directions: traces of this twofold tendency are found in the Homeric poems: Tragedy and Comedy exhibit the distinction in a developed form.

The successive steps in the history of Tragedy are enumerated.

V. Definition of the Ludicrous (τὸ γελοῖον), and a brief sketch of the rise of Comedy. Points of comparison between Epic Poetry and Tragedy. (The chapter is fragmentary.)

B

VI. Definition of Tragedy. Six elements in Tragedy : three external, —namely, Scenic Presentment (ὁ τῆς ὄψεως κόσμος or ὄψις), Lyrical Song (μελοποιία), Diction (λέξις) ; three internal,— namely, Plot (μῦθος), Character (ἦθος), and Thought (διάνοια). Plot, or the representation of the action, is of primary import‐ ance ; Character and Thought come next in order.

VII. The Plot must be a Whole, complete in itself, and of adequate magnitude.

VIII. The Plot must be a Unity. Unity of Plot consists not in Unity of Hero, but in Unity of Action.
The parts must be organically connected.

IX. (Plot continued.) Dramatic Unity can be attained only by the observance of Poetic as distinct from Historic Truth ; for Poetry is an expression of the Universal, History of the Par‐ ticular. The rule of probable or necessary sequence as applied to the incidents. Certain plots condemned for want of Unity. The best Tragic effects depend on the combination of the Inevitable and the Unexpected.

X. (Plot continued.) Definitions of Simple (ἁπλοῖ) and Complex (πεπλεγμένοι) Plots.

XI. (Plot continued.) Sudden Reversal or Recoil of the Action (περι‐ πέτεια), Recognition (ἀναγνώρισις), and Tragic or disastrous Incident (πάθος) defined and explained.

XII. The 'quantitative parts' (μέρη κατὰ τὸ ποσόν) of Tragedy de‐ fined :—Prologue, Episode, etc. (Probably an interpolation.)

XIII. (Plot continued.) What constitutes Tragic Action. The change of fortune and the character of the hero as requisite to an ideal Tragedy. The unhappy ending more truly tragic than the 'poetic justice' which is in favour with a popular audience, and belongs rather to Comedy.

XIV. (Plot continued.) The tragic emotions of pity and fear should spring out of the Plot itself. To produce them by Scenery or Spectacular effect is entirely against the spirit of Tragedy. Examples of Tragic Incidents designed to heighten the emotional effect.

XV. The element of Character (as the manifestation of moral purpose) in Tragedy. Requisites of ethical portraiture. The rule of necessity or probability applicable to Character as to Plot. The 'Deus ex Machina' (a passage out of place here). How Character is idealised.

XVI. (Plot continued.) Recognition : its various kinds, with examples.

ABBREVIATIONS IN THE CRITICAL NOTES

$A^c =$ the Parisian manuscript (1741) of the 11th century : generally, but perhaps too confidently, supposed to be the archetype from which all other extant MSS. directly or indirectly are derived.

Apogr. =   one or more of the MSS. other than A^c.

Arabs =   the Arabic version of the *Poetics* (Paris 882 A), of the middle of the 10th century, a version independent of our extant MSS. It is not directly taken from the Greek, but is a translation of a Syriac version of the *Poetics* by an unknown author, now lost. (The quotations in the critical notes are from the literal Latin translation of the Arabic, as given in Margoliouth's *Analecta Orientalia*.)

$\Sigma =$ the Greek manuscript, far older than A^c and no longer extant, which was used by the Syriac translator. (This symbol already employed by Susemihl I have taken for the sake of brevity.) It must be remembered, therefore, that the readings ascribed to Σ are those which we *infer* to have existed in the Greek exemplar, from which the Syriac translation was made.

Ald. =   the Aldine edition of *Rhetores Graeci*, published in 1508.

Vahlen =   Vahlen's text of the *Poetics* Ed. 3.

Vahlen coni. =   a conjecture of Vahlen, not admitted by him into the text.

[ ] =   words with manuscript authority (including A^c), which should be deleted from the text.

< > =   a conjectural supplement to the text.

* * =   a lacuna in the text.

† =   words which are corrupt and have not been satisfactorily restored.

ΑΡΙΣΤΟΤΕΛΟΥΣ
ΠΕΡΙ ΠΟΙΗΤΙΚΗΣ

ΑΡΙΣΤΟΤΕΛΟΥΣ ΠΕΡΙ ΠΟΙΗΤΙΚΗΣ

I Περὶ ποιητικῆς αὐτῆς τε καὶ τῶν εἰδῶν αὐτῆς, ἥν τινα
1447ᵃ δύναμιν ἕκαστον ἔχει, καὶ πῶς δεῖ συνίστασθαι τοὺς μύθους
10 εἰ μέλλει καλῶς ἕξειν ἡ ποίησις, ἔτι δὲ ἐκ πόσων καὶ
ποίων ἐστὶ μορίων, ὁμοίως δὲ καὶ περὶ τῶν ἄλλων ὅσα τῆς
αὐτῆς ἐστι μεθόδου, λέγωμεν ἀρξάμενοι κατὰ φύσιν πρῶτον ἀπὸ τῶν πρώτων. ἐποποιία δὴ καὶ ἡ τῆς τραγῳδίας 2
ποίησις ἔτι δὲ κωμῳδία καὶ ἡ διθυραμβοποιητικὴ καὶ τῆς
15 αὐλητικῆς ἡ πλείστη καὶ κιθαριστικῆς πᾶσαι τυγχάνουσιν
οὖσαι μιμήσεις τὸ σύνολον, διαφέρουσι δὲ ἀλλήλων τρισίν, 3
ἢ γὰρ τῷ ἐν ἑτέροις μιμεῖσθαι ἢ τῷ ἕτερα ἢ τῷ ἑτέ-
ρως καὶ μὴ τὸν αὐτὸν τρόπον. ὥσπερ γὰρ καὶ χρώμασι 4
καὶ σχήμασι πολλὰ μιμοῦνταί τινες ἀπεικάζοντες (οἱ μὲν
20 διὰ τέχνης οἱ δὲ διὰ συνηθείας), ἕτεροι δὲ διὰ τῆς φωνῆς,
οὕτω κἀν ταῖς εἰρημέναις τέχναις· ἅπασαι μὲν ποιοῦνται
τὴν μίμησιν ἐν ῥυθμῷ καὶ λόγῳ καὶ ἁρμονίᾳ, τούτοις δ᾽
ἢ χωρὶς ἢ μεμιγμένοις· οἷον ἁρμονίᾳ μὲν καὶ ῥυθμῷ χρώ-

1447 a 9. ἕκαστον apogr.: ἔκαστο Ν Aᶜ.   12. λέγωμεν apogr.: λέγομεν
Aᶜ: habuit iam Σ var. lect., 'et dicamus et dicimus' Arabs.   17. τῷ
ἐν Forchhammer: 'imitatur rebus diversis' Arabs: τῶι γένει Aᶜ.   20.
φωνῆς: 'per sonos' Arabs: φύσεως Maggi: δι᾽ αὐτῆς τῆς φύσεως Spengel.
21. καὶ ἐν apogr.: καὶ Aᶜ: κἂν Ald.

I
1447 a   I propose to treat of Poetry in itself and of its various
kinds, noting the essential quality of each; to inquire
into the structure of the plot as requisite to a good poem;
into the number and nature of the parts of which a
poem is composed; and similarly into whatever else falls
within the same inquiry. Following, then, the order of
nature, let us begin with the principles which come
first.

Epic poetry and Tragedy, Comedy also and dithyrambic 2
poetry, and the music of the flute and of the lyre in
most of their forms, are all in their general conception
modes of imitation. They differ, however, from one 3
another in three respects,—the medium, the objects, the
manner or mode of imitation, being in each case
distinct.

For as there are persons who, by conscious art or 4
mere habit, imitate and represent various objects through
the medium of colour and form, or again by the voice;
so in the arts above mentioned, taken as a whole, the
imitation is produced by rhythm, language, or 'harmony,'
either singly or combined.

μέναι μόνον ἥ τε αὐλητικὴ καὶ ἡ κιθαριστικὴ κἂν εἴ τινες
25 ἕτεραι τυγχάνουσιν οὖσαι τοιαῦται τὴν δύναμιν, οἷον ἡ τῶν
συρίγγων, αὐτῷ δὲ τῷ ῥυθμῷ [μιμοῦνται] χωρὶς ἁρμονίας 5
ἡ τῶν ὀρχηστῶν, καὶ γὰρ οὗτοι διὰ τῶν σχηματιζομένων
ῥυθμῶν μιμοῦνται καὶ ἤθη καὶ πάθη καὶ πράξεις· ἡ δὲ 6
[ἐποποιία] μόνον τοῖς λόγοις ψιλοῖς ἢ τοῖς μέτροις καὶ τού-
1447 b τοις εἴτε μιγνῦσα μετ᾽ ἀλλήλων εἴθ᾽ ἑνί τινι γένει χρωμένη
τῶν μέτρων, <ἀνώνυμος> τυγχάνουσα μέχρι τοῦ νῦν· 7
10 οὐδὲν γὰρ ἂν ἔχοιμεν ὀνομάσαι κοινὸν τοὺς Σώφρονος καὶ
Ξενάρχου μίμους καὶ τοὺς Σωκρατικοὺς λόγους, οὐδὲ εἴ
τις διὰ τριμέτρων ἢ ἐλεγείων ἢ τῶν ἄλλων τινῶν τῶν τοιούτων ποιοῖτο τὴν μίμησιν· πλὴν οἱ ἄνθρωποί γε συνάπτοντες
τῷ μέτρῳ τὸ ποιεῖν ἐλεγειοποιούς, τοὺς δὲ ἐποποιοὺς ὀνομά-
15 ζουσιν, οὐχ ὡς κατὰ τὴν μίμησιν ποιητὰς ἀλλὰ κοινῇ κατὰ
τὸ μέτρον προσαγορεύοντες. καὶ γὰρ ἂν ἰατρικὸν ἢ φυσικόν 8
τι διὰ τῶν μέτρων ἐκφέρωσιν, οὕτω καλεῖν εἰώθασιν· οὐδὲν
δὲ κοινόν ἐστιν Ὁμήρῳ καὶ Ἐμπεδοκλεῖ πλὴν τὸ μέτρον· διὸ
τὸν μὲν ποιητὴν δίκαιον καλεῖν, τὸν δὲ φυσιολόγον μᾶλλον
20 ἢ ποιητήν· ὁμοίως δὲ κἂν εἴ τις ἅπαντα τὰ μέτρα μιγνύων 9
ποιοῖτο τὴν μίμησιν καθάπερ Χαιρήμων ἐποίησε Κένταυ-
ρον μικτὴν ῥαψῳδίαν ἐξ ἁπάντων τῶν μέτρων, καὶ τοῦτον

25. τυγχάνουσιν apogr.: τυγχάνωσιν Aᶜ. τοιαῦται add. apogr.: habuit
codex Σ, unde Syrus-Arabs 'aliae artes similes vi.' 26. τῷ αὐτῷ
δὲ Σ male (Margoliouth). μιμοῦνται del. Spengel, quod confirmat
Arabs. 27. ἡ apogr.: 'ars instrumenti saltationis' Arabs: οἱ Aᶜ:
οἱ <χαριέστεροι> Gomperz: οἱ <χαριέντες> Zeller. ὀρχηστρῶν Σ
male (Margoliouth). 29. ἐποποιία seclus. Ueberweg, om. iam Σ.
ψιλοῖς ἢ τοῖς μέτροις: ἢ τοῖς ψιλοῖς μέτροις coni. Vahlen. 1447 b 9.
ἀνώνυμος add. Bernays, confirmante Arabe 'quae sine nomine est adhuc.'
15. κατὰ τὴν apogr.: τὴν κατὰ Aᶜ. 16. φυσικόν Heinsius: 're
physica' Arabs. 'Idem praestat Averroes' (Margoliouth): μουσικόν
codd. 22. μικτὴν om. Σ: μικτὴν ῥαψῳδίαν delere voluit Tyrwhitt.
καὶ τοῦτον apogr.: καὶ Aᶜ, Vahlen: καὶ om. Σ: καίτοι Rassow, Gomperz.
Loci difficultatem transpositione verborum tollere vult Susemihl; 20-22
ὁμοίως δὲ . . . τῶν μέτρων post 12 τοιούτων collocat, commate ad τοιούτων

Thus in the music of the flute and the lyre, 'harmony' and rhythm alone are employed; also in other arts, such as that of the shepherd's pipe, which are essentially similar to these. In dancing, rhythm alone is used 5 without 'harmony'; for even dancing imitates character, emotion, and action, by rhythmical movement. There 6 is another art which imitates by means of language alone, and that either in prose or verse — which 1447 b verse, again, may either combine different metres or consist of but one kind—but this has hitherto been without a name.

For there is no common term we could apply to 7 the mimes of Sophron and Xenarchus and the Socratic dialogues on the one hand; and, on the other, to poetic imitations in iambic, elegiac, or any similar metre. People do, indeed, add the word 'maker' or 'poet' to the name of the metre, and speak of elegiac poets, or epic (that is, hexameter) poets, as if it were not the imitation that makes the poet, but the verse that entitles them all indiscriminately to the name. Even 8 when a treatise on medicine or natural science is brought out in verse, the name of poet is by custom given to the author; and yet Homer and Empedocles have nothing in common but the metre, so that it would be right to call the one poet, the other physicist rather than poet. On the same principle, even if a writer in his poetic 9 imitation were to combine all metres, as Chaeremon did in his Centaur, which is a medley composed of metres

ποιητὴν προσαγορευτέον.   περὶ μὲν οὖν τούτων διωρίσθω
τοῦτον τὸν τρόπον· εἰσὶ δέ τινες αἳ πᾶσι χρῶνται τοῖς εἰρη- 10
25 μένοις, λέγω δὲ οἷον ῥυθμῷ καὶ μέλει καὶ μέτρῳ, ὥσπερ
ἥ τε τῶν διθυραμβικῶν ποίησις καὶ ἡ τῶν νόμων καὶ ἥ
τε τραγῳδία καὶ ἡ κωμῳδία· διαφέρουσι δὲ ὅτι αἱ μὲν
ἅμα πᾶσιν αἱ δὲ κατὰ μέρος.   ταύτας μὲν οὖν λέγω τὰς
διαφορὰς τῶν τεχνῶν, ἐν οἷς ποιοῦνται τὴν μίμησιν.

II   ἐπεὶ δὲ μιμοῦνται οἱ μιμούμενοι πράττοντας, ἀνάγκη δὲ
1448 a τούτους ἢ σπουδαίους ἢ φαύλους εἶναι (τὰ γὰρ ἤθη σχεδὸν
ἀεὶ τούτοις ἀκολουθεῖ μόνοις, κακίᾳ γὰρ καὶ ἀρετῇ τὰ ἤθη
διαφέρουσι πάντες), ἤτοι βελτίονας ἢ καθ᾽ ἡμᾶς ἢ χείρονας
5 ἢ καὶ τοιούτους, ὥσπερ οἱ γραφεῖς· Πολύγνωτος μὲν γὰρ
κρείττους, Παύσων δὲ χείρους, Διονύσιος δὲ ὁμοίους εἴκαζεν·
δῆλον δὲ ὅτι καὶ τῶν λεχθεισῶν ἑκάστη μιμήσεων ἕξει 2
ταύτας τὰς διαφορὰς καὶ ἔσται ἑτέρα τῷ ἕτερα μιμεῖσθαι
τοῦτον τὸν τρόπον.   καὶ γὰρ ἐν ὀρχήσει καὶ αὐλήσει καὶ 3
10 κιθαρίσει ἔστι γενέσθαι ταύτας τὰς ἀνομοιότητας· καὶ [τὸ]
περὶ τοὺς λόγους δὲ καὶ τὴν ψιλομετρίαν, οἷον Ὅμηρος
μὲν βελτίους, Κλεοφῶν δὲ ὁμοίους, Ἡγήμων δὲ ὁ Θάσιος ὁ
τὰς παρῳδίας ποιήσας πρῶτος καὶ Νικοχάρης ὁ τὴν Δηλι-
άδα χείρους· ὁμοίως δὲ καὶ περὶ τοὺς διθυράμβους καὶ περὶ 4
15 τοὺς νόμους, ὥσπερ οἱ τοὺς Κύκλωπας Τιμόθεος καὶ Φιλό-

posito, deleto 13 ποιοῖτο τὴν μίμησιν et 22 καὶ ποιητὴν: sic efficitur ut
verbis φυσιολόγον μᾶλλον ἢ ποιητὴν προσαγορευτέον concluditur locus:
οὐκ ἤδη καὶ Ald., Bekker.   24. αἴ Gryph.; αἱ apogr.: οἱ Aᶜ:
'homines qui' Arabs.   26. διθυράμβων apogr.   28. πᾶσαι apogr.
οὖν apogr.: οὐ Aᶜ.   29. οἷς Vettori: αἷς Aᶜ.   1448 a 3. κακίᾳ
. . . ἀρετῇ apogr., Σ: κακία . . . ἀρετὴ Aᶜ.   7. δὴ Morel.   8.
τῷ apogr.: τὸ Aᶜ.   12. ὁ ante τὰς add. apogr.   13. τραγῳδίας ut
videtur Σ, 'qui primus faciebat tragoediam' Arabs.   Δειλιάδα Aᶜ
pr. man., fort. recte, ut in Iliadis parodia (Tyrrell: cf. Castelvetro).   15.
ὥσπερ οἱ τοὺς coni. Margoliouth: ὥσπερ οὕτως Σ ut videtur: ὥσπερ γᾶς
codd.: ὥσπερ Ἀργᾶς Castelvetro: ὡς Πέρσας Vettori: ὥσπερ γὰρ coni.
Vahlen.

of all kinds, we should bring him too under the general term poet. So much then for these distinctions.

There are, again, some arts which employ all the 10 means above mentioned,—namely, rhythm, tune and metre. Such are dithyrambic and nomic poetry, and also Tragedy and Comedy; but between them the difference is, that in the first two cases these means are all employed in combination, in the latter, now one means is employed, now another.

Such, then, are the differences of the arts with respect to the medium of imitation.

II   Since the objects of imitation are men in action, and
1448 a these men must be either of a higher or a lower type (for moral character mainly answers to these divisions, goodness and badness being the distinguishing marks of moral differences), it follows that we must represent men either as better than in real life, or as worse, or as they are. It is the same in painting. Polygnotus depicted men as nobler than they are, Pauson as less noble, Dionysius drew them true to life.

Now it is evident that each of the modes of imitation 2 above mentioned will exhibit these differences, and become a distinct kind in imitating objects that are thus distinct. Such diversities may be found even in dancing, 3 flute-playing, and lyre-playing. So again in language, whether prose or verse unaccompanied by music. Homer, for example, makes men better than they are; Cleophon as they are; Hegemon the Thasian, the inventor of parodies, and Nicochares, the author of the Deliad, worse than they are. The same thing holds good of dithyrambs 4 and nomes; here too one may portray different types, as

ξενος[, μιμήσαιτο ἄν τις]· ἐν τῇ αὐτῇ δὲ διαφορᾷ καὶ ἡ
τραγῳδία πρὸς τὴν κωμῳδίαν διέστηκεν, ἡ μὲν γὰρ χείρους ἡ δὲ βελτίους μιμεῖσθαι βούλεται τῶν νῦν.
III ἔτι δὲ τούτων τρίτη διαφορὰ τὸ ὡς ἔκαστα τούτων
20 μιμήσαιτο ἄν τις. καὶ γὰρ ἐν τοῖς αὐτοῖς καὶ τὰ αὐτὰ
μιμεῖσθαι ἔστιν ὁτὲ μὲν ἀπαγγέλλοντα (ἢ ἕτερόν τι γιγνόμενον, ὥσπερ Ὅμηρος ποιεῖ, ἢ ὡς τὸν αὐτὸν καὶ μὴ μετα-
βάλλοντα), ἢ πάντας ὡς πράττοντας καὶ ἐνεργοῦντας [τοὺς
μιμουμένους]. ἐν τρισὶ δὴ ταύταις διαφοραῖς ἡ μίμησίς 2
25 ἐστιν, ὡς εἴπομεν κατ' ἀρχάς, ἐν οἷς τε καὶ ἃ καὶ ὥς. ὥστε
τῇ μὲν ὁ αὐτὸς ἂν εἴη μιμητὴς Ὁμήρῳ Σοφοκλῆς, μιμοῦνται
γὰρ ἄμφω σπουδαίους, τῇ δὲ Ἀριστοφάνει, πράττοντας γὰρ
μιμοῦνται καὶ δρῶντας ἄμφω. ὅθεν καὶ δράματα καλεῖ- 3
σθαί τινες αὐτά φασιν, ὅτι μιμοῦνται δρῶντας. διὸ καὶ
30 ἀντιποιοῦνται τῆς τε τραγῳδίας καὶ τῆς κωμῳδίας οἱ Δω-
ριεῖς (τῆς μὲν γὰρ κωμῳδίας οἱ Μεγαρεῖς οἵ τε ἐνταῦθα
ὡς ἐπὶ τῆς παρ' αὐτοῖς δημοκρατίας γενομένης, καὶ οἱ ἐκ
Σικελίας, ἐκεῖθεν γὰρ ἦν Ἐπίχαρμος ὁ ποιητὴς πολλῷ
πρότερος ὢν Χιωνίδου καὶ Μάγνητος, καὶ τῆς τραγῳδίας
35 ἔνιοι τῶν ἐν Πελοποννήσῳ)· ποιούμενοι τὰ ὀνόματα σημεῖον·
αὐτοὶ μὲν γὰρ κώμας τὰς περιοικίδας. καλεῖν φασιν, Ἀθηναίους δὲ δήμους, ὡς κωμῳδοὺς οὐκ ἀπὸ τοῦ κωμάζειν λε-

16. [μιμήσαιτο ἄν τις] secl. coni. Vahlen.   τῇ αὐτῇ δὲ Vettori : 'in
eadem discrepantia' Arabs : ταύτῃ δὲ τῇ M. Casaubon : αὐτῇ δὲ τῇ codd.
18. τῶν νῦν om. ut videtur Σ.   21. ὁτὲ μὲν . . . γιγνόμενον : <ἢ>
ὁτὲ μὲν ἀπαγγέλλοντα <ὁτὲ δ'> ἕτερόν τι γιγνόμενον Bywater secutus
Gumposch, recte, ut opinor. Eodem fere pervenit Arabem secutus
Margoliouth.   τι seclus. Zeller, Spengel.   23. πάντας fort.
secludendum (Bywater) : πάντα I. Casaubon.   τοὺς μιμουμένους
seclusi : olim seclus. Vahlen : tuetur Σ.   25. Pro καὶ ἃ καὶ ὥς,
ἀναγκαίως Σ (Margoliouth) : καὶ ἃ add. apogr.   35. <δ'> ἔνιοι
Bywater.   36. αὐτοὶ et Ἀθηναίους Spengel (cf. 1460 b 38) : Ἀθηναίους
iam editio Oxoniensis 1760 : οὗτοι et ἀθηναῖοι codd. : Ἀθηναῖοι tuentur
Wilamowitz, Gomperz.

Timotheus and Philoxenus differed in representing the
Cyclopes. The same distinction marks off Tragedy from
Comedy ; for Comedy aims at representing men as worse,
Tragedy as better than in actual life.

III   There is still a third difference—the manner in which
each of these objects may be imitated. For the medium
being the same, and the objects the same, the poet may
imitate by narration—in which case he can either take
another personality as Homer does, or speak in his own
person, unchanged—or he may present all his characters
as living and moving before us.

These, then, as we said at the beginning, are the 2
three differences which distinguish artistic imitation,—
the medium, the objects, and the manner. So that from
one point of view, Sophocles is an imitator of the same
kind as Homer — for both imitate higher types of
character ; from another point of view, of the same kind
as Aristophanes—for both imitate persons acting and
doing. Hence, some say, the name of 'drama' is given 3
to such poems, as representing action. For the same
reason the Dorians claim the invention both of Tragedy
and Comedy. The claim to Comedy is put forward by
the Megarians,—not only by those of Greece proper, who
allege that it originated under their democracy, but also by
the Megarians of Sicily, for the poet Epicharmus, who is
much earlier than Chionides and Magnes, belonged to that
country. Tragedy too is claimed by certain Dorians of
the Peloponnese. In each case they appeal to the
evidence of language. Villages, they say, are by them
called κῶμαι, by the Athenians δῆμοι : and they assume
that Comedians were so named not from κωμάζειν, 'to

χθέντας ἀλλὰ τῇ κατὰ κώμας πλάνῃ ἀτιμαζομένους ἐκ
1448 b τοῦ ἄστεως, καὶ τὸ ποιεῖν αὐτοὶ μὲν δρᾶν, Ἀθηναίους δὲ
πράττειν προσαγορεύειν. περὶ μὲν οὖν τῶν διαφορῶν 4
καὶ πόσαι καὶ τίνες τῆς μιμήσεως εἰρήσθω ταῦτα.

IV   ἐοίκασι δὲ γεννῆσαι μὲν ὅλως τὴν ποιητικὴν αἰτίαι δύο
5 τινὲς καὶ αὗται φυσικαί. τό τε γὰρ μιμεῖσθαι σύμφυτον 2
τοῖς ἀνθρώποις ἐκ παίδων ἐστί, καὶ τούτῳ διαφέρουσι
τῶν ἄλλων ζῴων ὅτι μιμητικώτατόν ἐστι καὶ τὰς μαθή-
σεις ποιεῖται διὰ μιμήσεως τὰς πρώτας, καὶ τὸ χαίρειν
τοῖς μιμήμασι πάντας. ʼ σημεῖον δὲ τούτου τὸ συμβαῖνον 3
10 ἐπὶ τῶν ἔργων· ἃ γὰρ αὐτὰ λυπηρῶς ὁρῶμεν, τούτων τὰς
εἰκόνας τὰς μάλιστα ἠκριβωμένας χαίρομεν θεωροῦντες, οἷον
θηρίων τε μορφὰς τῶν ἀτιμοτάτων καὶ νεκρῶν. αἴτιον δὲ 4
καὶ τούτου, ὅτι μανθάνειν οὐ μόνον τοῖς φιλοσόφοις ἥδιστον
ἀλλὰ καὶ τοῖς ἄλλοις ὁμοίως, ἀλλ᾽ ἐπὶ βραχὺ κοινωνοῦσιν
15 αὐτοῦ. διὰ γὰρ τοῦτο χαίρουσι τὰς εἰκόνας ὁρῶντες, ὅτι 5
συμβαίνει θεωροῦντας μανθάνειν καὶ συλλογίζεσθαι τί ἕκαστον, οἷον ὅτι οὗτος ἐκεῖνος, ἐπεὶ ἐὰν μὴ τύχῃ προεωρακώς,
οὐχ ᾗ μίμημα ποιήσει τὴν ἡδονὴν ἀλλὰ διὰ τὴν ἀπερ-
γασίαν ἢ τὴν χροιὰν ἢ διὰ τοιαύτην τινὰ ἄλλην αἰτίαν.
20 κατὰ φύσιν δὴ ὄντος ἡμῖν τοῦ μιμεῖσθαι καὶ τῆς ἁρμονίας 6
καὶ τοῦ ῥυθμοῦ, τὰ γὰρ μέτρα ὅτι μόρια τῶν ῥυθμῶν
ἐστι φανερόν, ἐξ ἀρχῆς πεφυκότες καὶ αὐτὰ μάλιστα κατὰ
μικρὸν προάγοντες ἐγέννησαν τὴν ποίησιν ἐκ τῶν αὐτοσχε-

1448 b 1. καὶ τὸ ποιεῖν . . . προσαγορεύειν om. Arabs.   4. ὅλως om.
Arabs.   5. αὗται apogr. : αὐταί A^c.   13. τούτου apogr. : confirmat
Arabs : τοῦτο A^c : [καὶ τούτου] Zeller : καὶ [τούτου] Spengel : καὶ <λόγος>
τούτου Bonitz.   18. οὐχ ᾗ Hermann, iam Σ, ut videtur : οὐχὶ codd.
τὴν ἡδονὴν om. Arabs.   20. δὴ coni. Vahlen (Beitr.) : δὲ codd.
22. καὶ αὐτὰ : πρὸς αὐτὰ Ald., Bekker : εἰς αὐτὰ καὶ Gomperz : καὶ αὐτὰ
post μάλιστα traiciendum esse coni. Susemihl.

revel,' but because they wandered from village to village (κατὰ κώμας), being excluded contemptuously from the 1448 b city. They add also that the Dorian word for 'doing' is δρᾶν, and the Athenian, πράττειν.

This may suffice as to the number and nature of the 4 various modes of imitation.

IV   Poetry in general seems to have sprung from two causes, each of them lying deep in our nature. First, the 2 instinct of imitation is implanted in man from childhood, one difference between him and other animals being that he is the most imitative of living creatures; and through imitation he learns his earliest lessons; and no less universal is the pleasure felt in things imitated. We 3 have evidence of this in the facts of experience. Objects which in themselves we view with pain, we delight to contemplate when reproduced with minute fidelity: such as the forms of the most ignoble animals and of dead bodies. The cause of this again is, that to 4 learn gives the liveliest pleasure, not only to philosophers but to men in general; whose capacity, however, of learning is more limited. Thus the reason why men 5 enjoy seeing a likeness is, that in contemplating it they find themselves learning or inferring, and saying perhaps, 'Ah, that is he.' For if you happen not to have seen the original, the pleasure will be due not to the imitation as such, but to the execution, the colouring, or some such other cause.

Imitation, then, is one instinct of our nature. Next, 6 there is the instinct for 'harmony' and rhythm, metres being manifestly sections of rhythm. Persons, therefore, starting with this natural gift developed by degrees their

διασμάτων. διεσπάσθη δὲ κατὰ τὰ οἰκεῖα ἤθη ἡ ποίησις· 7
25 οἱ μὲν γὰρ σεμνότεροι τὰς καλὰς ἐμιμοῦντο πράξεις καὶ
τὰς τῶν τοιούτων, οἱ δὲ εὐτελέστεροι τὰς τῶν φαύλων, πρῶτον ψόγους ποιοῦντες, ὥσπερ ἅτεροι ὕμνους καὶ ἐγκώμια.
τῶν μὲν οὖν πρὸ Ὁμήρου οὐδενὸς ἔχομεν εἰπεῖν τοιοῦτον 8
ποίημα, εἰκὸς δὲ εἶναι πολλούς, ἀπὸ δὲ Ὁμήρου ἀρξαμένοις
30 ἔστιν, οἷον ἐκείνου ὁ Μαργίτης καὶ τὰ τοιαῦτα. ἐν οἷς καὶ
τὸ ἁρμόττον [ἰαμβεῖον] ἦλθε μέτρον, διὸ καὶ ἰαμβεῖον κα-
λεῖται νῦν, ὅτι ἐν τῷ μέτρῳ τούτῳ ἰάμβιζον ἀλλήλους· καὶ 9
ἐγένοντο τῶν παλαιῶν οἱ μὲν ἡρωικῶν οἱ δὲ ἰάμβων ποιη-
ταί. ὥσπερ δὲ καὶ τὰ σπουδαῖα μάλιστα ποιητὴς Ὅμηρος
35 ἦν, μόνος γὰρ οὐχ ὅτι εὖ ἀλλ<ὰ> [ὅτι] καὶ μιμήσεις δραματικὰς ἐποίησεν, οὕτως καὶ τὰ τῆς κωμῳδίας σχήματα
πρῶτος ὑπέδειξεν, οὐ ψόγον ἀλλὰ τὸ γελοῖον δραματο-
ποιήσας· ὁ γὰρ Μαργίτης ἀνάλογον ἔχει, ὥσπερ Ἰλιὰς
1449 a καὶ ἡ Ὀδύσσεια πρὸς τὰς τραγῳδίας, οὕτω καὶ οὗτος πρὸς
τὰς κωμῳδίας. παραφανείσης δὲ τῆς τραγῳδίας καὶ κω- 10
μῳδίας οἱ ἐφ᾽ ἑκατέραν τὴν ποίησιν ὁρμῶντες κατὰ τὴν
οἰκείαν φύσιν οἱ μὲν ἀντὶ τῶν ἰάμβων κωμῳδοποιοὶ ἐγέ-
5 νοντο, οἱ δὲ ἀντὶ τῶν ἐπῶν τραγῳδοδιδάσκαλοι διὰ τὸ
μείζονα καὶ ἐντιμότερα τὰ σχήματα εἶναι ταῦτα ἐκείνων.
τὸ μὲν οὖν ἐπισκοπεῖν εἰ ἄρ᾽ ἔχει ἤδη ἡ τραγῳδία τοῖς 11

27. ἅτεροι Spengel : ἕτεροι codd.   30. καὶ τὸ ἁρμόττον [ἰαμβεῖον]
Gomperz: καὶ Ἀld. : κατὰ Ac.   31. ἰαμβεῖον seclus. Stahr.   35.
Alterum ὅτι seclus. Bonitz, quod confirm. Arabs.   δραματικὰς Ac, Σ :
δραματικῶς apogr.   1449 a 7. εἰ ἄρα ἔχει apogr. : παρέχει Ac : ἄρ᾽
ἔχει Vahlen.

special aptitudes, till their rude improvisations gave birth to Poetry.

Poetry now diverged in two directions, according to 7 the individual character of the writers. The graver spirits imitated noble actions, and the actions of good men. The more trivial sort imitated the actions of meaner persons, at first composing satires, as the former did hymns to the gods and the praises of famous men. A poem of the satirical kind cannot 8 indeed be put down to any author earlier than Homer; though many such writers probably there were. But from Homer onward, instances can be cited,—his own Margites, for example, and other similar compositions. The appropriate metre was also here introduced; hence the measure is still called the iambic or lampooning measure, being that in which people lampooned one another. Thus the older poets were distinguished as 9 writers of heroic or of lampooning verse.

As, in the serious style, Homer is preeminent among poets, standing alone not only in the excellence, but also in the dramatic form of his imitations, so he too first laid down the main lines of Comedy, by dramatising the ludicrous instead of writing personal satire. His Margites 1449 a bears the same relation to Comedy that the Iliad and Odyssey do to Tragedy. But when Tragedy and Comedy 10 came to light, the two classes of poets still followed their natural bent: the lampooners became writers of Comedy, and the Epic poets were succeeded by Tragedians, since the drama was a larger and higher form of art.

Whether Tragedy has as yet perfected its proper 11

c

εἴδεσιν ἱκανῶς ἢ οὔ, αὐτό τε καθ᾽ αὑτὸ κρίνεται ἢ [ναὶ]
καὶ πρὸς τὰ θέατρα, ἄλλος λόγος.   γενομένη <δ᾽> οὖν ἀπ᾽ 12
10 ἀρχῆς αὐτοσχεδιαστική, καὶ αὐτὴ καὶ ἡ κωμῳδία, καὶ ἡ μὲν
ἀπὸ τῶν ἐξαρχόντων τὸν διθύραμβον, ἡ δὲ ἀπὸ τῶν τὰ φαλ-
λικὰ ἃ ἔτι καὶ νῦν ἐν πολλαῖς τῶν πόλεων διαμένει νο-
μιζόμενα, κατὰ μικρὸν ηὐξήθη προαγόντων ὅσον ἐγίγνετο
φανερὸν αὐτῆς, καὶ πολλὰς μεταβολὰς μεταβαλοῦσα ἡ
15 τραγῳδία ἐπαύσατο, ἐπεὶ ἔσχε τὴν αὐτῆς φύσιν.   καὶ τό 13
τε τῶν ὑποκριτῶν πλῆθος ἐξ ἑνὸς εἰς δύο πρῶτος Αἰσχύλος ἤγαγε καὶ τὰ τοῦ χοροῦ ἠλάττωσε καὶ τὸν λόγον
πρωταγωνιστὴν παρεσκεύασεν, τρεῖς δὲ καὶ σκηνογραφίαν
Σοφοκλῆς.   ἔτι δὲ τὸ μέγεθος ἐκ μικρῶν μύθων καὶ λέ- 14
20 ξεως γελοίας διὰ τὸ ἐκ σατυρικοῦ μεταβαλεῖν ὀψὲ ἀπε-
σεμνύνθη.   τό τε μέτρον ἐκ τετραμέτρου ἰαμβεῖον ἐγένετο·
τὸ μὲν γὰρ πρῶτον τετραμέτρῳ ἐχρῶντο διὰ τὸ σατυρικὴν
καὶ ὀρχηστικωτέραν εἶναι τὴν ποίησιν, λέξεως δὲ γενομένης
αὐτὴ ἡ φύσις τὸ οἰκεῖον μέτρον εὗρε, μάλιστα γὰρ λεκτι-
25 κὸν τῶν μέτρων τὸ ἰαμβεῖόν ἐστιν· σημεῖον δὲ τούτου·
πλεῖστα γὰρ ἰαμβεῖα λέγομεν ἐν τῇ διαλέκτῳ τῇ πρὸς
ἀλλήλους, ἑξάμετρα δὲ ὀλιγάκις καὶ ἐκβαίνοντες τῆς λεκ-
τικῆς ἁρμονίας.   ἔτι δὲ ἐπεισοδίων πλήθη.   καὶ τὰ ἄλλ᾽ 15

8. κρίνεται ἢ ναί. | καὶ Aᶜ: κρίνεται εἶναι καὶ apogr. : κρῖναι καὶ Forch-
hammer : κρίνεται ἢ [ναί.] καὶ Bursian : fort. leg. κρίνεται εἶναι ἢ καί.
Habuit Σ, ut videtur, αὐτώ τε κατ᾽ αὐτό εἶναι κρεῖττον ἢ πρὸς θάτερα (Margoliouth).   9. γενομένη οὖν apogr. : γενομένης οὖν Aᶜ : γενομένη δ᾽
οὖν Bekker.   10. αὐτοσχεδιαστικὴ apogr., Bekker: αὐτοσχεδιαστικῆς
Aᶜ.   11. φαλλικά apogr.: φαϋλλικά Aᶜ: φαυλικά vel φαῦλα Σ.   12.
διαμένει apogr.: διαμένειν Aᶜ.   19. λέξεως: 'orationes' Arabs, i.e.
λέξεις Σ : <ἡ λέξις ἐκ> λέξεως Christ.   Omissum vocab. collato Arabe id
esse Margoliouth suspic. cuius vice Graeculi ὑψηγορία usurpant.   27.
ἑξάμετρα : τετράμετρα Winstanley.   εἰς λεκτικὴν ἁρμονίαν Wecklein (cf.
Rhet. iii. 8. 1408 b 32): codicum lect. tutatur Arabs.   Hunc locum 25
σημεῖον—28 ἁρμονίας suadente Usener seclus. Susemihl.   28. Post
πλήθη punctum del. Gomperz.   ἄλλα ὡς apogr.: ἄλλως Aᶜ:
ἄλλα οἷς Hermann.

types or not; and whether it is to be judged in itself, or
in relation also to the audience,—this raises another
question. Be that as it may, Tragedy—as also Comedy 12
—was at first mere improvisation. The one originated
with the leaders of the dithyramb, the other with those
of the phallic songs, which are still in use in many of
our cities. Tragedy advanced by slow degrees; each
new element that showed itself was in turn developed.
Having passed through many changes, it found its natural
form, and there it stopped.

Aeschylus first introduced a second actor; he dimin- 13
ished the importance of the Chorus, and assigned the
leading part to the dialogue. Sophocles raised the number
of actors to three, and added scene-painting. It was not 14
till late that the short plot was discarded for one of
greater compass, and the grotesque diction of the earlier
satyric form for the stately manner of Tragedy. The
iambic measure then replaced the trochaic tetrameter,
which was originally employed when the poetry was of
the satyric order, and had greater affinities with dancing.
Once dialogue had come in, Nature herself discovered the
appropriate measure. For the iambic is, of all measures,
the most colloquial: we see it in the fact that con-
versational speech runs into iambic form more frequently
than into any other kind of verse; rarely into hexameters,
and only when we drop the colloquial intonation. The
number of 'episodes' or acts was also increased, and the
other embellishments added, of which tradition tells.

ὡς ἕκαστα κοσμηθῆναι λέγεται ἔστω ἡμῖν εἰρημένα·
30 πολὺ γὰρ ἂν ἴσως ἔργον εἴη διεξιέναι καθ' ἕκαστον.

V   ἡ δὲ κωμῳδία ἐστὶν ὥσπερ εἴπομεν μίμησις φαυ-
λοτέρων μέν, οὐ μέντοι κατὰ πᾶσαν κακίαν, ἀλλὰ τοῦ
αἰσχροῦ ἐστι τὸ γελοῖον μόριον· τὸ γὰρ γελοῖόν ἐστιν
ἁμάρτημά τι καὶ αἶσχος ἀνώδυνον καὶ οὐ φθαρτικόν, οἷον
35 εὐθὺς τὸ γελοῖον πρόσωπον αἰσχρόν τι καὶ διεστραμμένον
ἄνευ ὀδύνης.   αἱ μὲν οὖν τῆς τραγῳδίας μεταβάσεις καὶ 2
δι' ὧν ἐγένοντο οὐ λελήθασιν, ἡ δὲ κωμῳδία διὰ τὸ μὴ
1449 b σπουδάζεσθαι ἐξ ἀρχῆς ἔλαθεν· καὶ γὰρ χορὸν κωμῳδῶν
ὀψέ ποτε ὁ ἄρχων ἔδωκεν, ἀλλ' ἐθελονταὶ ἦσαν.   ἤδη δὲ
σχήματά τινα αὐτῆς ἐχούσης οἱ λεγόμενοι αὐτῆς ποιηταὶ
μνημονεύονται.   τίς δὲ πρόσωπα ἀπέδωκεν ἢ προλόγους 3
5 ἢ πλήθη ὑποκριτῶν καὶ ὅσα τοιαῦτα, ἠγνόηται.   τὸ δὲ
μύθους ποιεῖν ['Επίχαρμος καὶ Φόρμις] τὸ μὲν ἐξ ἀρχῆς
ἐκ Σικελίας ἦλθε, τῶν δὲ 'Αθήνησιν Κράτης πρῶτος ἦρξεν
ἀφέμενος τῆς ἰαμβικῆς ἰδέας καθόλου ποιεῖν λόγους καὶ
μύθους.   ἡ μὲν οὖν ἐποποιία τῇ τραγῳδίᾳ μέχρι μὲν τοῦ 4
10 μετὰ μέτρου [μεγάλου] μίμησις εἶναι σπουδαίων ἠκολού-
θησεν· τῷ δὲ τὸ μέτρον ἁπλοῦν ἔχειν καὶ ἀπαγγελίαν

29. περὶ μὲν οὖν τούτων τοσαῦτα add. Ald. ante ἔστω.   32. ἀλλ'
ἢ τοῦ αἰσχροῦ Friedreich: ἀλλὰ <κατὰ τὸ γελοῖον,> τοῦ<δ'> αἰσχροῦ
Christ: 'sed tantum res ridicula est de genere foedi quae est portio
et ridicula' Arabs (Margoliouth), i.e. ἀλλὰ μόνον τὸ γελοῖόν ἐστι τοῦ
αἰσχροῦ ὃ μόριόν ἐστι καὶ τὸ γελοῖον Σ (Susemihl), quod ex duabus
lect. conflatum esse censet Susemihl (1) ἀλλὰ μόριον μόνον τὸ γελοῖόν ἐστι
τοῦ αἰσχροῦ, (2) ἀλλὰ τοῦ αἰσχροῦ μόριόν ἐστι καὶ τὸ γελοῖον.   1449 b 3.
οἱ λεγόμενοι: ὀλίγοι μὲν οἱ Castelvetro: ὀλίγοι μὲν [οἱ] Usener.   4.
προλόγους Aᶜ: πρόλογον Christ: λόγους Hermann.   6. 'Επίχαρμος καὶ
Φόρμις seclus. Susemihl: <ἐκεῖθεν γὰρ ᾔστην> 'Επίχαρμος καὶ Φόρμις post
ἦλθε Bywater, collato Themistio, Or. xxvii. p. 337 A, recte, ut opinor.
9. μέχρι μόνου μέτρου μεγάλου codd.: μέχρι μὲν τοῦ μετὰ μέτρου Thurot (cf.
Arab.): μέχρι μὲν τοῦ μέτρῳ <ἐν μήκει> μεγάλῳ coni. Susemihl: μέχρι
μὲν τοῦ μέτρῳ Tyrwhitt: μέχρι μόνου <τοῦ διὰ λόγου ἐμ>μέτρου μεγάλου
Ueberweg.   10. Pro μεγάλου codd., μετὰ λόγου Ald. et, ut videtur, Σ.

These we need not here discuss; to enter into them in 15
detail would, doubtless, be a large undertaking.

V   Comedy is, as we have said, an imitation of characters
of a lower type,—not, however, in the full sense of the
word bad, the Ludicrous being merely a subdivision of
the ugly. It consists in some defect or ugliness which
is not painful or destructive. To take an obvious
example, the comic mask is ugly and distorted, but does
not imply pain.

The successive changes through which Tragedy passed, 2
and the authors of these changes, are well known, whereas
Comedy has had no history, because it was not at first
1449 b treated seriously. It was late before the Archon granted
a comic chorus to a poet; the performers were till then
voluntary. Comedy had already taken definite shape
when comic poets, distinctively so called, are heard of.
Who introduced masks, or prologues, or increased the 3
number of actors,—these and other similar details re-
main unknown. As for the plot, it came originally from
Sicily; but of Athenian writers Crates was the first who,
abandoning the 'iambic' or lampooning form, generalised
his themes and plots.

Epic poetry agrees with Tragedy in so far as it is an 4
imitation in verse of characters of a higher type. They
differ, in that Epic poetry admits but one kind of metre,
and is narrative in form. They differ, again, in the

εἶναι, ταύτῃ διαφέρουσιν· ἔτι δὲ τῷ μήκει, <ἐπεὶ> ἡ μὲν
ὅτι μάλιστα πειρᾶται ὑπὸ μίαν περίοδον ἡλίου εἶναι ἢ
μικρὸν ἐξαλλάττειν, ἡ δὲ ἐποποιία ἀόριστος τῷ χρόνῳ,
15 καὶ τούτῳ διαφέρει· καίτοι τὸ πρῶτον ὁμοίως ἐν ταῖς
τραγῳδίαις τοῦτο ἐποίουν καὶ ἐν τοῖς ἔπεσιν. μέρη δ' 5
ἐστὶ τὰ μὲν ταὐτά, τὰ δὲ ἴδια τῆς τραγῳδίας. διόπερ
ὅστις περὶ τραγῳδίας οἶδε σπουδαίας καὶ φαύλης,
οἶδε καὶ περὶ ἐπῶν· ἃ μὲν γὰρ ἐποποιία ἔχει,
20 ὑπάρχει τῇ τραγῳδίᾳ, ἃ δὲ αὐτῇ, οὐ πάντα ἐν τῇ
ἐποποιίᾳ.

VI περὶ οὖν τῆς ἐν ἑξαμέτροις μιμητικῆς καὶ περὶ
κωμῳδίας ὕστερον ἐροῦμεν, περὶ δὲ τραγῳδίας λέγωμεν
ἀναλαβόντες αὐτῆς ἐκ τῶν εἰρημένων τὸν γινόμενον ὅρον
25 τῆς οὐσίας. ἔστιν οὖν τραγῳδία μίμησις πράξεως σπου- 2
δαίας καὶ τελείας μέγεθος ἐχούσης, ἡδυσμένῳ λόγῳ χωρὶς
ἑκάστῳ τῶν εἰδῶν ἐν τοῖς μορίοις, δρώντων καὶ οὐ δι'
ἀπαγγελίας, δι' ἐλέου καὶ φόβου περαίνουσα τὴν τῶν
τοιούτων παθημάτων κάθαρσιν. λέγω δὲ ἡδυσμένον μὲν 3
30 λόγον τὸν ἔχοντα ῥυθμὸν καὶ ἁρμονίαν καὶ μέλος, τὸ δὲ
χωρὶς τοῖς εἴδεσι τὸ διὰ μέτρων ἔνια μόνον περαίνεσθαι
καὶ πάλιν ἕτερα διὰ μέλους. ἐπεὶ δὲ πράττοντες ποιοῦν- 4
ται τὴν μίμησιν, πρῶτον μὲν ἐξ ἀνάγκης ἂν εἴη τι μόριον
τραγῳδίας ὁ τῆς ὄψεως κόσμος, εἶτα μελοποιία καὶ λέξις,
35 ἐν τούτοις γὰρ ποιοῦνται τὴν μίμησιν. λέγω δὲ λέξιν

---

12. διαφέρει Hermann, confirmat Arabs.   <ἐπεὶ> ἡ μὲν Gomperz:
<ῇ> ἡ μὲν coni. Vahlen : ἡ μὲν γὰρ apogr.   15. διαφέρουσιν Christ.
16. ἔπεσιν et ἅπασι var. lect. Σ (Diels), 'in omnibus epesi' Arabs.
20. αὐτῆι Aᶜ: αὐτὴ apogr.: αὕτη Reiz.   24. ἀναλαβόντες Bernays :
ἀπολαβόντες codd.   27. ἑκάστῳ Tyrwhitt : ἑκάστου codd.   29.
παθημάτων corr. apogr., habuit iam Σ : μαθημάτων Aᶜ.   30. μέλος :
μέτρον Vettori : καὶ μέλος seclus. Tyrwhitt.   31. μόνον : μόρια Σ
('partes' Arabs).

length of the action : for Tragedy endeavours, as far as possible, to confine itself to a single revolution of the sun, or but slightly to exceed this limit; whereas the Epic action has no limits of time. This, then, is a second point of difference; though at first the same freedom was admitted in Tragedy as in Epic poetry.

Of their constituent parts some are common to both, 5 some peculiar to Tragedy. Whoever, therefore, knows what is good or bad Tragedy, knows also about Epic poetry : for all the elements of an Epic poem are found in Tragedy, but the elements of a Tragedy are not all found in the Epic poem.

VI   Of the poetry which imitates in hexameter verse, and of Comedy, we will speak hereafter. Let us now discuss Tragedy, resuming its formal definition, as resulting from what has been already said.

Tragedy, then, is an imitation of an action that is 2 serious, complete, and of a certain magnitude ; in language embellished with each kind of artistic ornament, the several kinds being found in separate parts of the play ; in the form of action, not of narrative ; through pity and fear effecting the proper purgation of these emotions. By 3 'language embellished,' I mean language into which rhythm, 'harmony,' and song enter. By 'the several kinds in separate parts,' I mean, that some parts are rendered through the medium of verse alone, others again with the aid of song.

Now as tragic imitation implies persons acting, it 4 necessarily follows, in the first place, that Scenic equipment will be a part of Tragedy. Next, Song and Diction, for these are the medium of imitation. By 'Diction'

μὲν αὐτὴν τὴν τῶν μέτρων σύνθεσιν, μελοποιίαν δὲ ὁ
τὴν δύναμιν φανερὰν ἔχει πᾶσιν. ἐπεὶ δὲ πράξεως ἐστὶ 5
μίμησις, πράττεται δὲ ὑπὸ τινῶν πραττόντων, οὓς ἀνάγκη
ποιούς τινας εἶναι κατά τε τὸ ἦθος καὶ τὴν διάνοιαν
1450 a (διὰ γὰρ τούτων καὶ τὰς πράξεις εἶναί φαμεν ποιάς
τινας, πέφυκεν δὲ αἰτίας δύο τῶν πράξεων εἶναι,
διάνοιαν καὶ ἦθος, καὶ κατὰ ταύτας καὶ τυγχάνουσι
καὶ ἀποτυγχάνουσι πάντες), ἔστιν δὴ τῆς μὲν πράξεως 6
5 ὁ μῦθος ἡ μίμησις· λέγω γὰρ μῦθον τοῦτον τὴν σύνθεσιν
τῶν πραγμάτων, τὰ δὲ ἤθη, καθ' ὃ ποιούς τινας εἶναί
φαμεν τοὺς πράττοντας, διάνοιαν δέ, ἐν ὅσοις λέγοντες
ἀποδεικνύασίν τι ἢ καὶ ἀποφαίνονται γνώμην. ἀνάγκη 7
οὖν πάσης τραγῳδίας μέρη εἶναι ἕξ, καθ' ἃ ποιά τις
10 ἐστὶν ἡ τραγῳδία· ταῦτα δ' ἐστὶ μῦθος καὶ ἤθη καὶ
λέξις καὶ διάνοια καὶ ὄψις καὶ μελοποιία. οἷς μὲν
γὰρ μιμοῦνται, δύο μέρη ἐστίν, ὡς δὲ μιμοῦνται, ἕν, ἃ
δὲ μιμοῦνται, τρία, καὶ παρὰ ταῦτα οὐδέν. τούτοις μὲν 8
οὖν <πάντες> ὡς εἰπεῖν κέχρηνται τοῖς εἴδεσιν· καὶ γὰρ
15 ὄψεις ἔχει πᾶν καὶ ἦθος καὶ μῦθον καὶ λέξιν καὶ μέλος
καὶ διάνοιαν ὡσαύτως. μέγιστον δὲ τούτων ἐστὶν ἡ τῶν 9

36. μέτρων: ὀνομάτων Hermann, collato 1450 b 16.   37. πᾶσιν Maggi:
πᾶσαν codd.   40. διὰ δὲ Zeller.   διὰ γὰρ τούτων ... πάντες in
parenthesi Thurot.   1450 a 2. πέφυκεν δὲ apogr.: πέφυκεν Aᶜ.
αἰτίας Christ: αἴτια codd.   3. καὶ κατὰ ... πάντες nescio an post ποιάς
τινας transponere praestet (Christ).   4. δὴ Eucken: δὲ codd.   5.
τοῦτον: τοῦτο Maggi: seclus. Christ (cf. Arab.).   6. καθὸ Aᶜ: καθ' ἃ
apogr.   9. καθοποία Aᶜ: καθ' ἃ ποιά apogr.   14. οὐκ ὀλίγοι αὐτῶν
ὡς εἰπεῖν codd.: ὀλίγου αὐτῶν <ἅπαντες> ὡς εἰπεῖν Bywater: οὐκ ὀλίγοι
αὐτῶν <ἀλλὰ πάντες> ὡς εἰπεῖν Bursian: οὐκ ὀλίγοι αὐτῶν om. Σ, sed
πάντως (? = πάντες) add. Σ (vid. Margoliouth).   Deleto igitur tanquam
gloss. οὐκ ὀλίγοι αὐτῶν, scripsi <πάντες> ὡς εἰπεῖν: cf. Rhet. i. 1. 1354 a
12, ὀλίγου codd., οὐδὲν ὡς εἰπεῖν Aᶜ in marg., ubi ὀλίγου glossema esse
suspicor, veram lect. οὐδὲν ὡς εἰπεῖν.   Viam monstravit Diels, qui tamen
πάντες quoque omisso, τούτοις μὲν οὖν ὡς εἰπεῖν scripsit: οὐκ ὀλίγοι αὐτῶν
<ἀλλ' ἐν πᾶσι πάντες> Gomperz: οὐκ ὀλίγοι αὐτῶν <ἀλλὰ πάντες πᾶσι>
Zeller: <πάντες ἐν πᾶσιν αὐτῆς> Susemihl.   15. πᾶν iure suspexeris.

I mean the mere metrical arrangement of the words: as for 'Song,' it is a term whose sense every one understands.

Again, Tragedy is the imitation of an action; and an 5 action implies personal agents, who necessarily possess certain distinctive qualities both of character and thought. It is these that determine the qualities of actions themselves; these—thought and character—are the two natural causes from which actions spring: on these causes, again, all success or failure depends.   Hence, the 6 Plot is the imitation of the action:—for by plot I here mean the arrangement of the incidents.   By Character I mean that in virtue of which we ascribe certain qualities to the agents.   Thought is required wherever a statement is proved, or, it may be, a general truth enunciated. Every Tragedy, therefore, must have six parts, which 7 parts determine its quality—namely, Plot, Character, Diction, Thought, Scenery, Song.   Two of the parts constitute the medium of imitation, one the manner, and three the objects of imitation.   And these complete the list. These elements have been employed, we may say, by 8 the poets to a man; in fact, every play contains Scenic accessories as well as Character, Plot, Diction, Song, and Thought.

But most important of all is the structure of the 9

πραγμάτων σύστασις· ἡ γὰρ τραγῳδία μίμησίς ἐστιν
οὐκ ἀνθρώπων ἀλλὰ πράξεως καὶ βίου· <ὁ δὲ βίος> ἐν
πράξει ἐστὶν καὶ τὸ τέλος πρᾶξίς τις ἐστίν, οὐ ποιότης·
20 εἰσὶν δὲ κατὰ μὲν τὰ ἤθη ποιοί τινες, κατὰ δὲ τὰς 10
πράξεις εὐδαίμονες ἢ τοὐναντίον. οὔκουν ὅπως τὰ ἤθη
μιμήσωνται πράττουσιν, ἀλλὰ τὰ ἤθη συμπαραλαμβά-
νουσιν διὰ τὰς πράξεις· ὥστε τὰ πράγματα καὶ ὁ μῦθος
τέλος τῆς τραγῳδίας, τὸ δὲ τέλος μέγιστον ἁπάντων.
25 ἔτι ἄνευ μὲν πράξεως οὐκ ἂν γένοιτο τραγῳδία, ἄνευ 11
δὲ ἠθῶν γένοιτ᾽ ἄν. αἱ γὰρ τῶν νέων τῶν πλείστων
ἀήθεις τραγῳδίαι εἰσὶν καὶ ὅλως ποιηταὶ πολλοὶ τοιοῦτοι,
οἷον καὶ τῶν γραφέων Ζεῦξις πρὸς Πολύγνωτον πέπον-
θεν· ὁ μὲν γὰρ Πολύγνωτος ἀγαθὸς ἠθογράφος, ἡ δὲ
30 Ζεύξιδος γραφὴ οὐδὲν ἔχει ἦθος. ἔτι ἐάν τις ἐφεξῆς 12
θῇ ῥήσεις ἠθικὰς καὶ λέξει καὶ διανοίᾳ εὖ πεποιημένας,
οὐ ποιήσει ὃ ἦν τῆς τραγῳδίας ἔργον, ἀλλὰ πολὺ
μᾶλλον ἡ καταδεεστέροις τούτοις κεχρημένη τραγῳδία,
ἔχουσα δὲ μῦθον καὶ σύστασιν πραγμάτων. πρὸς 13
35 δὲ τούτοις τὰ μέγιστα οἷς ψυχαγωγεῖ ἡ τραγῳδία,
τοῦ μύθου μέρη ἐστίν, αἵ τε περιπέτειαι καὶ ἀναγνωρίσεις. ἔτι σημεῖον ὅτι καὶ οἱ ἐγχειροῦντες ποιεῖν 14
πρότερον δύνανται τῇ λέξει καὶ τοῖς ἤθεσιν ἀκριβοῦν
ἢ τὰ πράγματα συνιστάναι, οἷον καὶ οἱ πρῶτοι ποιηταὶ
40 σχεδὸν ἅπαντες. ἀρχὴ μὲν οὖν καὶ οἷον ψυχὴ ὁ μῦθος

18. ἀλλὰ πράξεως καὶ βίου καὶ ἡ εὐδαιμονία καὶ ἡ κακοδαιμονία ἐν πράξει codd.,
sed alio spectat Arabs ('sed in operibus et vita. Et <vita> est in
opere'); unde Margoliouth ἀλλὰ πράξεως καὶ βίου, <ὁ δὲ βίος> ἐν πράξει,
quod probant Diels, Zeller, Susemihl. Codicum lect. ita supplet Vahlen,
καὶ εὐδαιμονίας <καὶ κακοδαιμονίας, ἡ δὲ εὐδαιμονία> καὶ ἡ κακοδαιμονία.

22. πράττουσιν : πράττοντας ποιοῦσιν coni. Vahlen.   συμπαραλαμβάνουσι
Guelf. : συμπαραλαμβάνουσι Spengel : συμπεριλαμβάνουσιν Aᶜ.   29.
ἀγαθῶν Ald.   31. λέξει καὶ διανοίᾳ Vahlen : habuit iam Σ : λέξεις καὶ
διανοίας codd.   32. οὐ add. apogr. : 'nequaquam' Arabs : fort. οὐ-
δαμῶς Margoliouth.   39. συνιστάναι Thurot : συνίστασθαι codd.

incidents.   For Tragedy is an imitation, not of men, but of an action and of life, and life consists in action, and its end is a mode of action, not a quality.   Now 10 character determines men's qualities, but it is by their actions that they are happy or the reverse.   Dramatic action, therefore, is not with a view to the representation of character: character comes in as subsidiary to the action.   Hence the incidents and the plot are the end of a tragedy; and the end is the chief thing of all.   Again, 11 without action there cannot be a tragedy; there may be without character.   The tragedies of most of our modern poets fail in the rendering of character; and of poets in general this is often true.   It is the same in painting; and here lies the difference between Zeuxis and Polygnotus. Polygnotus delineates character well: the style of Zeuxis is devoid of ethical quality.   Again, if you string 12 together a set of speeches expressive of character, and well finished in point of diction and thought, you will not produce the essential tragic effect nearly so well as with a play which, however deficient in these respects, yet has a plot and artistically constructed incidents. Besides which, the most powerful elements of emotional 13 interest in Tragedy—Reversal or Recoil of the Action, and Recognition scenes—are parts of the plot.   A further 14 proof is, that novices in the art attain to finish of diction and precision of portraiture before they can construct the plot.   It is the same with almost all the early poets.

The Plot, then, is the first principle, and, as it were,

τῆς τραγῳδίας, δεύτερον δὲ τὰ ἤθη.   παραπλήσιον γάρ 15
1450 b ἐστιν καὶ ἐπὶ τῆς γραφικῆς· εἰ γάρ τις ἐναλείψειε τοῖς
καλλίστοις φαρμάκοις χύδην, οὐκ ἂν ὁμοίως εὐφράνειεν
καὶ λευκογραφήσας εἰκόνα.   ἔστιν τε μίμησις πράξεως
καὶ διὰ ταύτην μάλιστα τῶν πραττόντων.   τρίτον δὲ ἡ
5 διάνοια.   τοῦτο δέ ἐστιν τὸ λέγειν δύνασθαι τὰ ἐνόντα 16
καὶ τὰ ἁρμόττοντα, ὅπερ ἐπὶ τῶν λόγων τῆς πολιτικῆς
καὶ ῥητορικῆς ἔργον ἐστίν· οἱ μὲν γὰρ ἀρχαῖοι πολι-
τικῶς ἐποίουν λέγοντας, οἱ δὲ νῦν ῥητορικῶς.   ἔστιν δὲ 17
ἦθος μὲν τὸ τοιοῦτον ὃ δηλοῖ τὴν προαίρεσιν ὁποῖά τις
10 [προ]αιρεῖται ἢ φεύγει· διόπερ οὐκ ἔχουσιν ἦθος τῶν.
λόγων ἐν οἷς οὐκ ἔστι δῆλον ἢ ἐν οἷς μηδ' ὅλως ἔστιν
ὅ τι [προ]αιρεῖται ἢ φεύγει ὁ λέγων.   διάνοια δέ, ἐν
οἷς ἀποδεικνύουσί τι ὡς ἔστιν ἢ ὡς οὐκ ἔστιν ἢ καθόλου
τι ἀποφαίνονται.   τέταρτον δὲ τῶν λεγομένων ἡ λέξις· 18
15 λέγω δέ, ὥσπερ πρότερον εἴρηται, λέξιν εἶναι τὴν διὰ
τῆς ὀνομασίας ἑρμηνείαν, ὃ καὶ ἐπὶ τῶν ἐμμέτρων καὶ
ἐπὶ τῶν λόγων ἔχει τὴν αὐτὴν δύναμιν.   τῶν δὲ λοιπῶν 19
[πέντε] ἡ μελοποιία μέγιστον τῶν ἡδυσμάτων, ἡ δὲ ὄψις
ψυχαγωγικὸν μέν, ἀτεχνότατον δὲ καὶ ἥκιστα οἰκεῖον
20 τῆς ποιητικῆς· <ἴσ>ως γὰρ τῆς τραγῳδίας δύναμις καὶ
ἄνευ ἀγῶνος καὶ ὑποκριτῶν ἔστιν, ἔτι δὲ κυριωτέρα περὶ

41. παραπλήσιον . . . εἰκόνα supra collocavit post πραγμάτων v. 34 Castelvetro.   1450 b 3. τε codd. : γὰρ Hermann.   6. ἐπὶ τῶν λόγων secl.
M. Schmidt.   9. ὁποῖά τις ἐν οἷς οὐκ ἔστι δῆλον ἢ προαιρεῖται ἢ φεύγει·
διόπερ οὐκ ἔχουσιν ἦθος τῶν λόγων ἐν οἷς μηδ' ὅλως ἔστιν ὅ τις (ὅ τι apogr.)
προαιρεῖται ἢ φεύγει ὁ λέγων Aᶜ.   Lectionem in textu receptam dedit
Gomperz, alios secutus (cf. Christ).   Deerant in Σ ἐν οἷς οὐκ ἔστι δῆλον ἢ
προαιρεῖται ἢ φεύγει, unde coni. Margoliouth ὃ δηλοῖ τὴν προαίρεσιν, ὁποία
τις· omissis verbis ἐν οἷς . . . φεύγει·   Susp. Susemihl ἐν οἷς οὐκ ἔστι . . .
ἢ φεύγει et ἐν οἷς μηδ' ὅλως ἔστιν . . . ἢ φεύγει var. lect. esse.   12. ὅ τι
apogr. : ὅ τις Aᶜ.   14. τῶν λεγομένων Gomperz : τῶν μὲν λόγων codd.
quod aut corrigendum aut delendum esse censeo.   18. πέντε Aᶜ :
seclus. Spengel : om. iam Σ : πέμπτον apogr.   20. ἴσως Meiser : ὅλως
Gomperz : ὡς Aᶜ : ἡ apogr.

the soul of a tragedy: Character holds the second place.
1450 b A similar fact is seen in painting. The most beautiful 15
colours, laid on confusedly, will not give as much pleasure
as the chalk outline of a portrait. Thus Tragedy is the
imitation of an action, and of the agents, mainly with a
view to the action.

Third in order is Thought,—that is, the faculty of 16
saying what is possible and pertinent in given circumstances. In the case of oratory, this is the function of
the political art and of the art of rhetoric: and so indeed
the older poets make their characters speak the language
of civic life; the poets of our time, the language of the
rhetoricians. Character is that which reveals moral 17
purpose, showing what kind of things a man chooses or
avoids. Speeches, therefore, which do not make this
manifest, or in which the speaker does not choose or
avoid anything whatever, are not expressive of character.
Thought, on the other hand, is found where something is ✓
proved to be or not to be, or a general maxim is
enunciated.

Fourth among the elements enumerated comes 18
Diction; by which I mean, as has been already said, the
expression of our meaning in words; and its essence is
the same both in verse and prose.

Of the remaining elements Song holds the chief place 19
among the embellishments.

Scenery has, indeed, an emotional attraction of its
own, but, of all the parts, it is the least artistic, and
connected least with the art of poetry. For the power
of Tragedy, we may be sure, is felt even apart from
representation and actors. Besides, the production of

τὴν ὑπεργασίαν τῶν ὄψεων ἡ τοῦ σκευοποιοῦ τέχνη τῆς
τῶν ποιητῶν ἐστιν.

VII   διωρισμένων δὲ τούτων, λέγωμεν μετὰ ταῦτα ποίαν
25 τινὰ δεῖ τὴν σύστασιν εἶναι τῶν πραγμάτων, ἐπειδὴ
τοῦτο καὶ πρῶτον καὶ μέγιστον τῆς τραγῳδίας ἐστίν.
κεῖται δὴ ἡμῖν τὴν τραγῳδίαν τελείας καὶ ὅλης πράξεως 2
εἶναι μίμησιν ἐχούσης τι μέγεθος· ἔστιν γὰρ ὅλον καὶ
μηδὲν ἔχον μέγεθος. ὅλον δέ ἐστιν τὸ ἔχον ἀρχὴν καὶ 3
30 μέσον καὶ τελευτήν. ἀρχὴ δέ ἐστιν ὃ αὐτὸ μὲν μὴ ἐξ
ἀνάγκης μετ᾽ ἄλλο ἐστίν, μετ᾽ ἐκεῖνο δ᾽ ἕτερον πέφυκεν
εἶναι ἢ γίνεσθαι, τελευτὴ δὲ τοὐναντίον ὃ αὐτὸ μετ᾽
ἄλλο πέφυκεν εἶναι ἢ ἐξ ἀνάγκης ἢ ὡς ἐπὶ τὸ πολύ,
μετὰ δὲ τοῦτο ἄλλο οὐδέν, μέσον δὲ ὃ καὶ αὐτὸ μετ᾽
35 ἄλλο καὶ μετ᾽ ἐκεῖνο ἕτερον. δεῖ ἄρα τοὺς συνεστῶτας
εὖ μύθους μήθ᾽ ὁπόθεν ἔτυχεν ἄρχεσθαι μήθ᾽ ὅπου
ἔτυχε τελευτᾶν, ἀλλὰ κεχρῆσθαι ταῖς εἰρημέναις ἰδέαις.
ἔτι δ᾽ ἐπεὶ τὸ καλὸν καὶ ζῷον καὶ ἅπαν πρᾶγμα ὃ 4
συνέστηκεν ἐκ τινῶν οὐ μόνον ταῦτα τεταγμένα δεῖ
40 ἔχειν ἀλλὰ καὶ μέγεθος ὑπάρχειν μὴ τὸ τυχόν· τὸ γὰρ
καλὸν ἐν μεγέθει καὶ τάξει ἐστίν, διὸ οὔτε πάμμικρον
ἄν τι γένοιτο καλὸν ζῷον, συγχεῖται γὰρ ἡ θεωρία
ἐγγὺς τοῦ ἀναισθήτου χρόνου γινομένη, οὔτε παμμέγεθες,
1451 a οὐ γὰρ ἅμα ἡ θεωρία γίνεται ἀλλ᾽ οἴχεται τοῖς θεωροῦσι
τὸ ἓν καὶ τὸ ὅλον ἐκ τῆς θεωρίας, οἷον εἰ μυρίων σταδίων
εἴη ζῷον· ὥστε δεῖ καθάπερ ἐπὶ τῶν σωμάτων καὶ ἐπὶ 5
τῶν ζῴων ἔχειν μὲν μέγεθος, τοῦτο δὲ εὐσύνοπτον εἶναι,

---

27. δὴ Bywater: δ᾽ Aᶜ.   30. μὴ ἐξ ἀνάγκης codd.: ἐξ ἀνάγκης μὴ
Pazzi.   41. πᾶν μικρὸν Aᶜ: πάμμικρον Riccardianus 16: πάνυ μικρὸν
Laurentianus lx. 16.   43. χρόνου seclus. Bonitz, Spengel: tutatur
Arabs.   πᾶν μέγεθος Aᶜ: παμμέγεθες Riccardianus 16: πάνυ μέγα
Laurentianus lx. 16.   1451 a 3. σωμάτων: συστημάτων Bywater.

spectacular effects depends more on the art of the stage machinist than on that of the poet.

VII   These principles being established, let us now discuss the proper structure of the Plot, since this is the first and most important part of Tragedy.

Now, according to our definition, Tragedy is an 2 imitation of an action that is complete, and whole, and of a certain magnitude; for there may be a whole that is wanting in magnitude. A whole is that which has 3 a beginning, a middle, and an end. A beginning is that which does not itself follow anything by causal necessity, but after which something naturally is or comes to be. An end, on the contrary, is that which itself naturally follows some other thing, either by necessity, or as a rule, but has nothing following it. A middle is that which follows something as some other thing follows it. A well constructed plot, therefore, must neither begin nor end at haphazard, but conform to these principles.

Again, a beautiful object, whether it be a picture of 4 a living organism or any whole composed of parts, must not only have an orderly arrangement of parts, but must also be of a certain magnitude; for beauty depends on magnitude and order. Hence an exceedingly small picture cannot be beautiful; for the view of it is confused, the object being seen in an almost imperceptible moment of time. Nor, again, can one of vast size be 1451 a beautiful; for as the eye cannot take it all in at once, the unity and sense of the whole is lost for the spectator; as for instance if there were a picture a thousand miles long. As, therefore, in the case of animate bodies and 5 pictures a certain magnitude is necessary, and a magni-

5 οὕτω καὶ ἐπὶ τῶν μύθων ἔχειν μὲν μῆκος, τοῦτο δὲ
εὐμνημόνευτον εἶναι. τοῦ μήκους ὅρος <ὁ> μὲν πρὸς 6
τοὺς ἀγῶνας καὶ τὴν αἴσθησιν οὐ τῆς τέχνης ἐστίν· εἰ
γὰρ ἔδει ἑκατὸν τραγῳδίας ἀγωνίζεσθαι, πρὸς κλεψύδρας
ἂν ἠγωνίζοντο, ὥσπερ ποτὲ καὶ ἄλλοτε εἰώθασιν. ὁ δὲ 7
10 κατ' αὐτὴν τὴν φύσιν τοῦ πράγματος ὅρος, ἀεὶ μὲν ὁ
μείζων μέχρι τοῦ σύνδηλος εἶναι καλλίων ἐστὶ κατὰ
τὸ μέγεθος· ὡς δὲ ἁπλῶς διορίσαντας εἰπεῖν, ἐν ὅσῳ
μεγέθει κατὰ τὸ εἰκὸς ἢ τὸ ἀναγκαῖον ἐφεξῆς γιγνομένων
συμβαίνει εἰς εὐτυχίαν ἐκ δυστυχίας ἢ ἐξ εὐτυχίας εἰς
15 δυστυχίαν μεταβάλλειν, ἱκανὸς ὅρος ἐστὶν τοῦ μεγέθους.

VIII μῦθος δ' ἐστὶν εἰς οὐχ ὥσπερ τινὲς οἴονται ἐὰν περὶ
ἕνα ᾖ· πολλὰ γὰρ καὶ ἄπειρα τῷ ἑνὶ συμβαίνει, ἐξ ὧν
[ἐνίων] οὐδέν ἐστιν ἕν· οὕτως δὲ καὶ πράξεις ἑνὸς
πολλαί εἰσιν, ἐξ ὧν μία οὐδεμία γίνεται πρᾶξις. διὸ 2
20 πάντες ἐοίκασιν ἁμαρτάνειν ὅσοι τῶν ποιητῶν Ἡρα-
κληΐδα Θησηΐδα καὶ τὰ τοιαῦτα ποιήματα πεποιήκασιν·
οἴονται γάρ, ἐπεὶ εἰς ἦν ὁ Ἡρακλῆς, ἕνα καὶ τὸν μῦθον
εἶναι προσήκειν. ὁ δ' Ὅμηρος ὥσπερ καὶ τὰ ἄλλα 3
διαφέρει καὶ τοῦτ' ἔοικεν καλῶς ἰδεῖν ἤτοι διὰ τέχνην
25 ἢ διὰ φύσιν· Ὀδύσσειαν γὰρ ποιῶν οὐκ ἐποίησεν
ἅπαντα ὅσα αὐτῷ συνέβη, οἷον πληγῆναι μὲν ἐν τῷ
Παρνασσῷ, μανῆναι δὲ προσποιήσασθαι ἐν τῷ ἀγερμῷ,

---

6. ὁ add. Bursian : πρὸς μὲν apogr.   8. κλεψύδραν apogr.   9.
εἰώθασιν M. Schmidt: 'sicut solemus dicere etiam aliquo tempore et
aliquando' Arabs: φασιν codd.   17. τῷ ἑνὶ apogr. : τῶι γένει Aᶜ (cf.
1447 a 17).   18. ἐνίων seclus. Spengel.

tude which may be easily embraced in one view; so in
the plot, a certain length is necessary, and a length
which can be easily embraced by the memory. The 6
limit of length in relation to dramatic competition· and
sensuous presentment, is no part of artistic theory. For
had it been the rule for a hundred tragedies to compete
together, the performance would have been regulated by
the water-clock,—as indeed is the practice in certain
other contests. But the limit as fixed by the nature
of the drama itself is this:—the greater the length, the
more beautiful will the piece be, so far as beauty depends
on size, provided that the whole be perspicuous. And
to define the matter roughly, we may say that the
proper magnitude is comprised within such limits, that
the sequence of events, according to the law of probability
or necessity, will admit of a change from bad fortune to
good, or from good fortune to bad.

VIII   Unity of plot does not, as some persons think, consist
in the unity of the hero. For infinitely various are the
incidents in one man's life, which cannot be reduced to
unity; and so, too, there are many actions of one man
out of which we cannot make one action. Hence the 2
error, as it appears, of all poets who have composed a
Heracleid, a Theseid, or other poems of the kind. They
imagine that as Heracles was one man, the story of
Heracles must also be a unity. But Homer, as in all 3
else he is of surpassing merit, here too—whether from
art or natural genius—seems to have happily discerned
the truth. In composing the Odyssey he did not include
all the adventures of Odysseus—such as his wound on
Parnassus, or his feigned madness at the mustering of

ὧν οὐδὲν θατέρου γενομένου ἀναγκαῖον ἦν ἢ εἰκὸς
θάτερον γενέσθαι, ἀλλὰ περὶ μίαν πρᾶξιν οἵαν λέγομεν
30 τὴν Ὀδύσσειαν συνέστησεν, ὁμοίως δὲ καὶ τὴν Ἰλιάδα.

χρὴ οὖν καθάπερ καὶ ἐν ταῖς ἄλλαις μιμητικαῖς ἡ μία 4
μίμησις ἑνός ἐστιν οὕτω καὶ τὸν μῦθον, ἐπεὶ πράξεως
μίμησίς ἐστι, μιᾶς τε εἶναι καὶ ταύτης ὅλης καὶ τὰ μέρη
συνεστάναι τῶν πραγμάτων οὕτως, ὥστε μετατιθεμένου
35 τινὸς μέρους ἢ ἀφαιρουμένου διαφέρεσθαι καὶ κινεῖσθαι
τὸ ὅλον· ὃ γὰρ προσὸν ἢ μὴ προσὸν μηδὲν ποιεῖ ἐπίδηλον, οὐδὲν μόριον τοῦ ὅλου ἐστίν.

IX φανερὸν δὲ ἐκ τῶν εἰρημένων καὶ ὅτι οὐ τὸ τὰ
γενόμενα λέγειν, τοῦτο ποιητοῦ ἔργον ἐστίν, ἀλλ' οἷα ἂν
40 γένοιτο καὶ τὰ δυνατὰ κατὰ τὸ εἰκὸς ἢ τὸ ἀναγκαῖον.
1451 b ὁ γὰρ ἱστορικὸς καὶ ὁ ποιητὴς οὐ τῷ ἢ ἔμμετρα λέγειν 2
ἢ ἄμετρα διαφέρουσιν, εἴη γὰρ ἂν τὰ Ἡροδότου εἰς
μέτρα τεθῆναι, καὶ οὐδὲν ἧττον ἂν εἴη ἱστορία τις μετὰ
μέτρου ἢ ἄνευ μέτρων, ἀλλὰ τούτῳ διαφέρει, τῷ τὸν
5 μὲν τὰ γενόμενα λέγειν, τὸν δὲ οἷα ἂν γένοιτο. διὸ καὶ 3
φιλοσοφώτερον καὶ σπουδαιότερον ποίησις ἱστορίας ἐστίν·
ἡ μὲν γὰρ ποίησις μᾶλλον τὰ καθόλου, ἡ δ' ἱστορία τὰ
καθ' ἕκαστον λέγει. ἔστιν δὲ καθόλου μέν, τῷ ποίῳ τὰ 4
ποῖα ἄττα συμβαίνει λέγειν ἢ πράττειν κατὰ τὸ εἰκὸς
10 ἢ τὸ ἀναγκαῖον, οὗ στοχάζεται ἡ ποίησις ὀνόματα
ἐπιτιθεμένη, τὸ δὲ καθ' ἕκαστον, τί Ἀλκιβιάδης ἔπραξεν
ἢ τί ἔπαθεν. ἐπὶ μὲν οὖν τῆς κωμῳδίας ἤδη τοῦτο, 5
δῆλον γέγονεν· συστήσαντες γὰρ τὸν μῦθον διὰ τῶν

28. ἦν ἢ apogr.: ἦν Ἀᶜ.   29. λέγομεν apogr.: λέγοιμεν Ἀᶜ: ἂν
λέγοιμεν Vahlen.   33. καὶ ταύτης: ταύτης καὶ Susemihl.   35.
διαφέρεσθαι: ? διαφορεῖσθαι, cf. de Div. 2, 464 b 13: διαφθείρεσθαι coni.
Margoliouth: habuit fort. utramque lect. Σ, 'corrumpatur et confundatur'
Arabs.   36. ποιεῖ, ἐπίδηλον ὡς apogr.   38. οὐ τὸ apogr.: οὕτω Ἀᶜ.
40. [καὶ τὰ δυνατὰ] Maggi.   1451 b 4. τούτῳ . . . τῷ apogr.: τοῦτο
. . . τῷ Ἀᶜ: τοῦτο . . . τὸ Spengel.   10. τὸ apogr.: τὸν Ἀᶜ.

the host—incidents between which there was no necessary
or probable connexion : but he made the Odyssey, and
likewise the Iliad, to centre round an action, that in our
sense of the word is one.   As therefore, in the other 4
imitative arts, the imitation is one, when the object imitated
is one, so the plot, being an imitation of an action, must
imitate one action and that a whole, the structural union
of the parts being such that, if any one of them is
displaced or removed, the whole will be disjointed and
disturbed.   For a thing whose presence or absence makes
no visible difference, is not an organic part of the
whole.

IX   It is, moreover, evident from what has been said,
that it is not the function of the poet to relate what
has happened, but what may happen,—what is possible
according to the law of probability or necessity.   The 2
1451 b poet and the historian differ not by writing in verse or
in prose.   The work of Herodotus might be put into
verse, and it would still be a species of history, with
metre no less than without it.   The true difference is
that one relates what has happened, the other what may
happen.   Poetry, therefore, is a more philosophical and 3
a higher thing than history : for poetry tends to express
the universal, history the particular.   By the universal 4
I mean how a person of given character will on occasion
speak or act, according to the law of probability or
necessity ; and it is this universality at which poetry
aims in the names she attaches to the personages.   The
particular is—for example—what Alcibiades did or
suffered.   In Comedy this is already apparent : for here 5
the poet first constructs the plot on the lines of prob-

εἰκότων οὐ τὰ τυχόντα ὀνόματα ὑποτιθέασιν, καὶ οὐχ
15 ὥσπερ οἱ ἰαμβοποιοὶ περὶ τὸν καθ' ἕκαστον ποιοῦσιν.
ἐπὶ δὲ τῆς τραγῳδίας τῶν γενομένων ὀνομάτων ἀντ- 6
έχονται. αἴτιον δ' ὅτι πιθανόν ἐστι τὸ δυνατόν. τὰ
μὲν οὖν μὴ γενόμενα οὔπω πιστεύομεν εἶναι δυνατά, τὰ
δὲ γενόμενα φανερὸν ὅτι δυνατά, οὐ γὰρ ἂν ἐγένετο, εἰ
20 ἦν ἀδύνατα. οὐ μὴν ἀλλὰ καὶ ἐν ταῖς τραγῳδίαις ἐν 7
ἐνίαις μὲν ἓν ἢ δύο τῶν γνωρίμων ἐστὶν ὀνομάτων, τὰ
δὲ ἄλλα πεποιημένα, ἐν ἐνίαις δὲ οὐδ' ἕν, οἷον ἐν τῷ
Ἀγάθωνος Ἄνθει· ὁμοίως γὰρ ἐν τούτῳ τά τε πράγματα
καὶ τὰ ὀνόματα πεποίηται, καὶ οὐδὲν ἧττον εὐφραίνει·
25 ὥστ' οὐ πάντως εἶναι ζητητέον τῶν παραδεδομένων 8
μύθων, περὶ οὓς αἱ τραγῳδίαι εἰσίν, ἀντέχεσθαι. καὶ
γὰρ γελοῖον τοῦτο ζητεῖν, ἐπεὶ καὶ τὰ γνώριμα ὀλίγοις
γνώριμά ἐστιν ἀλλ' ὅμως εὐφραίνει πάντας. δῆλον οὖν 9
ἐκ τούτων ὅτι τὸν ποιητὴν μᾶλλον τῶν μύθων εἶναι δεῖ
30 ποιητὴν ἢ τῶν μέτρων, ὅσῳ ποιητὴς κατὰ τὴν μίμησίν
ἐστιν, μιμεῖται δὲ τὰς πράξεις. κἂν ἄρα συμβῇ γενόμενα ποιεῖν, οὐδὲν ἧττον ποιητής ἐστι· τῶν γὰρ γενομένων ἔνια οὐδὲν κωλύει τοιαῦτα εἶναι οἷα ἂν εἰκὸς
γενέσθαι καὶ δυνατὰ γενέσθαι, καθ' ὃ ἐκεῖνος αὐτῶν
35 ποιητής ἐστιν.
    τῶν δὲ ἄλλων μύθων καὶ πράξεων αἱ ἐπεισοδιώδεις 10

14. οὐ (vel οὐχὶ) scripsi : 'nequaquam' Arabs: οὕτω codd., cf. 1451 a
38. ἐπιτιθέασι apogr., Bekker.   15. τὸν A^c: τῶν apogr.   20.
ἐν ἐνίαις apogr., Susemihl : ἐνίαις A^c.   22. ἐν τῷ Ἀγάθωνος ἄνθει :
'quemadmodum si quis unum esse bonum statuit' Arabs: male Syrus
legisse videtur ἐν τὸ ἀγαθὸν ὃς ἂν θῇ (Margoliouth). Pro ἄνθει coni. Ἀνθεῖ
(dat. Ἀνθεύς), cf. Parthenius περὶ ἐρωτικῶν παθημάτων, Mackail.   25.
εἶναι seclus. Spengel.   26. αἱ <εὐδοκιμοῦσαι> τραγῳδίαι coni.
Vahlen.   34. καὶ <οὐκ ἄλλως> δυνατὰ Susemihl: καὶ δυνατὰ γενέσθαι seclus. Vorländer, om. Arabs.   36. τῶν δὲ ἄλλων Tyrwhitt : τῶν
δὲ ἁπλῶν codd. : ἁπλῶς δὲ τῶν Castelvetro.

ability, and then inserts characteristic names;—unlike
the lampooners who write about particular individuals.
But tragedians still keep to real names, the reason being 6
that what is possible is credible: what has not happened
we do not at once feel sure to be possible : but what has
happened is manifestly possible; otherwise it would not
have happened.   Still there are some tragedies in which 7
there are only one or two well known names, the rest
being fictitious.   In others, none are well known,—as
in Agathon's Flower, where incidents and names alike
are fictitious, and yet they give none the less pleasure.
We must not, therefore, at all costs keep to the received 8
legends, which are the usual subjects of Tragedy.   Indeed,
it would be absurd to attempt it; for even familiar subjects are familiar only to a few, and yet give pleasure
to all.   It clearly follows that the poet or 'maker' 9
should be the maker of plots rather than of verses;
since he is a poet because he imitates,. and what he
imitates are actions.   And even if he chances to take
an historical subject, he is none the less a poet; for
there is no reason why some events that have actually
happened should not conform to the law of the probable
and possible, and in virtue of that quality in them he is
their poet or maker.

Of all plots and actions the epeisodic are the worst. 10

εἰσὶν χείρισται. λέγω δ᾽ ἐπεισοδιώδη μῦθον ἐν ᾧ τὰ
ἐπεισόδια μετ᾽ ἄλληλα οὔτ᾽ εἰκὸς οὔτ᾽ ἀνάγκη εἶναι.
τοιαῦται δὲ ποιοῦνται ὑπὸ μὲν τῶν φαύλων ποιητῶν δι᾽
40 αὐτούς, ὑπὸ δὲ τῶν ἀγαθῶν διὰ τοὺς ὑποκριτάς· ἀγωνί-
σματα γὰρ ποιοῦντες καὶ παρὰ τὴν δύναμιν παρατεί-
1452 a νοντες μῦθον πολλάκις διαστρέφειν ἀναγκάζονται τὸ
ἐφεξῆς. ἐπεὶ δὲ οὐ μόνον τελείας ἐστὶ πράξεως ἡ μίμησις 11
ἀλλὰ καὶ φοβερῶν καὶ ἐλεεινῶν, ταῦτα δὲ γίνεται [καὶ]
μάλιστα ὅταν γένηται παρὰ τὴν δόξαν, καὶ μᾶλλον
5 <ὅταν> δι᾽ ἄλληλα· τὸ γὰρ θαυμαστὸν οὕτως ἕξει 12
μᾶλλον ἢ εἰ ἀπὸ τοῦ αὐτομάτου καὶ τῆς τύχης, ἐπεὶ καὶ
τῶν ἀπὸ τύχης ταῦτα θαυμασιώτατα δοκεῖ ὅσα ὥσπερ
ἐπίτηδες φαίνεται γεγονέναι, οἷον ὡς ὁ ἀνδριὰς ὁ τοῦ
Μίτυος ἐν Ἄργει ἀπέκτεινεν τὸν αἴτιον τοῦ θανάτου τῷ
10 Μίτυι, θεωροῦντι ἐμπεσών· ἔοικε γὰρ τὰ τοιαῦτα οὐκ
εἰκῇ γενέσθαι. ὥστε ἀνάγκη τοὺς τοιούτους εἶναι
καλλίους μύθους.

X   εἰσὶ δὲ τῶν μύθων οἱ μὲν ἁπλοῖ οἱ δὲ πεπλεγμένοι,
καὶ γὰρ αἱ πράξεις ὧν μιμήσεις οἱ μῦθοί εἰσιν ὑπάρχου-
15 σιν εὐθὺς οὖσαι τοιαῦται. λέγω δὲ ἁπλῆν μὲν πρᾶξιν 2
ἧς γινομένης ὥσπερ ὥρισται συνεχοῦς καὶ μιᾶς ἄνευ
περιπετείας ἢ ἀναγνωρισμοῦ ἡ μετάβασις γίνεται,
πεπλεγμένη δ᾽ ἐστὶν ἧς μετὰ ἀναγνωρισμοῦ ἢ περιπετείας ἢ ἀμφοῖν ἡ μετάβασίς ἐστιν. ταῦτα δὲ δεῖ 3
20 γίνεσθαι ἐξ αὐτῆς τῆς συστάσεως τοῦ μύθου, ὥστε ἐκ

40. ὑποκριτὰς Aᶜ: κριτὰς apogr.   41. παρατείνοντες apogr., Bekker:
παρατείναντες Aᶜ.   1452 a 2. ἡ seclus. Gomperz.   3. καὶ seclus.
Susemihl.   καὶ μάλιστα καὶ μᾶλλον ὅταν γένηται παρὰ τὴν δόξαν codd.:
correxit Reiz: codd. lect. tuetur Tucker, καὶ κάλλιον scripto pro καὶ μᾶλλον:
[καὶ μᾶλλον] vel [καὶ μάλιστα] Spengel.   18. δ᾽ ἐστὶν ἧς Susemihl: δὲ
λέξις Aᶜ: δέ ἐστιν ἐξ ἧς (h. e. δέ ᾽Λ᾽ εξης) Vahlen: δὲ ἐξ ἧς vel δὲ πρᾶξις
apogr. : δὲ πρᾶξις ἧς Ueberweg.

I call a plot ' epeisodic ' in which the episodes or acts suc-
ceed one another without probable or necessary sequence.
Bad poets compose such pieces by their own fault, good
poets, to please the players; for, as they write show
pieces for competition, they stretch the plot beyond its
1452 a capacity, and are often forced to break the natural con-
tinuity.

But again, Tragedy is an imitation not only of a 11
complete action, but of events terrible and pitiful. Such
an effect is best produced when the events come on us
by surprise; and the effect is heightened when, at the
same time, they follow from one another. The tragic 12
wonder will then be greater than if they happened of
themselves or by accident; for even coincidences are most
striking when they have an air of design. We may
instance the statue of Mitys at Argos, which fell upon his
murderer while he was a spectator at a festival, and killed
him. Such events seem not to be due to mere chance.
Plots, therefore, constructed on these principles are
necessarily the best.

X   Plots are either Simple or Complex, for the actions
in real life, of which the plots are an imitation, obviously
show a similar distinction. An action which is one and 2
continuous in the sense above defined, I call Simple, when
the change of fortune takes place without Reversal (or
Recoil) of the Action and without Recognition.

A Complex action is one in which the change is
accompanied by such Reversal, or by Recognition, or
by both. These last should arise from the internal 3
structure of the plot, so that what follows should be the

τῶν προγεγενημένων συμβαίνειν ἢ ἐξ ἀνάγκης ἢ κατὰ
τὸ εἰκὸς γίγνεσθαι ταῦτα· διαφέρει γὰρ πολὺ τὸ γίγνεσθαι τάδε διὰ τάδε ἢ μετὰ τάδε.

XI ἔστι δὲ περιπέτεια μὲν ἡ εἰς τὸ ἐναντίον τῶν πρατ-
25 τομένων μεταβολή, [καθάπερ εἴρηται,] καὶ τοῦτο δὲ
ὥσπερ λέγομεν κατὰ τὸ εἰκὸς ἢ ἀναγκαῖον· ὥσπερ ἐν
τῷ Οἰδίποδι ἐλθὼν ὡς εὐφρανῶν τὸν Οἰδίπουν καὶ
ἀπαλλάξων τοῦ πρὸς τὴν μητέρα φόβου, δηλώσας ὃς
ἦν, τοὐναντίον ἐποίησεν· καὶ ἐν τῷ Λυγκεῖ ὁ μὲν ἀγό-
30 μενος ὡς ἀποθανούμενος, ὁ δὲ Δαναὸς ἀκολουθῶν ὡς
ἀποκτενῶν, τὸν μὲν συνέβη ἐκ τῶν πεπραγμένων ἀποθανεῖν, τὸν δὲ σωθῆναι. ἀναγνώρισις δέ, ὥσπερ καὶ 2
τοὔνομα σημαίνει, ἐξ ἀγνοίας εἰς γνῶσιν μεταβολὴ ἢ
εἰς φιλίαν ἢ εἰς ἔχθραν τῶν πρὸς εὐτυχίαν ἢ δυστυχίαν
35 ὡρισμένων· καλλίστη δὲ ἀναγνώρισις, ὅταν ἅμα περιπέτειαι γίνωνται, οἷον ἔχει ἡ ἐν τῷ Οἰδίποδι. εἰσὶν 3
μὲν οὖν καὶ ἄλλαι ἀναγνωρίσεις· καὶ γὰρ πρὸς ἄψυχα
καὶ τὰ τυχόντα ἔστιν ὡς <ὅ>περ εἴρηται συμβαίνει, καὶ
εἰ πέπραγέ τις ἢ μὴ πέπραγεν ἔστιν ἀναγνωρίσαι· ἀλλ'
40 ἡ μάλιστα τοῦ μύθου καὶ ἡ μάλιστα τῆς πράξεως ἡ
εἰρημένη ἐστίν· ἡ γὰρ τοιαύτη ἀναγνώρισις καὶ περι- 4
1452 b πέτεια ἢ ἔλεον ἕξει ἢ φόβον, οἵων πράξεων ἡ τραγῳδία
μίμησις ὑπόκειται· ἔτι δὲ καὶ τὸ ἀτυχεῖν καὶ τὸ εὐτυχεῖν

---

22. ταῦτα: τἀναντία Bonitz: τὰ ὕστερα Gomperz.   25. καθάπερ εἴρηται,
tanquam gloss. ad ὥσπερ λέγομεν seclus. Zeller, Gomperz: <ἢ> καθ' ἃ
προῄρηται deleto commate post μεταβολή Essen, probante Susemihl.
34. Post ἔχθραν add. ἢ ἄλλο τι Gomperz.   35. ἅμα περιπετείᾳ Gomperz.
36. Fort. οἵαν Bywater.   38. ἔστιν ὥσπερ Aᶜ: ἔστιν ὅτε ὥσπερ Riccardianus: ἔστιν ὡς <ὅ>περ Spengel: ἔστιν ὅθ' <ὅ>περ Gomperz.
συμβαίνειν apogr.: συμβαίνει Aᶜ.   39. ἢ μὴ apogr.: εἰ μὴ Aᶜ.   41.
καὶ περιπέτεια seclus. Susemihl.   καὶ <μάλιστ' ἐὰν καὶ> περιπέτεια
ἢ ἔλεον coni. Vahlen.   1452 b 1. οἵων apogr.: οἷον Aᶜ.   2. ἔτι
δὲ: ἐπειδὴ Susemihl, pos. commate post ὑπόκειται.

necessary or probable result of the preceding action.   It
makes all the difference whether any given event is a
case of *propter hoc* or *post hoc*.

XI   Reversal (or Recoil) is a change by which a train of
action produces the opposite of the effect intended, subject
always to our rule of probability or necessity.   Thus in
the Oedipus, the messenger comes to cheer Oedipus and
free him from his alarms about his mother, but by reveal-
ing who he is, he produces the opposite effect.   Again in
the Lynceus, Lynceus is being led away to his death, and
Danaus goes with him, meaning to slay him; but the
outcome of the action is, that Danaus is killed and
Lynceus saved.

Recognition, as the name indicates, is a change from 2
ignorance to knowledge, producing love or hate between
the persons destined by the poet for good or bad fortune.
The best form of recognition is coincident with a Reversal
(or Recoil), as in the Oedipus.   There are indeed other forms. 3
Even inanimate things of the most trivial kind may sometimes be objects of recognition.   Again, we may recognise
or discover whether a person has done a thing or not.   But
the recognition which is most intimately connected with
the plot and action is, as we have said, the recognition of
persons.   This recognition, combined with Reversal, will 4
1452 b produce either pity or fear; and actions producing these
effects are those which, by our definition, Tragedy represents.   Moreover, it is upon such issues that fortune or

ἐπὶ τῶν τοιούτων συμβήσεται. ἐπεὶ δὴ ἡ ἀναγνώρισις 5
τινῶν ἐστιν ἀναγνώρισις, αἱ μὲν θατέρου πρὸς τὸν ἕτερον
5 μόνον, ὅταν ᾖ δῆλος ἅτερος τίς ἐστιν, ὁτὲ δὲ ἀμφοτέρους
δεῖ ἀναγνωρίσαι, οἷον ἡ μὲν Ἰφιγένεια τῷ Ὀρέστῃ
ἀνεγνωρίσθη ἐκ τῆς πέμψεως τῆς ἐπιστολῆς, ἐκείνου δὲ
πρὸς τὴν Ἰφιγένειαν ἄλλης ἔδει ἀναγνωρίσεως.
    δύο μὲν οὖν τοῦ μύθου μέρη περὶ ταῦτ' ἐστί, περι- 6
10 πέτεια καὶ ἀναγνώρισις, τρίτον δὲ πάθος. [τούτων δὲ
περιπέτεια μὲν καὶ ἀναγνώρισις εἴρηται,] πάθος δέ ἐστι
πρᾶξις φθαρτικὴ ἢ ὀδυνηρά, οἷον οἵ τε ἐν τῷ φανερῷ
θάνατοι καὶ αἱ περιωδυνίαι καὶ τρώσεις καὶ ὅσα
τοιαῦτα.

XII [μέρη δὲ τραγῳδίας οἷς μὲν ὡς εἴδεσι δεῖ χρῆσθαι
16 πρότερον εἴπομεν, κατὰ δὲ τὸ ποσὸν καὶ εἰς ἃ διαιρεῖται
κεχωρισμένα τάδε ἐστίν, πρόλογος ἐπεισόδιον ἔξοδος
χορικόν, καὶ τούτου τὸ μὲν πάροδος τὸ δὲ στάσιμον·
κοινὰ μὲν ἁπάντων ταῦτα, ἴδια δὲ τὰ ἀπὸ τῆς σκηνῆς
20 καὶ κόμμοι. ἔστιν δὲ πρόλογος μὲν μέρος ὅλον τραγῳ- 2
δίας τὸ πρὸ χοροῦ παρόδου, ἐπεισόδιον δὲ μέρος ὅλον
τραγῳδίας τὸ μεταξὺ ὅλων χορικῶν μελῶν, ἔξοδος δὲ
μέρος ὅλον τραγῳδίας μεθ' ὃ οὐκ ἔστι χοροῦ μέλος,
χορικοῦ δὲ πάροδος μὲν ἡ πρώτη λέξις ὅλη χοροῦ,
25 στάσιμον δὲ μέλος χοροῦ τὸ ἄνευ ἀναπαίστου καὶ
τροχαίου, κόμμος δὲ θρῆνος κοινὸς χοροῦ καὶ <τῶν>
ἀπὸ σκηνῆς. μέρη δὲ τραγῳδίας οἷς μὲν ὡς εἴδεσι δεῖ 3

3. ἐπεὶ δὴ ἡ Aᶜ: ἐπειδὴ apogr.: ἐπεὶ δ' ἡ Bekker.   4. ἕτερον: ἑταῖρον
Σ, ut videtur.   5. ἅτερος Bernays: ἕτερος codd.   7. ἐκείνου
Bywater: ἐκείνῳ codd.   9. περὶ seclus. Maggi: περὶ non habuisse
videtur Σ (Margoliouth): περὶ ταῦτα Twining.   10. τούτων δὲ—εἴρηται
seclus. Susemihl, om. Arabs.   12. οἵ τε apogr.: ὅτε Aᶜ.   15.
Totum hoc cap. seclus. Ritter, recte, ut opinor.   19. κοινὰ μὲν . . .
κόμμοι del. Susemihl.   24. ὅλη Westphal: ὅλου Aᶜ.   26. τῶν add.
Christ praeeunte Ritter.   27. οἷς μὲν ὡς εἴδεσι δεῖ apogr.: οἷς μὲν δεῖ Aᶜ.

misfortune will turn. Recognition, then, being between 5
persons, it may happen that one person only is recognised
by the other—when the latter is already known—or it
may be necessary that the recognition should be on both
sides. Thus Iphigenia is revealed to Orestes by the
sending of the letter ; but another act of recognition is
required to make Orestes known to Iphigenia.

Two parts, then, of the Plot—Reversal and Recogni- 6
tion—turn upon surprises. A third part is the Tragic
Incident. The Tragic Incident is a destructive or painful
action, such as death on the stage, bodily agony, wounds
and the like.

XII   [The parts of Tragedy, which must be treated as
elements of the whole, have been already mentioned.
We now come to the quantitative parts—the separate
parts into which Tragedy is divided—namely, Prologue,
Episode, Exodos, Choric song ; this last being divided
into Parodos and Stasimon. These are common to all
plays : peculiar to some are the songs of actors from the
stage and the Commoi.

The Prologos is that entire part of a tragedy which 2
precedes the Parodos of the Chorus. The Episode is
that entire part of a tragedy which is between complete
choric songs. The Exodos is that entire part of a tragedy
which has no choric song after it. Of the Choric part
the Parodos is the first undivided utterance of the
Chorus : the Stasimon is a Choric ode without anapaests
or trochees : the Commos is a joint lamentation of Chorus
and actors. The parts of Tragedy which must be treated 3

χρῆσθαι πρότερον εἴπαμεν, κατὰ δὲ τὸ ποσὸν καὶ εἰς
ἃ διαιρεῖται κεχωρισμένα ταῦτ᾽ ἐστίν.]

XIII ὧν δὲ δεῖ στοχάζεσθαι καὶ ἃ δεῖ εὐλαβεῖσθαι συν-
31 ιστάντας τοὺς μύθους καὶ πόθεν ἔσται τὸ τῆς τραγῳδίας
ἔργον, ἐφεξῆς ἂν εἴη λεκτέον τοῖς νῦν εἰρημένοις.. ἐπειδὴ 2
οὖν δεῖ τὴν σύνθεσιν εἶναι τῆς καλλίστης τραγῳδίας μὴ
ἁπλῆν ἀλλὰ πεπλεγμένην καὶ ταύτην φοβερῶν καὶ
35 ἐλεεινῶν εἶναι μιμητικήν, τοῦτο γὰρ ἴδιον τῆς τοιαύτης
μιμήσεως ἐστίν, πρῶτον μὲν δῆλον ὅτι οὔτε τοὺς ἐπιεικεῖς
ἄνδρας δεῖ μεταβάλλοντας φαίνεσθαι ἐξ εὐτυχίας εἰς
δυστυχίαν, οὐ γὰρ φοβερὸν οὐδὲ ἐλεεινὸν τοῦτο ἀλλὰ
μιαρόν ἐστιν· οὔτε τοὺς μοχθηροὺς ἐξ ἀτυχίας εἰς
40 εὐτυχίαν, ἀτραγῳδότατον γὰρ τοῦτ᾽ ἐστὶ πάντων· οὐδὲν
1453 a γὰρ ἔχει ὧν δεῖ, οὔτε γὰρ φιλάνθρωπον οὔτε ἐλεεινὸν
οὔτε φοβερόν ἐστιν· οὐδ᾽ αὖ τὸν σφόδρα πονηρὸν ἐξ
εὐτυχίας εἰς δυστυχίαν μεταπίπτειν· τὸ μὲν γὰρ φιλάνθρωπον ἔχοι ἂν ἡ τοιαύτη σύστασις ἀλλ᾽ οὔτε ἔλεον
5 οὔτε φόβον, ὁ μὲν γὰρ περὶ τὸν ἀνάξιόν ἐστιν δυστυ-
χοῦντα, ὁ δὲ περὶ τὸν ὅμοιον, ἔλεος μὲν περὶ τὸν ἀνάξιον,
φόβος δὲ περὶ τὸν ὅμοιον, ὥστε οὔτε ἐλεεινὸν οὔτε
φοβερὸν ἔσται τὸ συμβαῖνον. ὁ μεταξὺ ἄρα τούτων 3
λοιπός. ἔστι δὲ τοιοῦτος ὁ μήτε ἀρετῇ διαφέρων καὶ
10 δικαιοσύνῃ, μήτε διὰ κακίαν καὶ μοχθηρίαν μεταβάλλων
εἰς τὴν δυστυχίαν ἀλλὰ δι᾽ ἁμαρτίαν τινά, τῶν ἐν
μεγάλῃ δόξῃ ὄντων καὶ εὐτυχίᾳ, οἷον Οἰδίπους καὶ

---

30. ὧν apogr. : ὡς Aᶜ.   34. πεπλεγμένην seclus. Susemihl.   1453 a
2. αὖ τὸν apogr.: αὖ τὸ Aᶜ.   6. ἔλεος μὲν . . . τὸν ὅμοιον seclus.
Ritter, quod non confirm. Arabs (Margoliouth).   12. Οἰδίπους apogr. :
δίπους Aᶜ.

as elements of the whole have been already mentioned.
The quantitative parts—the separate parts into which it
is divided—are here enumerated.]

XIII   As the sequel to what has already been said, we must
proceed to consider what the poet should aim at, and
what he should avoid, in constructing his plots; and by
what means the specific effect of Tragedy will be produced.

A perfect tragedy should, as we have seen, be arranged 2
not on the simple but on the complex plan. It should,
moreover, imitate actions which excite pity and fear, this
being the distinctive mark of tragic imitation. It follows
plainly, in the first place, that the change of fortune
presented must not be the spectacle of a virtuous man
brought from prosperity to adversity: for this moves
neither pity nor fear; it merely shocks us. Nor, again,
that of a bad man passing from adversity to prosperity;
for nothing can be more alien to the spirit of Tragedy; it
1453 a possesses no single tragic quality; it neither satisfies
the moral sense, nor calls forth pity or fear. Nor,
again, should the downfall of the utter villain be exhibited. A plot of this kind would, doubtless, satisfy
the moral sense, but it would inspire neither pity nor
fear; for pity is aroused by unmerited misfortune, fear
by the misfortune of a man like ourselves. Such an
event, therefore, will be neither pitiful nor terrible.
There remains, then, the character between these two 3
extremes,—that of a man who is not eminently good and
just, yet whose misfortune is brought about not by vice
or depravity, but by some error or frailty. He must
be one who is highly renowned and prosperous,—a

Θυέστης καὶ οἱ ἐκ τῶν τοιούτων γενῶν ἐπιφανεῖς ἄνδρες.
ἀνάγκη ἄρα τὸν καλῶς ἔχοντα μῦθον ἁπλοῦν εἶναι 4
15 μᾶλλον ἢ διπλοῦν, ὥσπερ τινές φασι, καὶ μεταβάλλειν
οὐκ εἰς εὐτυχίαν ἐκ δυστυχίας ἀλλὰ τοὐναντίον ἐξ
εὐτυχίας εἰς δυστυχίαν, μὴ διὰ μοχθηρίαν ἀλλὰ δι᾽
ἁμαρτίαν μεγάλην ἢ οἵου εἴρηται ἢ βελτίονος μᾶλλον
ἢ χείρονος.   σημεῖον δὲ καὶ τὸ γιγνόμενον· πρῶτον μὲν 5
20 γὰρ οἱ ποιηταὶ τοὺς τυχόντας μύθους ἀπηρίθμουν, νῦν
δὲ περὶ ὀλίγας οἰκίας αἱ [κάλλισται] τραγῳδίαι συντί-
θενται, οἷον περὶ Ἀλκμαίωνα καὶ Οἰδίπουν καὶ Ὀρέστην
καὶ Μελέαγρον καὶ Θυέστην καὶ Τήλεφον καὶ ὅσοις
ἄλλοις συμβέβηκεν ἢ παθεῖν δεινὰ ἢ ποιῆσαι.   ἡ μὲν
25 οὖν κατὰ τὴν τέχνην καλλίστη τραγῳδία ἐκ ταύτης
τῆς συστάσεως ἐστί.   διὸ καὶ οἱ Εὐριπίδῃ ἐγκαλοῦντες 6
τοῦτ᾽ αὐτὸ ἁμαρτάνουσιν, ὅτι τοῦτο δρᾷ ἐν ταῖς τραγῳδίαις καὶ πολλαὶ αὐτοῦ εἰς δυστυχίαν τελευτῶσιν.
τοῦτο γάρ ἐστιν ὥσπερ εἴρηται ὀρθόν.   σημεῖον δὲ
30 μέγιστον· ἐπὶ γὰρ τῶν σκηνῶν καὶ τῶν ἀγώνων τραγι-
κώταται αἱ τοιαῦται φαίνονται, ἂν κατορθωθῶσιν, καὶ
ὁ Εὐριπίδης εἰ καὶ τὰ ἄλλα μὴ εὖ οἰκονομεῖ ἀλλὰ
τραγικώτατός γε τῶν ποιητῶν φαίνεται.   δευτέρα δ᾽ ἡ 7
πρώτη λεγομένη ὑπὸ τινῶν ἐστιν [σύστασις] ἡ διπλῆν
35 τε τὴν σύστασιν ἔχουσα, καθάπερ ἡ Ὀδύσσεια, καὶ
τελευτῶσα ἐξ ἐναντίας τοῖς βελτίοσι καὶ χείροσιν.
δοκεῖ δὲ εἶναι πρώτη διὰ τὴν τῶν θεάτρων ἀσθένειαν·
ἀκολουθοῦσι γὰρ οἱ ποιηταὶ κατ᾽ εὐχὴν ποιοῦντες τοῖς
θεαταῖς.   ἔστιν δὲ οὐχ αὕτη <ἡ> ἀπὸ τραγῳδίας ἡδονὴ 8

21. κάλλισται seclus. Christ, om. iam Σ.   27. τοῦτ᾽ αὐτὸ Thurot : αὐτοὶ
Reiz : τὸ αὐτὸ codd. Vahlen, secludendum coni. Margoliouth collato Arabe.
28. <αἱ> πολλαὶ Knebel : ἢ πολλαὶ <αἱ> Tyrrell.   34. σύστασις
seclus. Twining.   37. θεάτρων Aᶜ et Σ, ut videtur (cf. 1449 a 9,
Herod. vi. 21 ἐς δάκρυα ἔπεσε τὸ θέητρον, Aristoph. Eq. 233 τὸ γὰρ θέατρον
δεξιόν) : θεατῶν apogr.   39. αὕτη <ἡ> coni. Vahlen.

personage like Oedipus, Thyestes, or other illustrious men of such families.

A well constructed plot should, therefore, be single 4 in its issue, rather than double as some maintain. The change of fortune should be not from bad to good, but, reversely, from good to bad. It should come about as the result not of vice, but of some great error or frailty, in a character either such as we have described, or better rather than worse. The practice of the stage bears out 5 our view. At first the poets recounted any legend that came in their way. Now, tragedies are founded on the story of a few houses,—on the fortunes of Alcmaeon, Oedipus, Orestes, Meleager, Thyestes, Telephus, and those others who have done or suffered something terrible. A tragedy, then, to be perfect according to the rules of art should be of this construction. Hence they are in error 6 who censure Euripides just because he follows this principle in his plays, many of which end unhappily. It is, as we have said, the right ending. The best proof is that on the stage and in dramatic competition, such plays, if they are well represented, are the most tragic in effect; and Euripides, faulty as he is in the general management of his subject, yet is felt to be the most tragic of the poets.

In the second rank comes the kind of tragedy which 7 some place first. Like the Odyssey, it has a double thread of plot, and also an opposite catastrophe for the good and for the bad. It is accounted the best because of the weakness of the spectators; for the poet is guided in what he writes by the wishes of his audience. The 8 pleasure, however, thence derived is not the true tragic

40 ἀλλὰ μᾶλλον τῆς κωμῳδίας οἰκεία· ἐκεῖ γὰρ οἳ ἂν
ἔχθιστοι ὦσιν ἐν τῷ μύθῳ, οἷον Ὀρέστης καὶ Αἴγισθος,
φίλοι γενόμενοι ἐπὶ τελευτῆς ἐξέρχονται καὶ ἀποθνήσκει
οὐδεὶς ὑπ' οὐδενός.

XIV   ἔστιν μὲν οὖν τὸ φοβερὸν καὶ ἐλεεινὸν ἐκ τῆς ὄψεως
1453 b γίγνεσθαι, ἔστιν δὲ καὶ ἐξ αὐτῆς τῆς συστάσεως τῶν
πραγμάτων, ὅπερ ἐστὶ πρότερον καὶ ποιητοῦ ἀμείνονος.
δεῖ γὰρ καὶ ἄνευ τοῦ ὁρᾶν οὕτω συνεστάναι τὸν μῦθον,
5 ὥστε τὸν ἀκούοντα τὰ πράγματα γινόμενα καὶ φρίττειν
καὶ ἐλεεῖν ἐκ τῶν συμβαινόντων· ἅπερ ἂν πάθοι τις
ἀκούων τὸν τοῦ Οἰδίπου μῦθον. τὸ δὲ διὰ τῆς ὄψεως 2
τοῦτο παρασκευάζειν ἀτεχνότερον καὶ χορηγίας δεόμενόν
ἐστιν. οἱ δὲ μὴ τὸ φοβερὸν διὰ τῆς ὄψεως ἀλλὰ τὸ
10 τερατῶδες μόνον παρασκευάζοντες οὐδὲν τραγῳδίᾳ κοινω-
νοῦσιν· οὐ γὰρ πᾶσαν δεῖ ζητεῖν ἡδονὴν ἀπὸ τραγῳδίας
ἀλλὰ τὴν οἰκείαν. ἐπεὶ δὲ τὴν ἀπὸ ἐλέου καὶ φόβου 3
διὰ μιμήσεως δεῖ ἡδονὴν παρασκευάζειν τὸν ποιητήν,
φανερὸν ὡς τοῦτο ἐν τοῖς πράγμασιν ἐμποιητέον. ποῖα
15 οὖν δεινὰ ἢ ποῖα οἰκτρὰ φαίνεται τῶν συμπιπτόντων,
λάβωμεν. ἀνάγκη δὴ ἡ φίλων εἶναι πρὸς ἀλλήλους 4
τὰς τοιαύτας πράξεις ἢ ἐχθρῶν ἢ μηδετέρων. ἂν μὲν
οὖν ἐχθρὸς ἐχθρόν, οὐδὲν ἐλεεινὸν οὔτε ποιῶν οὔτε
μέλλων, πλὴν κατ' αὐτὸ τὸ πάθος· οὐδ' ἂν μηδετέρως
20 ἔχοντες· ὅταν δ' ἐν ταῖς φιλίαις ἐγγένηται τὰ πάθη,

---

40. οἱ ἂν Bonitz: ἂν οἱ codd.: κἂν οἱ Spengel.   **1453 b 8.** ἀτεχνότερον apogr.: ἀτεχνώτερον Aᶜ.   16. δὴ Spengel: δὲ codd.   18.
ἐχθρόν: ἐχθρὸν ἀποκτείνῃ Bekk. praeeunte Pazzi.   ἐλεεινὸν: <φοβερὸν
οὐδ'> ἐλεεινὸν Ueberweg.

pleasure. It is proper rather to Comedy, where those
who, in the piece, are the deadliest enemies—like Orestes
and Aegisthus—quit the stage as friends at the close,
and no one slays or is slain.

XIV   Fear and pity may be aroused by spectacular means;
1453 b but they may also result from the inner structure of the
piece, which is the better way, and indicates a superior
poet.   For the plot ought to be so constructed that, even
without the aid of the eye, he who hears the tale told
will thrill with horror and melt to pity at what takes
place.   This is the impression we should receive from
hearing the story of the Oedipus.   But to produce this 2
effect by the mere spectacle is a less artistic method,
and dependent on extraneous aids.   Those who employ
spectacular means to create a sense not of the terrible
but of the monstrous, are strangers to the purpose of
Tragedy; for we must not demand of Tragedy any and
every kind of pleasure, but only that which is proper
to it.   And since the pleasure which the poet should 3
afford is that which comes from pity and fear through
imitation, it is evident that this quality must be impressed
upon the incidents.

Let us then determine what are the circumstances
which strike us as terrible or pitiful.

Actions capable of this effect must happen between 4
persons who are either friends or enemies or indifferent
to one another.   If an enemy kills an enemy, there is
nothing to excite pity either in the act or the intention,
—except so far as the suffering in itself is pitiful.   So
again with indifferent persons.   But when the tragic
incident occurs between those who are near or dear to

E

οἶον εἰ ἀδελφὸς ἀδελφὸν ἢ υἱὸς πατέρα ἢ μήτηρ υἱὸν ἢ υἱὸς μητέρα ἀποκτείνει ἢ μέλλει ἢ τι ἄλλο τοιοῦτον ἐρᾷ, ταῦτα ζητητέον. τοῖς μὲν οὖν παρειλημμένους 5 μύθοις λύειν οὐκ ἔστιν, λέγω δὲ οἶον τὴν Κλυταιμνήστραν ἀποθανοῦσαν ὑπὸ τοῦ Ὀρέστου καὶ τὴν Ἐριφύλην ὑπὸ τοῦ Ἀλκμαίωνος, αὐτὸν δὲ εὑρίσκειν δεῖ καὶ τοῖς παραδεδομένοις χρῆσθαι καλῶς. τὸ δὲ καλῶς τί λέγομεν, εἴπωμεν σαφέστερον. ἔστι μὲν γὰρ οὕτω γίνεσθαι τὴν 6 πρᾶξιν, ὥσπερ οἱ παλαιοὶ ἐποίουν εἰδότας καὶ γιγνώσκοντας, καθάπερ καὶ Εὐριπίδης ἐποίησεν ἀποκτείνουσαν τοὺς παῖδας τὴν Μήδειαν. ἔστιν δὲ πρᾶξαι μέν, ἀγνοοῦντας δὲ πρᾶξαι τὸ δεινόν, εἶθ᾽ ὕστερον ἀναγνωρίσαι τὴν φιλίαν, ὥσπερ ὁ Σοφοκλέους Οἰδίπους· τοῦτο μὲν οὖν ἔξω τοῦ δράματος, ἐν δ᾽ αὐτῇ τῇ τραγῳδίᾳ οἶον ὁ Ἀλκμαίων ὁ Ἀστυδάμαντος ἢ ὁ Τηλέγονος ὁ ἐν τῷ τραυματίᾳ Ὀδυσσεῖ. ἔτι δὲ τρίτον παρὰ ταῦτα το 7 μέλλοντα ποιεῖν τι τῶν ἀνηκέστων δι᾽ ἄγνοιαν ἀναγνωρίσαι πρὶν ποιῆσαι. καὶ παρὰ ταῦτα οὐκ ἔστιν ἄλλως. ἢ γὰρ πρᾶξαι ἀνάγκη ἢ μὴ καὶ εἰδότας ἢ μὴ εἰδότας. τούτων δὲ τὸ μὲν γινώσκοντα μελλῆσαι καὶ μὴ πρᾶξαι χείριστον· τό τε γὰρ μιαρὸν ἔχει, καὶ οὐ τραγικόν· ἀπαθές γάρ. διόπερ οὐδεὶς ποιεῖ ὁμοίως, εἰ μὴ ὀλιγάκις, οἶον ἐν Ἀντιγόνῃ τον Κρέοντα ὁ Αἵμων. τὸ δὲ πρᾶξαι 8 δεύτερον. βέλτιον δὲ τὸ ἀγνοοῦντα μὲν πρᾶξαι, πράξαντα

21. εἰ ἀδελφὸς Sylburg: ἢ ἀδελφὸν codd. 22. ἐρᾷ ἀρυσ.. ὁρᾷ Αᶜ. 24. εἴπωμεν ἀρυσ.: εἴπομεν Αᶜ. 34. ὁ Ἀλκμαίων ὁ Guel.: ὁ Ἀλκμαίων codd. 34. Post παρὰ ταῦτα, <τὸ μελλῆσαι γινώσκοντα καὶ μὴ ταῦτα, ex τετραχμα> codd Vahlen: παρὰ ταῦτα seclus. M. Schmidt. ... Bonitz: ... Αᶜ. 1454 a 3-7. Huius loci ordinem ita restituendum censet Susemihl: βέλτιον δὲ τὸ ἀγνοοῦντα, λέγω δὲ ὡς ... ἀλλ᾽ ἀναγνωρίσαι· ... δὲ τι ἀγνοοῦντα μὲν ... ἀναγνωρίσαι· τό τε γὰρ μιαρὸν ... τετύηνται.

one another—if, for example, a brother kills, or intends to kill, a brother, a son his father, a mother her son, a son his mother, or any other deed of the kind is done—these are the situations to be looked for by the poet. He may not indeed destroy the framework of the received legends—the 5 fact, for instance, that Clytemnestra was slain by Orestes and Eriphyle by Alcmaeon—but he ought to show invention of his own, and skilfully handle the traditional material. Let us explain more clearly what is meant by skilful handling.

The action may be done consciously and with know- 6 ledge of the persons, in the manner of the older poets. It is thus indeed that Euripides makes Medea slay her children. Or, again, the deed of horror may be done, but done in ignorance, and the tie of kinship or friendship be discovered afterwards. The Oedipus of Sophocles is an example. Here, indeed, the incident is outside the drama proper; but cases occur where it falls within the action of the play: one may cite the Alcmaeon of Astydamas, or Telegonus in the Wounded Odysseus. Again, there is a third case, where some one is just 7 about to do some irreparable deed through ignorance, and makes the discovery before it is done. These are the only possible ways. For the deed must either be done or not done,—and that wittingly or unwittingly. But of all these ways, to be about to act knowing the persons, and then not to act, is the worst. It is shocking without being tragic, for no disaster follows. It is, 1454 a therefore, never, or very rarely, found in poetry. One instance, however, is in the Antigone, where Haemon threatens to kill Creon. The next and better way is 8 that the deed should be perpetrated. Still better, that

δὲ ἀναγνωρίσαι· τό τε γὰρ μιαρὸν οὐ πρόσεστιν καὶ ἡ
5 ἀναγνώρισις ἐκπληκτικόν. κράτιστον δὲ τὸ τελευταῖον, 9
λέγω δὲ οἷον ἐν τῷ Κρεσφόντῃ ἡ Μερόπη μέλλει τὸν
υἱὸν ἀποκτείνειν, ἀποκτείνει δὲ οὔ, ἀλλ' ἀνεγνώρισεν,
καὶ ἐν τῇ Ἰφιγενείᾳ ἡ ἀδελφὴ τὸν ἀδελφόν, καὶ ἐν τῇ
Ἕλλῃ ὁ υἱὸς τὴν μητέρα ἐκδιδόναι μέλλων ἀνεγνώρισεν.
10 διὰ γὰρ τοῦτο, ὅπερ πάλαι εἴρηται, οὐ περὶ πολλὰ
γένη αἱ τραγῳδίαι εἰσίν. ζητοῦντες γὰρ οὐκ ἀπὸ
τέχνης ἀλλ' ἀπὸ τύχης εὗρον τὸ τοιοῦτον παρασκευάζειν
ἐν τοῖς μύθοις. ἀναγκάζονται οὖν ἐπὶ ταύτας τὰς οἰκίας
ἀπαντᾶν ὅσαις τὰ τοιαῦτα συμβέβηκε πάθη.
15 περὶ μὲν οὖν τῆς τῶν πραγμάτων συστάσεως καὶ
ποίους τινὰς εἶναι δεῖ τοὺς μύθους εἴρηται ἱκανῶς.
XV περὶ δὲ τὰ ἤθη τέτταρά ἐστιν ὧν δεῖ στοχάζεσθαι,
ἐν μὲν καὶ πρῶτον ὅπως χρηστὰ ᾖ. ἕξει δὲ ἦθος μὲν
ἐὰν ὥσπερ ἐλέχθη ποιῇ φανερὸν ὁ λόγος ἢ ἡ πρᾶξις
20 προαίρεσίν τινα [ᾖ], χρηστὸν δὲ ἐὰν χρηστήν. ἔστιν
δὲ ἐν ἑκάστῳ γένει· καὶ γὰρ γυνή ἐστιν χρηστὴ καὶ
δοῦλος, καίτοι γε ἴσως τούτων τὸ μὲν χεῖρον, τὸ δὲ ὅλως
φαῦλόν ἐστιν. δεύτερον δὲ τὰ ἁρμόττοντα· ἔστιν γὰρ 2
ἀνδρεῖον μέν τι ἦθος, ἀλλ' οὐχ ἁρμόττον γυναικὶ τὸ
25 ἀνδρείαν ἢ δεινὴν εἶναι. τρίτον δὲ τὸ ὅμοιον. τοῦτο 3

5. κρατεῖ <δὲ πλεῖ>στον Tucker.   9. Ἕλλῃ: Ἀντιόπῃ Valckenaer.
19. φανερὰν Ald., Bekker.   20. προαίρεσιν τινὰ ᾗι Aᶜ: ᾖ secludendum,
vel <ἢ τις ἂν> ᾖ coni. Vahlen (? cf. Arab.): <ἣν>τινα <δ>ἢ Bywater:
ἢ φυγήν Düntzer: προαίρεσίν τινα <ἔχοντα, ὁποία τις ἂν> ᾖ Gomperz:
προαίρεσίν τινα, φαῦλον μὲν ἐὰν φαύλη ᾖ, χρηστὸν κ.τ.λ. apogr.   23. τὸ
ἁρμόττοντα coni. Vahlen, probante Gomperz.   24. τι ἦθος Hermann:
τὸ ἦθος codd.   τὸ apogr.: *τῶι Aᶜ: οὕτως Vahl. collato Pol. iii. 4,
1277 b 20. Desunt in Arabe verba τῷ ἀνδρείαν . . . εἶναι, quorum vicem
supplet haec clausula, 'ne ut appareat quidem in ea omnino' (Margoliouth). Unde Diels τῷ ἀνδρείαν . . . εἶναι glossema esse arbitratus quod
veram lectionem ʼeiecerit, scribendum esse coni. ὥστε μηδὲ φαίνεσθαι

it should be perpetrated in ignorance, and the discovery made afterwards. There is then nothing to shock us, while the discovery produces a startling effect. The last 9 case is the best, as when in the Cresphontes Merope is about to slay her son, but, recognising who he is, spares his life. So in the Iphigenia, the sister recognises the brother just in time. Again in the Helle, the son recognises the mother when on the point of giving her up. This, then, is why a few families only, as has been already observed, furnish the subjects of tragedy. It was not art, but happy chance, that led poets to look for such situations and so impress the tragic quality upon their plots. They are compelled, therefore, to have recourse to those houses whose history contains moving incidents like these.

Enough has now been said concerning the structure of the incidents, and the proper constitution of the plot.

XV   In respect of Character there are four things to be aimed at. First, and most important, it must be good. Now any speech or action that manifests moral purpose of any kind will be expressive of character: the character will be good if the purpose is good. This rule is relative to each class. Even a woman may be good, and also a slave; though the woman may be said to be an inferior being, and the slave quite worthless. The second thing 2 to aim at is propriety. There is a type of manly valour; but for a woman to be valiant, or terrible, would be inappropriate. Thirdly, character must be true to life: for 3

γὰρ ἕτερον τοῦ χρηστὸν τὸ ἦθος καὶ ἁρμόττον ποιῆσαι
ὥσπερ εἴρηται. τέταρτον δὲ τὸ ὁμαλόν. κἂν γὰρ 4
ἀνώμαλός τις ᾖ ὁ τὴν μίμησιν παρέχων καὶ τοιοῦτον
ἦθος ὑποτιθείς, ὅμως ὁμαλῶς ἀνώμαλον δεῖ εἶναι. ἔστιν 5
30 δὲ παράδειγμα πονηρίας μὲν ἤθους μὴ ἀναγκαίας οἷον ὁ
Μενέλαος ὁ ἐν τῷ Ὀρέστῃ, τοῦ δὲ ἀπρεποῦς καὶ μὴ
ἁρμόττοντος ὅ τε θρῆνος Ὀδυσσέως ἐν τῇ Σκύλλῃ καὶ
ἡ τῆς Μελανίππης ῥῆσις, τοῦ δὲ ἀνωμάλου ἡ ἐν Αὐλίδι
Ἰφιγένεια· οὐδὲν γὰρ ἔοικεν ἡ ἱκετεύουσα τῇ ὑστέρᾳ.
35 χρὴ δὲ καὶ ἐν τοῖς ἤθεσιν ὥσπερ καὶ ἐν τῇ τῶν πραγ- 6
μάτων συστάσει ἀεὶ ζητεῖν ἢ τὸ ἀναγκαῖον ἢ τὸ εἰκός,
ὥστε τὸν τοιοῦτον τὰ τοιαῦτα λέγειν ἢ πράττειν ἢ
ἀναγκαῖον ἢ εἰκός, καὶ τοῦτο μετὰ τοῦτο γίνεσθαι ἢ
ἀναγκαῖον ἢ εἰκός. φανερὸν οὖν ὅτι καὶ τὰς λύσεις τῶν 7
1454 b μύθων ἐξ αὐτοῦ δεῖ τοῦ μύθου συμβαίνειν καὶ μὴ ὥσπερ
ἐν τῇ Μηδείᾳ ἀπὸ μηχανῆς καὶ ἐν τῇ Ἰλιάδι τὰ περὶ
τὸν ἀπόπλουν· ἀλλὰ μηχανῇ χρηστέον ἐπὶ τὰ ἔξω τοῦ
δράματος, ἢ ὅσα πρὸ τοῦ γέγονεν ἃ οὐχ οἷόν τε ἄνθρωπον
5 εἰδέναι, ἢ ὅσα ὕστερον, ἃ δεῖται προαγορεύσεως καὶ

καθόλου: 'The manly character is indeed sometimes found even in a woman
(ἔστιν γὰρ ἀνδρεῖον μὲν τὸ ἦθος), but it is not appropriate to her, so that it
never appears as a general characteristic of the sex.' Sed hoc aliter
dicendum fuisse suspicari licet; itaque Susemihl huiusmodi aliquid tentavit,
ὥστε μηδὲ φαίνεσθαι ἐν αὐτῇ ὡς ἐπίπαν, vel ὡς ἐπίπαν εἰπεῖν: 'There is
indeed a character (τι ἦθος) of manly courage, but it is not appropriate to
a woman, and as a rule is not found in her at all.'   27. ὥσπερ εἴρηται
fort. secludendum: ἅπερ εἴρηται Hermann: lacunam ante ὥσπερ statuit
Spengel, quem seq. Susemihl.   30. ἀναγκαῖον Aᶜ: ἀναγκαίου apogr.,
Bywater: ἀναγκαίας Thurot: [μὴ ἀναγκαῖον] Gomperz.   οἷον seclus.
E. Müller, Sus. ed. 1, Christ.   32. <τοῦ> Ὀδυσσέως Bywater.
33. Exemplum τοῦ ἀνομοίου post ῥῆσις intercidisse coni. Vettori; cf.
Susemihl, Christ.   37 et 38. ἢ ἀναγκαῖον Hermann.   38. <ὡς>
καὶ τοῦτο Bywater, fort. recte.   39. τῶν μύθων: τῶν ἠθῶν Σ, ut videtur
(Margoliouth).   1454 b 3. ἀπόπλουν apogr., Σ: ἀπλοῦν Aᶜ.   5.
Commate post ὕστερον disting. W. R. Hardie, qui ἀγγελίας ad ὅσα πρὸ τοῦ
refert, προαγορεύσεως ad ὅσα ὕστερον.

this is a distinct thing from goodness and propriety, as here described. The fourth point is consistency : for though 4 the subject of the imitation, who suggested the type, be inconsistent, still he must be consistently inconsistent. As an example of character gratuitously bad, we have 5 Menelaus in the Orestes : of character indecorous and inappropriate, the lament of Odysseus in the Scylla, and the speech of Melanippe : of inconsistency, the Iphigenia at Aulis,—for Iphigenia the suppliant in no way resembles her later self.

As in the structure of the plot, so too in the por- 6 traiture of character, the poet should always aim either at the necessary or the probable. Thus a person of a given character should speak or act in a given way, by the rule either of necessity or of probability ; just as this event should follow that by necessary or probable sequence. It is therefore evident that the unravelling 7 of the plot, no less than the complication, must arise out 1454 b of the plot itself, it must not be brought about by the *Deus ex Machina*,—as in the Medea, or in the Return of the Greeks in the Iliad. The *Deus ex Machina* should be employed only for events external to the drama,— for antecedent or subsequent events, which lie beyond the range of human knowledge, and which require to be

56 XV. 7—XVI. 3. 1454 b 6—29

ἀγγελίας· ἅπαντα γὰρ ἀποδίδομεν τοῖς θεοῖς ὁρᾶν.
ἄλογον δὲ μηδὲν εἶναι ἐν τοῖς πράγμασιν, εἰ δὲ μή, ἔξω
τῆς τραγῳδίας, οἷον τὸ ἐν τῷ Οἰδίποδι τῷ Σοφοκλέους.
ἐπεὶ δὲ μίμησίς ἐστιν ἡ τραγῳδία βελτιόνων <ἢ καθ'> 8
10 ἡμᾶς, δεῖ μιμεῖσθαι τοὺς ἀγαθοὺς εἰκονογράφους· καὶ
γὰρ ἐκεῖνοι ἀποδιδόντες τὴν ἰδίαν μορφὴν ὁμοίους ποιοῦντες καλλίους γράφουσιν· οὕτω καὶ τὸν ποιητὴν μιμού-
μενον καὶ ὀργίλους καὶ ῥαθύμους καὶ τἆλλα τὰ τοιαῦτα
ἔχοντας ἐπὶ τῶν ἠθῶν, τοιούτους ὄντας ἐπιεικεῖς ποιεῖν·
15 [παράδειγμα σκληρότητος] οἷον τὸν Ἀχιλλέα Ἀγάθων
καὶ Ὅμηρος. ταῦτα δὴ δεῖ διατηρεῖν καὶ πρὸς τούτοις 9
τὰς παρὰ τὰ ἐξ ἀνάγκης ἀκολουθούσας αἰσθήσεις τῇ
ποιητικῇ· καὶ γὰρ κατ' αὐτὰς ἔστιν ἁμαρτάνειν πολλάκις, εἴρηται δὲ περὶ αὐτῶν ἐν τοῖς ἐκδεδομένοις λόγοις
20 ἱκανῶς.

XVI   ἀναγνώρισις δὲ τί μέν ἐστιν, εἴρηται πρότερον· εἴδη
δὲ ἀναγνωρίσεως, πρώτη μὲν ἡ ἀτεχνοτάτη καὶ ᾗ πλείστῃ
χρῶνται δι' ἀπορίαν, ἡ διὰ τῶν σημείων. τούτων δὲ τὰ 2
μὲν σύμφυτα, οἷον "λόγχην ἣν φοροῦσι Γηγενεῖς" ἢ
25 ἀστέρας οἵους ἐν τῷ Θυέστῃ Καρκίνος, τὰ δὲ ἐπίκτητα,
καὶ τούτων τὰ μὲν ἐν τῷ σώματι, οἷον οὐλαί, τὰ δὲ ἐκτός,
τὰ περιδέραια καὶ οἷον ἐν τῇ Τυροῖ διὰ τῆς σκάφης.
ἔστιν δὲ καὶ τούτοις χρῆσθαι ἢ βέλτιον ἢ χεῖρον, οἷον 3
Ὀδυσσεὺς διὰ τῆς οὐλῆς ἄλλως ἀνεγνωρίσθη ὑπὸ τῆς

8. τὸ vel τῷ apogr.: τὸ ?Aᶜ: τὰ Ald.   9. ἢ καθ' ἡμᾶς Stahr, Margoliouth collato Arabe: ἡμᾶς codd.   15. παράδειγμα σκληρότητος seclus.
Bywater.   16. δὴ δεῖ Ald., Bekker: δὴ Aᶜ: δεῖ apogr.   17. τὰς παρὰ
τὰ vel τὰ παρὰ τὰς apogr.: τὰς παρὰ τὰς Aᶜ.   22. ἀτεχνωτάτη apogr.
pauca.   ᾗ πλείστῃ apogr.: ἡ πλείστη Λᶜ.   23. ἡ apogr.: ἢ Aᶜ.
27. περιδέραια Pazzi et apogr. pauca: περιδέρρεα Aᶜ: περὶ δέραια Ald.
οἷον apogr.: οἱ Aᶜ.   σκάφης: 'ensis' Arabs, σπάθης Σ, ut videtur
(R. Ellis).   29. <ὁ> Ὀδυσσεὺς Bywater.

reported or foretold; for to the gods we ascribe the power of seeing all things. Within the action there must be nothing irrational. If the irrational cannot be excluded, it should be outside the scope of the tragedy. Such is the irrational element in the Oedipus of Sophocles.

Again, since Tragedy is an imitation of persons who 8 are above the common level, the example of good portrait-painters should be followed. They, while reproducing the distinctive form of the original, make a likeness which is true to life and yet more beautiful. So too the poet, in representing men who are irascible or indolent, or have other defects of character, should preserve the type and yet ennoble it. In this way Achilles is portrayed by Agathon and Homer.

These are rules the poet should observe. Nor should 9 he neglect those appeals to the senses, which, though not among the essentials, are the concomitants of poetry; for here too there is much room for error. But of this enough has been said in the published treatises.

XVI   What Recognition is has been already explained. We will now enumerate its kinds.

First, the least artistic form, which, from poverty of wit, is most commonly employed—recognition by signs. Of these some are congenital,—such as 'the spear which 2 the earth-born race bear on their bodies,' or the stars introduced by Carcinus in his Thyestes. Others are acquired after birth; and of these some are bodily marks, as scars; some external tokens, as necklaces, or the little ark in the Tyro by which the discovery is effected. Even 3 these admit of more or less skilful treatment. Thus in the recognition of Odysseus by his scar, the discovery is

30 τροφοῦ καὶ ἄλλως ὑπὸ τῶν συβοτῶν· εἰσὶ γὰρ αἱ μὲν
πίστεως ἕνεκα ἀτεχνότεραι, καὶ αἱ τοιαῦται πᾶσαι, αἱ δὲ
ἐκ περιπετείας, ὥσπερ ἡ ἐν τοῖς Νίπτροις, βελτίους.
δεύτεραι δὲ αἱ πεποιημέναι ὑπὸ τοῦ ποιητοῦ, διὸ ἄτεχνοι. 4
οἷον Ὀρέστης ἐν τῇ Ἰφιγενείᾳ ἀνεγνώρισεν ὅτι Ὀρέστης·
35 ἐκείνη μὲν γὰρ διὰ τῆς ἐπιστολῆς, ἐκεῖνος δὲ αὐτὸς λέγει
ἃ βούλεται ὁ ποιητὴς ἀλλ' οὐχ ὁ μῦθος· διὸ ἐγγύς τι
τῆς εἰρημένης ἁμαρτίας ἐστίν, ἐξῆν γὰρ ἂν ἔνια καὶ
ἐνεγκεῖν. καὶ ἐν τῷ Σοφοκλέους Τηρεῖ ἡ τῆς κερκίδος
1455 a φωνή. ἡ τρίτη διὰ μνήμης τῷ αἰσθέσθαι τι ἰδόντα, 5
ὥσπερ ἡ ἐν Κυπρίοις τοῖς Δικαιογένους, ἰδὼν γὰρ τὴν
γραφὴν ἔκλαυσεν, καὶ ἡ ἐν Ἀλκίνου ἀπολόγῳ, ἀκούων
γὰρ τοῦ κιθαριστοῦ καὶ μνησθεὶς ἐδάκρυσεν, ὅθεν ἀνεγνω-
5 ρίσθησαν. τετάρτη δὲ ἡ ἐκ συλλογισμοῦ, οἷον ἐν 6
Χοηφόροις, ὅτι ὅμοιός τις ἐλήλυθεν, ὅμοιος δὲ οὐθεὶς
ἀλλ' ἢ ὁ Ὀρέστης, οὗτος ἄρα ἐλήλυθεν. καὶ ἡ Πολυείδου τοῦ σοφιστοῦ περὶ τῆς Ἰφιγενείας· εἰκὸς γὰρ τὸν
Ὀρέστην συλλογίσασθαι, ὅτι ἥ τ' ἀδελφὴ ἐτύθη καὶ
10 αὐτῷ συμβαίνει θύεσθαι. καὶ ἐν τῷ Θεοδέκτου Τυδεῖ,
ὅτι ἐλθὼν ὡς εὑρήσων υἱὸν αὐτὸς ἀπόλλυται. καὶ ἡ ἐν
τοῖς Φινείδαις, ἰδοῦσαι γὰρ τὸν τόπον συνελογίσαντο τὴν

34. <ὁ> Ὀρέστης Bywater: Ὀρέστης seclus. Diels sec. Arabem.   ἀνεγνωρίσθη Spengel.   36. διὸ ἐγγύς τι Vahlen, cf. Arab. 'quam ob causam
fit vicinum': διότι ἐγγὺς Aᶜ.   38. Alia Σ legisse videtur, 'haec sunt in
eo quod dixit Sophocles se audiisse vocem radii contempti' (Arabs); fort-
τοιαύτη δ' ἐν τῷ Σοφοκλέους Τηρεῖ ἡ τῆς κερκίδος φωνὴ "ἄτιμος": unde
W. R. Hardie coni. τοιαύτη δ' ἡ ἐν τῷ [Σοφοκλέους?] Τηρεῖ "τῆς ἀναύδου,"
φησί, "κερκίδος φωνὴν κλύω."   39. ἡ τρίτη Spengel: ἤτοι τηι Aᶜ:
τρίτη ἡ apogr.   ἄχθεσθαι Gomperz.   1455 a 2. τοῖς apogr.: τῆς
Aᶜ.   3. ἀπολόγῳ apogr.: ἀπὸ λόγων Aᶜ.   6. Χοηφόροις Vettori:
χλοηφόροις Aᶜ.   7. Πολυείδου apogr.: Πολυείδους Aᶜ.   12. Φινείδαις
Reiz: φινίδαις Aᶜ.

made in one way by the nurse, in another by the herds-men. The use of tokens for the express purpose of proof —and, indeed, any formal proof with or without tokens —is a less artistic mode of recognition. A better kind is that which comes about by a turn of incident, as in the Bath Scene in the Odyssey.

Next come the recognitions invented at will by the 4 poet, and on that account wanting in art. For example, Orestes in the Iphigenia reveals the fact that he is Orestes. She, indeed, makes herself known by the letter; but he, by speaking himself, and saying what the poet, not what the plot requires. This, therefore, is nearly allied to the fault above mentioned :—for Orestes might as well have brought tokens with him. Another similar instance is the 'voice of the shuttle' in the Tereus of Sophocles.

1455 a   The third kind depends on memory when the sight of 5 some object awakens a feeling : as in the Cyprians of Dicaeogenes, where the hero breaks into tears on seeing the picture ; or again in the 'Lay of Alcinous,' where Odysseus, hearing the minstrel play the lyre, recalls the past and weeps ; and hence the recognition.

The fourth kind is by process of reasoning. Thus in 6 the Choephori :—' Some one resembling me has come : no one resembles me but Orestes : therefore Orestes has come.' Such too is the discovery made by Iphigenia in the play of Polyeidus the Sophist. It was a natural reflection for Orestes to make, ' So I too must die at the altar like my sister.' So, again, in the Tydeus of Theodectes, the father says, ' I came to find my son, and I lose my own life.' So too in the Phineidae : the

εἱμαρμένην ὅτι ἐν τούτῳ εἵμαρτο ἀποθανεῖν αὐταῖς, καὶ
γὰρ ἐξετέθησαν ἐνταῦθα. ἔστιν δέ τις καὶ συνθετὴ ἐκ 7
15 παραλογισμοῦ τοῦ θατέρου, οἷον ἐν τῷ Ὀδυσσεῖ τῷ
ψευδαγγέλῳ· ὁ μὲν γὰρ τὸ τόξον ἔφη γνώσεσθαι ὃ οὐχ
ἑωράκει, τὸ δέ, ὡς δὴ ἐκείνου ἀναγνωριοῦντος διὰ τούτου,
ἐποίησε παραλογισμόν. πασῶν δὲ βελτίστη ἀναγνώ- 8
ρισις ἡ ἐξ αὐτῶν τῶν πραγμάτων τῆς ἐκπλήξεως γιγνο-
20 μένης δι' εἰκότων, οἷον [ὁ] ἐν τῷ Σοφοκλέους Οἰδίποδι
καὶ τῇ Ἰφιγενείᾳ· εἰκὸς γὰρ βούλεσθαι ἐπιθεῖναι γράμ-
ματα. αἱ γὰρ τοιαῦται μόναι ἄνευ τῶν πεποιημένων
σημείων καὶ περιδεραίων. δεύτεραι δὲ αἱ ἐκ συλλογισμοῦ.

XVII δεῖ δὲ τοὺς μύθους συνιστάναι καὶ τῇ λέξει συναπ-
25 εργάζεσθαι ὅτι μάλιστα πρὸ ὀμμάτων τιθέμενον· οὕτω
γὰρ ἂν ἐναργέστατα [ὁ] ὁρῶν ὥσπερ παρ' αὐτοῖς γιγνό-
μενος τοῖς πραττομένοις εὑρίσκοι τὸ πρέπον καὶ ἥκιστα
ἂν λανθάνοι [τὸ] τὰ ὑπεναντία. σημεῖον δὲ τούτου ὃ
ἐπετιμᾶτο Καρκίνῳ· ὁ γὰρ Ἀμφιάραος ἐξ ἱεροῦ ἀνῄει,
30 ὃ μὴ ὁρῶντα [τὸν θεατὴν] ἐλάνθανεν, ἐπὶ δὲ τῆς σκηνῆς
ἐξέπεσεν δυσχερανάντων τοῦτο τῶν θεατῶν. ὅσα δὲ
δυνατὸν καὶ τοῖς σχήμασιν συναπεργαζόμενον. πιθανώ- 2
τατοι γὰρ ἀπὸ τῆς αὐτῆς φύσεως οἱ ἐν τοῖς πάθεσίν

15. τοῦ θατέρου Bursian, praeeunte Hermann: τοῦ θεάτρου codd.   16.
ὁ μὲν apogr.: τὸ μὲν A°.   17. ὡς δὴ Tyrwhitt: ὡς δι' codd.   18.
ἐποίησε Ald., Bekker: ποιῆσαι codd. Locus autem prope desperatus est.
'Multo plura legisse videtur Arabs quam nostri codices praebent' (Margoliouth).   19. ἐκπλήξεως apogr.: πλήξεως A°: τῆς ἐκπλήξεως . . .
εἰκότων om. Arabs.   20. ὁ seclus. Vahlen : ἡ apogr. pauca.   22.
αἱ γὰρ τοιαῦται . . . περιδεραίων seclus. Gomperz.   23. περιδεραίων
apogr. (cf. 1454 b 27), Vahlen ed. 3 : δέρεων A°: δεραίων Vahlen ed. 2.
24. συναπεργάζεσθαι: ἀπεργάζεσθαι Susemihl.   26. ἐναργέστατα apogr.:
ἐνεργέστατα A°.   ὁ om. Ald.   28. τὸ om. apogr.   29. ἀνῄει
apogr.: ἂν εἴη A°.   30. ὁρῶντα codd. : ὁρῶντ' ἂν Vahlen.   τὸν
θεατὴν seclusi (simili errore Rhet. i. 2, 1358 a 8 τοὺς ἀκροατὰς in textum
irrepsit) : μὴ ὁρῶντ' α<ὑ>τὸν [θεατὴν] Gomperz, emendationis meae,
credo, inscius: τὸν ποιητὴν Dacier, Susemihl.   33. ἀπ' αὐτῆς τῆς
Tyrwhitt: codd. lect. confirmare videtur Arabs (Margoliouth).

women, on seeing the place, inferred their fate :—' Here
we are doomed to die, for here we were cast forth.'
Again, there is a recognition combined with a false in- 7
ference on the part of one of the characters, as in the
Odysseus Disguised as a Messenger. A man said he
would know the bow,—which, however, he had not seen.
This remark led Odysseus to imagine that the other
would recognise him through the bow, thus suggesting a
false inference.

But, of all recognitions, the best is that which arises 8
from the incidents themselves, where the startling discovery is made by natural means. Such is that in the
Oedipus of Sophocles, and in the Iphigenia; for it was
natural that Iphigenia should wish to despatch a letter.
These recognitions alone dispense with the artificial aid
of tokens or necklaces. Next come the recognitions by
process of reasoning.

XVII   In constructing the plot and working it out with
the proper diction, the poet should place the scene,
as far as possible, before his eyes. In this way, seeing
everything with the utmost vividness, as if he were a
spectator of the action, he will discover what is in keeping
with it, and be most unlikely to overlook inconsistencies.
The need of such a rule is shown by the fault found in
Carcinus. Amphiaraus was on his way from the temple.
This fact escaped the observation of one who did not see
the situation. On the stage, however, the piece failed,
the audience being offended at the oversight.

Again, the poet should work out his play, to the
best of his power, with appropriate gestures; for 2
those who feel emotion are most convincing by force of

εἰσιν καὶ χειμαίνει ὁ χειμαζόμενος καὶ χαλεπαίνει ὁ
35 ὀργιζόμενος ἀληθινώτατα. διὸ εὐφυοῦς ἡ ποιητική
ἐστιν ἢ μανικοῦ· τούτων γὰρ οἱ μὲν εὔπλαστοι οἱ
δὲ ἐκστατικοί εἰσιν. τούς τε λόγους καὶ τοὺς 3
1455 b πεποιημένους δεῖ καὶ αὐτὸν ποιοῦντα ἐκτίθεσθαι καθόλου, εἶθ' οὕτως ἐπεισοδιοῦν καὶ παρατείνειν. λέγω δὲ
οὕτως ἂν θεωρεῖσθαι τὸ καθόλου, οἷον τῆς Ἰφιγενείας·
τυθείσης τινὸς κόρης καὶ ἀφανισθείσης ἀδήλως τοῖς
5 θύσασιν, ἱδρυνθείσης δὲ εἰς ἄλλην χώραν, ἐν ᾗ νόμος
ἦν τοὺς ξένους θύειν τῇ θεῷ, ταύτην ἔσχε τὴν ἱερω-
σύνην· χρόνῳ δὲ ὕστερον τῷ ἀδελφῷ συνέβη ἐλθεῖν
τῆς ἱερείας (τὸ δὲ ὅτι ἀνεῖλεν ὁ θεὸς διά τινα αἰτίαν,
ἔξω τοῦ καθόλου [ἐλθεῖν ἐκεῖ], καὶ ἐφ' ὅ τι δέ, ἔξω τοῦ
10 μύθου), ἐλθὼν δὲ καὶ ληφθεὶς θύεσθαι μέλλων ἀνεγνώρισεν, εἴθ' ὡς Εὐριπίδης εἴθ' ὡς Πολύειδος ἐποίησεν,
κατὰ τὸ εἰκὸς εἰπὼν ὅτι οὐκ ἄρα μόνον τὴν ἀδελφὴν
ἀλλὰ καὶ αὐτὸν ἔδει τυθῆναι, καὶ ἐντεῦθεν ἡ σωτηρία.
μετὰ ταῦτα δὲ ἤδη ὑποθέντα τὰ ὀνόματα ἐπεισοδιοῦν, 4
15 ὅπως δὲ ἔσται οἰκεῖα τὰ ἐπεισόδια, οἷον ἐν τῷ Ὀρέστῃ
ἡ μανία δι' ἧς ἐλήφθη καὶ ἡ σωτηρία διὰ τῆς καθάρ-
σεως. ἐν μὲν οὖν τοῖς δράμασιν τὰ ἐπεισόδια σύντομα, 5

---

36. Var. lect. εὔπλαστοι et ἄπλαστοι habuisse videtur Σ (Diels).   37.
ἐκστατικοί cod. Vettori: ἐξεταστικοί codd.   τούτους τε τοὺς vel τούς
τε apogr.: τούτους τε Aᶜ (Vahlen, Christ), sed ne Graece quidem dicitur.
38. παρειλημμένοις coni. Vahlen.   1455 b 2. παρατείνειν Vettori: περι-
τείνειν Aᶜ.   9. καθόλου: fort. μύθου Vahlen.   10. μύθου: fort.
καθόλου Vahlen.   Secludendum videtur aut ἐλθεῖν ἐκεῖ (Bekker ed. 3) aut
ἔξω τοῦ καθόλου (Düntzer, Susemihl).   ἀνεγνωρίσθη M. Schmidt, et
olim Vahlen.   17. δράμασιν (vel ᾄσμασι) apogr.: ἄρμασιν Aᶜ.

sympathy.   One who is agitated storms, one who is angry rages, with the most life-like reality.   Hence poetry implies either a happy gift of nature or a strain of madness.   In the one case a man can take the mould of any character; in the other, he is lifted out of his proper self.

As for the story, whether the poet takes it ready 3
1455 b made or constructs it for himself, he should first sketch its general outline, and then fill in the episodes and amplify in detail.   The general plan may be illustrated by the Iphigenia.   A young girl is sacrificed; she disappears mysteriously from the eyes of those who sacrificed her; she is transported to another country, where the custom is to offer up all strangers to the goddess.   To this ministry she is appointed.   Some time later her brother chances to arrive.   The fact that the oracle for some reason ordered him to go there, is outside the general plan of the play.   The purpose, again, of his coming is outside the action proper.   However, he comes, he is seized, and, when on the point of being sacrificed, reveals who he is. The mode of recognition may be either that of Euripides or of Polyeidus, in whose play he exclaims very naturally :—' So it was not my sister only, but I too, who was doomed to be sacrificed'; and by that remark he is saved.

After this, the names being once given, it remains 4 to fill in the episodes.   We must see that they are relevant to the action.   In the case of Orestes, for example, there is the madness which led to his capture, and his deliverance by means of the purificatory rite. In the drama, the episodes are short, but it is these that 5

ἡ δ' ἐποποιία τούτοις μηκύνεται. τῆς γὰρ Ὀδυσσείας
<οὐ> μακρὸς ὁ λόγος ἐστίν· ἀποδημοῦντός τινος ἔτη
20 πολλὰ καὶ παραφυλαττομένου ὑπὸ τοῦ Ποσειδῶνος καὶ
μόνου ὄντος, ἔτι δὲ τῶν οἴκοι οὕτως ἐχόντων ὥστε τὰ
χρήματα ὑπὸ μνηστήρων ἀναλίσκεσθαι καὶ τὸν υἱὸν
ἐπιβουλεύεσθαι, αὐτὸς δὴ ἀφικνεῖται χειμασθεὶς καὶ
ἀναγνωρίσας ὅτι αὐτὸς ἐπιθέμενος αὐτὸς μὲν ἐσώθη τοὺς
25 δ' ἐχθροὺς διέφθειρε. τὸ μὲν οὖν ἴδιον τοῦτο, τὰ δ'
ἄλλα ἐπεισόδια.

XVIII ἔστι δὲ πάσης τραγῳδίας τὸ μὲν δέσις τὸ δὲ λύσις,
τὰ μὲν ἔξωθεν καὶ ἔνια τῶν ἔσωθεν πολλάκις ἡ δέσις,
τὸ δὲ λοιπὸν ἡ λύσις. λέγω δὲ δέσιν μὲν εἶναι τὴν
30 ἀπ' ἀρχῆς μέχρι τούτου τοῦ μέρους ὃ ἔσχατόν ἐστιν
ἐξ οὗ μεταβαίνειν <εἰς δυστυχίαν συμβαίνει ἢ> εἰς
εὐτυχίαν, λύσιν δὲ τὴν ἀπὸ τῆς ἀρχῆς τῆς μεταβάσεως
μέχρι τέλους· ὥσπερ ἐν τῷ Λυγκεῖ τῷ Θεοδέκτου δέσις
μὲν τά τε προπεπραγμένα καὶ ἡ τοῦ παιδίου λῆψις
35 καὶ πάλιν † ἡ αὐτῶν δὴ * * † <λύσις δ' ἡ> ἀπὸ τῆς
αἰτιάσεως τοῦ θανάτου μέχρι τοῦ τέλους. τραγῳδίας δὲ 2
εἴδη εἰσὶ τέσσαρα, [τοσαῦτα γὰρ καὶ τὰ μέρη ἐλέχθη,]
ἡ μὲν <ἁπλῆ ἡ δὲ> πεπλεγμένη, ἧς τὸ ὅλον ἐστὶν

19. μικρὸς apogr.: μακρὸς Aᶜ: 'sermo non est longus' Arabs, h. e. οὐ
μακρὸς (Margoliouth).   20. παραφυλαττομένου . . . Ποσειδῶνος seclus.
Castelvetro.   21. ἔτι apogr., Σ: ἐπεὶ Aᶜ.   23. δὴ coni. Vahlen:
δὲ codd.   24. τινὰς αὐτὸς codd.: ὅτι αὐτὸς Bywater: τινὰς αὐτὸς olim
seclusi: αὐτὸς seclus. Spengel.   28. πολλάκις post ἔξωθεν collocavit
Ueberweg: codd. lect. confirmat Arabs (Margoliouth).   31. <εἰς
δυστυχίαν συμβαίνει ἢ> Gomperz, alios secutus: <συμβαίνει ἢ ἐξ εὐτυχίας
εἰς δύστυχίαν> addenda esse coni. Vahlen.   35. ἡ αὐτῶν δὴ <ἀπαγωγή,
λύσις δ' ἡ> coni. Vahlen: ἡ αὐτῶν δή<λωσις, λύσις δ' ἡ> Christ, quod
confirmare videtur Arabs, 'et ea quae patefecit, solutio autem est quod
fiebat' etc. (Margoliouth).   36. τοῦ θανάτου: fort. τοῦ Δαναοῦ (Vahlen
et Spengel).   37. τοσαῦτα γὰρ . . . ἐλέχθη seclus. Susemihl ed. 1.
τὰ μέρη: τὰ μύθων Tyrwhitt: τὰ μύθου Sus. ed. 2 sec. Ueberweg.
38. ἡ μὲν <ἁπλῆ ἡ δὲ> Zeller (cf. Vahlen, qui post ἀναγνώρισις 39 <ἡ
δὲ ἁπλῆ> cum definitione deesse susp.).

give extension to Epic poetry. Thus the story of the Odyssey can be stated briefly. A certain man is absent from home for many years; he is jealously watched by Poseidon, and left desolate. Meanwhile his home is in a wretched plight—suitors are wasting his substance and plotting against his son. At length, tempest-tost, he arrives and reveals his true self; he attacks his enemies, destroys them and is himself preserved. This is the essence of the plot; the rest is episode.

XVIII   Every tragedy falls into two parts,—Complication and Unravelling (or *Dénouement*). Incidents extraneous to the action are frequently combined with a portion of the action proper, to form the Complication; the rest is the Unravelling. By the Complication I mean all that comes between the beginning of the action and the part which marks the turning-point to good or bad fortune. The Unravelling is that which comes between the beginning of the change and the end. Thus, in the Lynceus of Theodectes, the Complication consists of the incidents presupposed in the drama, the seizure of the child, and then again * * <The Unravelling> extends from the accusation of murder to the end.

There are four kinds of Tragedy,—first, the <Simple, 2 then> the Complex, depending entirely on Reversal and

περιπέτεια καὶ ἀναγνώρισις, ἡ δὲ παθητική, οἷον οἵ τε

1456 a Αἴαντες καὶ οἱ Ἰξίονες, ἡ δὲ ἠθική, οἷον αἱ Φθιώτιδες

καὶ ὁ Πηλεύς. † τὸ δὲ τέταρτον ὄης † οἷον αἵ τε

Φορκίδες καὶ Προμηθεὺς καὶ ὅσα ἐν ᾅδου. μάλιστα 3

μὲν οὖν ἅπαντα δεῖ πειρᾶσθαι ἔχειν, εἰ δὲ μή, τὰ

5 μέγιστα καὶ πλεῖστα, ἄλλως τε καὶ ὡς νῦν συκοφαν-

τοῦσιν τοὺς ποιητάς· γεγονότων γὰρ καθ' ἕκαστον μέρος

ἀγαθῶν ποιητῶν, ἑκάστου τοῦ ἰδίου ἀγαθοῦ ἀξιοῦσι τὸν

ἕνα ὑπερβάλλειν. δίκαιον δὲ καὶ τραγῳδίαν ἄλλην καὶ

τὴν αὐτὴν λέγειν οὐδεν<ὶ> ἴσως <ὡς> τῷ μύθῳ· τοῦτο

10 δέ, ὧν ἡ αὐτὴ πλοκὴ καὶ λύσις. πολλοὶ δὲ πλέξαντες

εὖ λύουσι κακῶς· δεῖ δὲ ἄμφω ἀεὶ κρατεῖσθαι. χρὴ 4

δὲ ὅπερ εἴρηται πολλάκις μεμνῆσθαι καὶ μὴ ποιεῖν

ἐποποιικὸν σύστημα τραγῳδίαν. ἐποποιικὸν δὲ λέγω

[δὲ] τὸ πολύμυθον, οἷον εἴ τις τὸν τῆς Ἰλιάδος ὅλον

15 ποιοῖ μῦθον. ἐκεῖ μὲν γὰρ διὰ τὸ μῆκος λαμβάνει τὰ

μέρη τὸ πρέπον μέγεθος, ἐν δὲ τοῖς δράμασι πολὺ παρὰ

τὴν ὑπόληψιν ἀποβαίνει. σημεῖον δέ, ὅσοι πέρσιν 5

Ἰλίου ὅλην ἐποίησαν καὶ μὴ κατὰ μέρος ὥσπερ Εὐ-

ριπίδης, <ἢ> Νιόβην καὶ μὴ ὥσπερ Αἰσχύλος, ἢ ἐκ-

20 πίπτουσιν ἢ κακῶς ἀγωνίζονται, ἐπεὶ καὶ Ἀγάθων ἐξ-

1456 a 2. τὸ δὲ τέταρτον ὄης : τὸ δὲ τερατῶδες Schrader : τὸ δὲ τερατῶδες <ἀλλότριον> Wecklein : τὸ δὲ τέταρτον <ἡ ἁπλῆ, οἷον * * παρέκβασις δὲ ἡ τερατώ>δης Susemihl : τὸ δὲ τέταρτον ὄψις (cf. 1458 a 6) Bywater ; sed τὰ εἴδη in hoc loco eadem utique esse debent quae in xxiv. 1.   5. τε apogr. : γε Aᶜ.   7. ἑκάστου apogr. : ἕκαστον Aᶜ.   9. οὐδενὶ ἴσως ὡς Bonitz : οὐδενὶ ὡς Zeller : οὐδὲν ἴσως τῷ codd.   τοῦτο : ταὐτὸ Teichmüller : τούτῳ Bursian.   11. κρατεῖσθαι (cf. Polit. iv. (vii.) 13, 1331 b 38) Vahlen : habuit iam Σ, 'prensarunt utrumque' Arabs : κρο-τεῖσθαι codd.   14. δὲ om. apogr.   19. ἢ add. Vahlen : ἢ Ἰοφῶν Susemihl, Spengel : pro Νιόβην, Ἑκάβην coni. Valla, unde Ἑκάβην [καὶ . . . Αἰσχύλος,] Reinach.

Recognition; next, the Pathetic (where the motive is 1456 apassion),—such as the tragedies on Ajax and Ixion; next, the Ethical (where the motives are ethical),—such as the Phthiotides and the Peleus. <We here exclude the supernatural kind>, such as the Phorcides, the Prometheus, and tragedies whose scene is in the lower world. The poet should endeavour, if possible, to 3 combine all poetic merits; or failing that, the greatest number and those the most important; the more so, in face of the cavilling criticism of the day. For whereas there have hitherto been good poets, each in his own branch, the critics now expect one man to surpass all others in their several lines of excellence.

In speaking of a tragedy as the same or different, the best test to take is the plot. Identity exists where the Complication and Unravelling are the same. Many poets tie the knot well, but unravel it ill. Both arts, however, should always be mastered.

Again, the poet should remember what has been often 4 said, and not make a Tragedy into an Epic structure. By an Epic structure I mean one with a multiplicity of plots: as if, for instance, you were to make a tragedy out of the entire story of the Iliad. In the Epic poem, owing to its length, each part assumes its proper magnitude. In the drama the result is far from answering to the poet's expectation. The proof is that 5 the poets who have dramatised the whole story of the Fall of Troy, instead of selecting portions, like Euripides; or who have taken the whole tale of Niobe, and not a part of her story, like Aeschylus, either fail utterly or meet with poor success on the stage. Even Agathon

ἔπεσεν ἐν τούτῳ μόνῳ· ἐν δὲ ταῖς περιπετείαις [καὶ ἐν
τοῖς ἁπλοῖς πράγμασι] στοχάζεται ὧν βούλονται θαυ-
μαστῶς· τραγικὸν γὰρ τοῦτο καὶ φιλάνθρωπον. ἔστιν 6
δὲ τοῦτο, ὅταν ὁ σοφὸς [μὲν] μετὰ πονηρίας ἐξαπατηθῇ,
25 ὥσπερ Σίσυφος, καὶ ὁ ἀνδρεῖος μὲν ἄδικος δὲ ἡττηθῇ.
ἔστιν δὲ τοῦτο <καὶ> εἰκὸς ὥσπερ Ἀγάθων λέγει, εἰκὸς
γὰρ γίνεσθαι πολλὰ καὶ παρὰ τὸ εἰκός. καὶ τὸν χορὸν 7
δὲ ἕνα δεῖ ὑπολαβεῖν τῶν ὑποκριτῶν, καὶ μόριον εἶναι
τοῦ ὅλου καὶ συναγωνίζεσθαι μὴ ὥσπερ Εὐριπίδη ἀλλ᾽
30 ὥσπερ Σοφοκλεῖ. τοῖς δὲ λοιποῖς τὰ ᾀδόμενα <οὐδὲν>
μᾶλλον τοῦ μύθου ἢ ἄλλης τραγῳδίας ἐστίν· διὸ ἐμβόλιμα ᾄδουσιν πρώτου ἄρξαντος Ἀγάθωνος τοῦ τοιούτου. καίτοι τί διαφέρει ἢ ἐμβόλιμα ᾄδειν ἢ εἰ ῥῆσιν ἐξ
ἄλλου εἰς ἄλλο ἁρμόττοι ἢ ἐπεισόδιον ὅλον;
XIX   περὶ μὲν οὖν τῶν ἄλλων ἤδη εἴρηται, λοιπὸν δὲ
36 περὶ λέξεως καὶ διανοίας εἰπεῖν. τὰ μὲν οὖν περὶ
τὴν διάνοιαν ἐν τοῖς περὶ ῥητορικῆς κείσθω, τοῦτο γὰρ
ἴδιον μᾶλλον ἐκείνης τῆς μεθόδου. ἔστι δὲ κατὰ τὴν
διάνοιαν ταῦτα, ὅσα ὑπὸ τοῦ λόγου δεῖ παρασκευασθῆναι.
40 μέρη δὲ τούτων τό τε ἀποδεικνύναι καὶ τὸ λύειν καὶ τὸ 2
1456 b πάθη παρασκευάζειν, οἷον ἔλεον ἢ φόβον ἢ ὀργὴν καὶ

21. καὶ ἐν . . . πράγμασι seclus. Susemihl: tuetur Arabs: pro ἁπλοῖς,
ἄλλοις Tucker, collato 1451 b 36: διπλοῖς Twining: καὶ ἁπλῶς ἐν
τοῖς πράγμασι Gomperz.   22. στοχάζεται Heinsius: στοχάζον-
ται codd.   24. Aut secludendum μὲν (Margoliouth cum Arabe)
aut legend. ὁ σοφὸς μὲν μετὰ πονηρίας δὲ cum apogr.   26. εἰκὸς:
<καὶ> εἰκὸς Susemihl, qui τραγικὸν . . . φιλάνθρωπον post ἡττηθῇ
collocat: καὶ ante εἰκὸς confirm. Arabs.   29. ὥσπερ . . . ὥσπερ:
ὥσπερ παρ' . . . ὥσπερ παρὰ Ald., Bekker.   30. λοιποῖς: πολλοῖς
Margoliouth cum Arabe.   ᾀδόμενα Maggi, 'quae canuntur' Arabs:
διδόμενα Aᶜ.   οὐδὲν add. Vahlen, habuit iam Σ ('nihil . . .
aliud amplius' Arabs): οὐ add. Maggi.   32. τοιούτου: 'poeta'
Arabs, ποιητοῦ Σ, ut videtur.   35. ἤδη apogr.: ἠδ' Aᶜ: εἰδεῶν ut
videtur Σ (Margoliouth).   36. καὶ Hermann: ἢ codd.   41. πάθη
seclus. Bernays, tuetur Arabs.

has been known to fail from this one defect.   In his
Reversals of the Action, however, he shows a marvellous
skill in the effort to hit the popular taste,—to produce a
tragic effect that satisfies the moral sense.   This effect is 6
produced when the clever rogue, like Sisyphus, is out-
witted, or the brave villain defeated.   Such an event is,
moreover, probable in Agathon's sense of the word : 'it
is probable,' he says, 'that many things should happen
contrary to probability.'

The Chorus too should be regarded as one of the 7
actors ; it should be an integral part of the whole, and
share in the action, in the manner not of Euripides but
of Sophocles.   As for the later poets, their choral songs
pertain as little to the subject of the piece as to that of
any other tragedy.   They are, therefore, sung as mere
interludes,—a practice first begun by Agathon.   Yet
what difference is there between introducing such choral
interludes, and transferring a speech, or even a whole act,
from one play to another ?

XIX   It remains to speak of Diction and Thought, the
other parts of Tragedy having been already discussed.
Concerning Thought, we may assume what is said in
the Rhetoric, to which inquiry the subject more
strictly belongs.   Under Thought is included every effect
which has to be produced by speech ; in particular,— 2
proof and refutation ; the excitation of the feelings, such
1456 b as pity, fear, anger, and the like ; the suggestion of

ὅσα τοιαῦτα, καὶ ἔτι μέγεθος καὶ μικρότητας.   δῆλον 3
δὲ ὅτι καὶ [ἐν] τοῖς πράγμασιν ἀπὸ τῶν αὐτῶν ἰδεῶν
δεῖ χρῆσθαι, ὅταν ἢ ἐλεεινὰ ἢ δεινὰ ἢ μεγάλα ἢ εἰκότα
5 δέῃ παρασκευάζειν· πλὴν τοσοῦτον διαφέρει, ὅτι τὰ μὲν
δεῖ φαίνεσθαι ἄνευ διδασκαλίας, τὰ δὲ ἐν τῷ λόγῳ ὑπὸ
τοῦ λέγοντος παρασκευάζεσθαι καὶ παρὰ τὸν λόγον
γίγνεσθαι.   τί γὰρ ἂν εἴη τοῦ λέγοντος ἔργον, εἰ φαίνοιτο
ἤδη ἃ δεῖ καὶ μὴ διὰ τὸν λόγον;   τῶν δὲ περὶ τὴν 4
10 λέξιν ἓν μέν ἐστιν εἶδος θεωρίας τὰ σχήματα τῆς
λέξεως, ἅ ἐστιν εἰδέναι τῆς ὑποκριτικῆς καὶ τοῦ τὴν
τοιαύτην ἔχοντος ἀρχιτεκτονικήν, οἷον τί ἐντολὴ καὶ
τί εὐχὴ καὶ διήγησις καὶ ἀπειλὴ καὶ ἐρώτησις καὶ
ἀπόκρισις καὶ εἴ τι ἄλλο τοιοῦτον.   παρὰ γὰρ τὴν 5
15 τούτων γνῶσιν ἢ ἄγνοιαν οὐδὲν εἰς τὴν ποιητικὴν
ἐπιτίμημα φέρεται ὅ τι καὶ ἄξιον σπουδῆς.   τί γὰρ
ἄν τις ὑπολάβοι ἡμαρτῆσθαι ἃ Πρωταγόρας ἐπιτιμᾷ,
ὅτι εὔχεσθαι οἰόμενος ἐπιτάττει εἰπὼν "μῆνιν ἄειδε
θεά," τὸ γὰρ κελεῦσαι φησὶν ποιεῖν τι ἢ μὴ ἐπίταξίς
20 ἐστιν.   διὸ παρείσθω ὡς ἄλλης καὶ οὐ τῆς ποιητικῆς
ὃν θεώρημα.

XX   [τῆς δὲ λέξεως ἁπάσης τάδ' ἐστὶ τὰ μέρη, στοιχεῖον
συλλαβὴ σύνδεσμος ὄνομα ῥῆμα [ἄρθρον] πτῶσις λόγος.
στοιχεῖον μὲν οὖν ἐστιν φωνὴ ἀδιαίρετος, οὐ πᾶσα δὲ ἀλλ' 2

1456 b 2. μικρότητας Aᶜ: σμικρότητα apogr.   3. ἐν seclus. Ueberweg
(cf. Spengel).   ἰδεῶν apogr.: εἰδεῶν Aᶜ.   8. φαίνοιτο scripsi:
φανοῖτο codd.   9. ἤδη ἃ δεῖ Tyrwhitt: ἤδη Castelvetro: ἤδη δι'
αὐτὰ Susemihl; ἤδη τῇ θέᾳ Gomperz (praeeunte Spengel): ἠδέα codd.,
Vahlen ed. 3: ᾗ δέοι Vahlen ed. 2.   23. ἄρθρον cum Hartung
seclusi (cf. Susemihl), sed eo dubitantius quod proprio loco post σύνδεσμος
hoc verbum statuisse videtur Σ (cf. Arab.): transposuit iam Spengel:
σύνδεσμος <ἢ> ἄρθρον ὄνομα ῥῆμα Steinthal.

importance or its opposite.   Further, it is evident that 3
the dramatic incidents must be treated from the same
points of view as the dramatic speeches, when the object
is to evoke the sense of pity, fear, importance, or probability.   The only difference is, that the incidents
should speak for themselves without verbal exposition;
while the effects aimed at in a speech should be produced by the speaker, and as a result of the speech.
For what were the need of a speaker, if the proper
impression were at once conveyed, quite apart from what
he says?

Next, as regards Diction.   One branch of the inquiry 4
treats of the Modes of Expression.   But this province
of knowledge belongs to the art of Declamation, and to
the masters of that science.   It includes, for instance,
—what is a command, a prayer, a narrative, a threat,
a question, an answer, and so forth.   To know or not 5
to know these things involves no serious censure upon
the poet's art.   For who can admit the fault imputed
to Homer by Protagoras,—that in the words, 'Sing,
goddess, of the wrath,' he gives a command under the
idea that he utters a prayer?   For to tell some one to
do a thing or not to do it is, he says, a command.   We
may, therefore, pass this over as an inquiry that belongs
to another art, not to poetry.

XX   [Language in general includes the following parts :—
the Letter, the Syllable, the Connecting word, the Noun,
the Verb, the Inflexion or Case, the Proposition or
Phrase.

A Letter is an indivisible sound, yet not every such 2
sound, but only one which can form part of a group of

25 ἐξ ἧς πέφυκε συνθετὴ γίγνεσθαι φωνή· καὶ γὰρ τῶν θηρίων
εἰσὶν ἀδιαίρετοι φωναὶ ὧν οὐδεμίαν λέγω στοιχεῖον.
ταύτης δὲ μέρη τό τε φωνῆεν καὶ τὸ ἡμίφωνον καὶ 3
ἄφωνον. ἔστιν δὲ φωνῆεν μὲν <τὸ> ἄνευ προσβολῆς
ἔχον φωνὴν ἀκουστήν, ἡμίφωνον δὲ τὸ μετὰ προσβολῆς
30 ἔχον φωνὴν ἀκουστήν, οἷον τὸ Σ καὶ τὸ Ρ, ἄφωνον δὲ
τὸ μετὰ προσβολῆς καθ' αὑτὸ μὲν οὐδεμίαν ἔχον φωνήν,
μετὰ δὲ τῶν ἐχόντων τινὰ φωνὴν γινόμενον ἀκουστόν,
οἷον τὸ Γ καὶ τὸ Δ. ταῦτα δὲ διαφέρει σχήμασίν τε 4
τοῦ στόματος καὶ τόποις καὶ δασύτητι καὶ ψιλότητι
35 καὶ μήκει καὶ βραχύτητι, ἔτι δὲ ὀξύτητι καὶ βαρύτητι
καὶ τῷ μέσῳ· περὶ ὧν καθ' ἕκαστον ἐν τοῖς μετρικοῖς
προσήκει θεωρεῖν. συλλαβὴ δέ ἐστιν φωνὴ ἄσημος 5
συνθετὴ ἐξ ἀφώνου * * καὶ φωνὴν ἔχοντος. καὶ γὰρ
τὸ ΓΡ <οὐκ> ἄνευ τοῦ Α συλλαβὴ ἀλλὰ μετὰ τοῦ Α,
40 οἷον τὸ ΓΡΑ. ἀλλὰ καὶ τούτων θεωρῆσαι τὰς διαφορὰς
τῆς μετρικῆς ἐστιν. σύνδεσμος δέ ἐστιν φωνὴ ἄσημος 6
1457 a ἢ οὔτε κωλύει οὔτε ποιεῖ φωνὴν μίαν σημαντικὴν ἐκ
πλειόνων φωνῶν, πεφυκυῖα [συν]τίθεσθαι καὶ ἐπὶ τῶν

25. συνθετὴ apogr., Arabs 'compositae voci': συνετὴ Aᶜ.   38. Post
ἀφώνου intercidisse videtur <ἢ ἐξ ἀφώνου καὶ ἡμιφώνου>.   Post φωνὴν
ἔχοντος coni. Christ <ἢ πλειόνων ἀφώνων καὶ φωνὴν ἔχοντος>.   καὶ
γὰρ τὸ ΓΡ ἄνευ τοῦ Α συλλαβὴ καὶ μετὰ τοῦ Α, Aᶜ: 'nam Γ et
P sine A non faciunt syllabam, quoniam tantum fiunt syllaba cum A'
Arabs (Margoliouth), unde restituit Susemihl quod in textum recepi:
καὶ γὰρ τὸ ΓΑ ἄνευ τοῦ Ρ συλλαβὴ καὶ μετὰ τοῦ Ρ Tyrwhitt: καὶ γὰρ
τὸ Α ἄνευ τοῦ ΓΡ συλλαβὴ καὶ μετὰ τοῦ ΓΡ M. Schmidt.   1457 a 1-8.
Locus valde impeditus. Codicum fide ita vulgo legitur: ἢ οὔτε κωλύει
οὔτε ποιεῖ φωνὴν μίαν σημαντικήν, ἐκ πλειόνων φωνῶν πεφυκυῖαν συντί-
θεσθαι, καὶ ἐπὶ τῶν ἄκρων καὶ ἐπὶ τοῦ μέσου, ἣν μὴ ἁρμόττει (ἣν μὴ
ἁρμόττῃ apogr., Bekker) ἐν ἀρχῇ τιθέναι καθ' αὑτόν (αὑτήν Tyrwhitt),
οἷον μέν, ἤτοι, δέ (vel δή). ἢ φωνὴ ἄσημος ἢ ἐκ πλειόνων μὲν φωνῶν
μιᾶς σημαντικῶν (σημαντικὸν Aᶜ) δὲ ποιεῖν πέφυκεν μίαν σημαντικὴν φωνήν.
ἄρθρον δ' ἐστὶ φωνὴ ἄσημος, ἢ λόγου ἀρχὴν ἢ τέλος ἢ διορισμὸν δηλοῖ,
οἷον τὸ ἀμφί (φ. μ. ῑ. Aᶜ: φημί Ald., Bekker) καὶ τὸ περί καὶ τὰ ἄλλα.

sounds. For even brutes utter indivisible sounds, none
of which I call a letter. The sound I mean may be 3
either a vowel, a semi-vowel, or a mute. A vowel is
that which without impact of tongue or lip has an
audible sound. A semi-vowel, that which with such
impact has an audible sound, as S and R. A mute,
that which with such impact has by itself no sound,
but joined to a vowel sound becomes audible, as G and
D. These are distinguished according to the form 4
assumed by the mouth, and the place where they are
produced; according as they are aspirated or smooth,
long or short; as they are acute, grave, or of an inter-
mediate tone; which inquiry belongs in detail to a
treatise on metre.

A Syllable is a non-significant sound, composed of a 5
mute and a vowel <or of a mute, a semi-vowel> and a
vowel: for GR without A is not a syllable, but with
A it is,—GRA. But the investigation of these differences
belongs also to metrical science.

A Connecting word is a non-significant sound, which 6
1457 a neither causes nor hinders the union of many sounds
into one significant sound; it may be placed at either

ἄκρων καὶ ἐπὶ τοῦ μέσου· ἡ φωνὴ ἄσημος ἢ ἐκ πλειόνων
μὲν φωνῶν μιᾶς, σημαντικῶν δέ, ποιεῖν πέφυκεν μίαν
5 σημαντικὴν φωνήν, οἷον τὸ ἀμφί καὶ τὸ περί καὶ τὰ
ἄλλα· <ἢ> φωνὴ ἄσημος ἢ λόγου ἀρχὴν ἢ τέλος ἢ 7
διορισμὸν δηλοῖ, ἣν μὴ ἁρμόττει ἐν ἀρχῇ λόγου τιθέναι
καθ' αὑτήν, οἷον μέν, ἤτοι, δέ. [ἡ φωνὴ ἄσημος ἡ
οὔτε κωλύει οὔτε ποιεῖ φωνὴν μίαν σημαντικὴν ἐκ
10 πλειόνων φωνῶν πεφυκυῖα τίθεσθαι καὶ ἐπὶ τῶν ἄκρων
καὶ ἐπὶ τοῦ μέσου.] ὄνομα δέ ἐστι φωνὴ συνθετὴ 8
σημαντικὴ ἄνευ χρόνου ἧς μέρος οὐδέν ἐστι καθ' αὑτὸ
σημαντικόν· ἐν γὰρ τοῖς διπλοῖς οὐ χρώμεθα ὡς καὶ
αὐτὸ καθ' αὑτὸ σημαῖνον, οἷον ἐν τῷ Θεοδώρῳ τὸ δῶρον
15 οὐ σημαίνει. ῥῆμα δὲ φωνὴ συνθετὴ σημαντικὴ μετὰ 9
χρόνου ἧς οὐδὲν μέρος σημαίνει καθ' αὑτό, ὥσπερ καὶ
ἐπὶ τῶν ὀνομάτων· τὸ μὲν γὰρ ἄνθρωπος ἢ λευκόν οὐ
σημαίνει τὸ πότε, τὸ δὲ βαδίζει ἢ βεβάδικεν προσ-
σημαίνει τὸ μὲν τὸν παρόντα χρόνον τὸ δὲ τὸν παρ-
20 εληλυθότα. πτῶσις δ' ἐστὶν ὀνόματος ἢ ῥήματος ἡ 10
μὲν τὸ κατὰ τὸ τούτου ἢ τούτῳ σημαῖνον καὶ ὅσα
τοιαῦτα, ἡ δὲ κατὰ τὸ ἑνὶ ἢ πολλοῖς, οἷον ἄνθρωποι
ἢ ἄνθρωπος, ἡ δὲ κατὰ τὰ ὑποκριτικά, οἷον κατ'
ἐρώτησιν, ἐπίταξιν· τὸ γὰρ <ἆρ'> ἐβάδισεν ἢ βάδιζε
25 πτῶσις ῥήματος κατὰ ταῦτα τὰ εἴδη ἐστίν. λόγος δὲ 11
φωνὴ συνθετὴ σημαντικὴ ἧς ἔνια μέρη καθ' αὑτὰ
σημαίνει τι· οὐ γὰρ ἅπας λόγος ἐκ ῥημάτων καὶ
ὀνομάτων σύγκειται, οἷον " ὁ τοῦ ἀνθρώπου ὁρισμός "·
ἀλλ' ἐνδέχεται <καὶ> ἄνευ ῥημάτων εἶναι λόγον. μέρος

8-11. ἡ . . . μέσου seclus. Reiz, Hermann.   18. ποτὲ Spengel.
βαδίζει apogr.: βαδίζειν Aᶜ.   21. Alterum τὸ add. apogr.   24.
ἆρ' add. Vahlen.   βάδιζε apogr.: ἐβάδιζεν Aᶜ.   29. καὶ add.
Gomperz, quem secutus sum etiam in loci interpunctione.

end or in the middle of a sentence. Or, a non-significant
sound, which out of several sounds, each of them significant, is capable of forming one significant sound,—as
ἀμφί, περί, and the like. Or, a non-significant sound, 7
which marks the beginning, end, or division of a sentence;
such, however, that it cannot correctly stand by itself at
the beginning of a sentence,—as μέν, ἤτοι, δέ.

A Noun is a composite significant sound, not marking 8
time, of which no part is in itself significant; for in
double or compound words we do not employ the
separate parts as if each were in itself significant. Thus
in Theodorus, 'god-given,' the δῶρον or 'gift' is not in
itself significant.

A Verb is a composite significant sound, marking 9
time, in which, as in the noun, no part is in itself significant. For 'man,' or 'white' does not express the idea
of 'when'; but 'he walks,' or 'he has walked' does
connote time, present or past.

Inflexion belongs both to the noun and verb, and 10
expresses either the relation 'of,' 'to,' or the like; or
that of number, whether one or many, as 'man' or
'men'; or the modes or tones in actual delivery, e.g. a
question or a command. 'Did he go?' and 'go' are
verbal inflexions of this kind.

A Proposition or Phrase is a composite significant 11
sound, some at least of whose parts are in themselves
significant; for not every such group of words consists
of verbs and nouns—'the definition of man,' for example
—but it may dispense even with the verb. Still it will

30 μέντοι ἀεί τι σημαῖνον ἔξει, οἶον " ἐν τῷ βαδίζειν,"
" Κλέων ὁ Κλέωνος." εἶς δέ ἐστι λόγος διχῶς, ἢ γὰρ 12
ὁ ἐν σημαίνων, ἢ ὁ ἐκ πλειόνων συνδέσμῳ, οἶον ἡ
Ἰλιὰς μὲν συνδέσμῳ εἶς, ὁ δὲ τοῦ ἀνθρώπου τῷ ἓν
σημαίνειν.]

XXI   ὀνόματος δὲ εἴδη τὸ μὲν ἁπλοῦν, ἁπλοῦν δὲ λέγω ὃ
36 μὴ ἐκ σημαινόντων σύγκειται, οἶον γῆ, τὸ δὲ διπλοῦν·
τούτου δὲ τὸ μὲν ἐκ σημαίνοντος καὶ ἀσήμου (πλὴν
οὐκ ἐν τῷ ὀνόματι σημαίνοντος [καὶ ἀσήμου]), τὸ δὲ ἐκ
σημαινόντων σύγκειται. εἴη δ' ἂν καὶ τριπλοῦν καὶ
40 τετραπλοῦν ὄνομα καὶ πολλαπλοῦν, οἶον τὰ πολλὰ
1457 b τῶν Μασσαλιωτῶν· Ἑρμοκαϊκόξανθος <ἐπευξάμενος Διὶ
πατρί>. ἅπαν δὲ ὄνομά ἐστιν ἢ κύριον ἢ γλῶττα ἢ 2
μεταφορὰ ἢ κόσμος ἢ πεποιημένον ἢ ἐπεκτεταμένον ἢ
ὑφῃρημένον ἢ ἐξηλλαγμένον. λέγω δὲ κύριον μὲν ᾧ 3
5 χρῶνται ἕκαστοι, γλῶτταν δὲ ᾧ ἕτεροι, ὥστε φανερὸν
ὅτι καὶ γλῶτταν καὶ κύριον εἶναι δυνατὸν τὸ αὐτό, μὴ
τοῖς αὐτοῖς δέ· τὸ γὰρ σίγυνον Κυπρίοις μὲν κύριον,
ἡμῖν δὲ γλῶττα. μεταφορὰ δέ ἐστιν ὀνόματος ἀλλοτρίου 4
ἐπιφορὰ ἢ ἀπὸ τοῦ γένους ἐπὶ εἶδος ἢ ἀπὸ τοῦ

30. βαδίζειν Aᶜ : βαδίζει apogr.   31. Κλέων ὁ Κλέων codd. : τὸ Κλέων
Bigg : οἶον ἐν τῷ " βαδίζει Κλέων" ὁ Κλέων plerique edd. : οἶον " ἐν τῳ
βαδίζειν," " Κλέων ὁ Κλέωνος " M. Schmidt: (habuit Σ Κλέωνος).   32.
συνδέσμῳ apogr. : συνδέσμων Aᶜ.   33. τῷ apogr. : τὸ Aᶜ.   38.
ἐντὸς τοῦ ὀνόματος Tucker.   ὀνόματι Vahlen, Σ : ὀνόματος Aᶜ.
καὶ ἀσήμου om. iam Σ, ut videtur ('non tamen indicans in nomine'
Arabs). Idem effecit Ussing deleto καὶ ἀσήμου in v. 33, mutata quoque
interpunctione, ἐκ σημαίνοντος, πλὴν οὐκ ἐν τῷ ὀνόματι σημαίνοντος, καὶ
ἀσήμου, . . .   41. μεγαλιωτῶν codd. : Μασσαλιωτῶν Diels, qui collato
Arabe ('sicut multa de Massiliotis Hermocaicoxanthus qui supplicabatur
dominum caelorum') totum versum Ἑρμοκ . . . πατρί tanquam epici
carminis, comice scripti, ex coniectura restituit. Ἑρμοκ. ad Phocacam
spectat, Massiliae μητρόπολιν, urbem inter Hermum et Caïcum sitam.
Ceteras emendationes licet iam missas facere, e.g. μεγαλείων ὡς Winstanley : μεγαλείων οἶον Bekker ed. 3 : μεγαλείων ὧν Vahlen.   1457 b 4.
ἀφῃρημένον Spengel (cf. 1458 a 1).

always have some significant part, as 'in walking,' or 'Cleon son of Cleon.' A proposition or phrase may form 12 a unity in two ways,—either as signifying one thing, or as consisting of several parts linked together. Thus the Iliad is one by the linking together of parts, the definition of man by the unity of the thing signified.]

XXI   Words are of two kinds, simple and double. By simple I mean those composed of non-significant elements, such as γῆ. By double or compound, those composed either of a significant and non - significant element (though within the whole word no element is significant), or of elements that are both significant. A word may likewise be triple, quadruple, or multiple in form, like 1457 b so many Massilian expressions, e.g. ' Hermo-caico-xanthus < who prayed to Father Zeus.' >

Every word is either current, or strange, or metaphorical, 2 or ornamental, or newly-coined, or lengthened, or contracted, or altered.

By a current or proper word I mean one which is 3 in general use among a people ; by a strange word, one which is in use in another country. Plainly, therefore, the same word may be at once strange and current, but not in relation to the same people. The word σίγυνον, ' lance,' is to the Cyprians a current term but to us a strange one.

Metaphor is the application of an alien name by 4 transference either from genus to species, or from species

10 εἴδους ἐπὶ τὸ γένος ἢ ἀπὸ τοῦ εἴδους ἐπὶ εἶδος ἢ
κατὰ τὸ ἀνάλογον. λέγω δὲ ἀπὸ γένους μὲν ἐπὶ εἶδος, 5
οἶον " νηῦς δέ μοι ἥδ' ἔστηκεν·" τὸ γὰρ ὁρμεῖν ἐστιν
ἑστάναι τι. ἀπ' εἴδους δὲ ἐπὶ γένος, "ἦ δὴ μυρί'
'Οδυσσεὺς ἐσθλὰ ἔοργεν·" τὸ γὰρ μυρίον πολύ <τί>
15 ἐστιν, ᾧ νῦν ἀντὶ τοῦ πολλοῦ κέχρηται. ἀπ' εἴδους δὲ
ἐπὶ εἶδος οἶον "χαλκῷ ἀπὸ ψυχὴν ἀρύσας" καὶ "ταμὼν
ἀτειρέι χαλκῷ." ἐνταῦθα γὰρ τὸ μὲν ἀρύσαι ταμεῖν, τὸ
δὲ ταμεῖν ἀρύσαι εἴρηκεν· ἄμφω γὰρ ἀφελεῖν τί ἐστιν.
τὸ δὲ ἀνάλογον λέγω, ὅταν ὁμοίως ἔχῃ τὸ δεύτερον 6
20 πρὸς τὸ πρῶτον καὶ τὸ τέταρτον πρὸς τὸ τρίτον· ἐρεῖ
γὰρ ἀντὶ τοῦ δευτέρου τὸ τέταρτον ἢ ἀντὶ τοῦ τετάρτου
τὸ δεύτερον, καὶ ἐνίοτε προστιθέασιν ἀνθ' οὗ λέγει πρὸς
ὅ ἐστι. λέγω δὲ οἶον ὁμοίως ἔχει φιάλη‾ πρὸς Διόνυσον
καὶ ἀσπὶς πρὸς ῞Αρη· ἐρεῖ τοίνυν τὴν φιάλην ἀσπίδα
25 Διονύσου καὶ τὴν ἀσπίδα φιάλην ῎Αρεως. ἢ ὃ γῆρας πρὸς
βίον, καὶ ἑσπέρα πρὸς ἡμέραν· ἐρεῖ τοίνυν τὴν ἑσπέραν
γῆρας ἡμέρας καὶ τὸ γῆρας ἑσπέραν βίου ἤ, ὥσπερ
'Εμπεδοκλῆς, δυσμὰς βίου. ἐνίοις δ' οὐκ ἔστιν ὄνομα 7
κείμενον τῶν ἀνάλογον, ἀλλ' οὐδὲν ἧττον ὁμοίως λεχθή-
30 σεται· οἶον τὸ τὸν καρπὸν μὲν ἀφιέναι σπείρειν, τὸ δὲ
τὴν φλόγα ἀπὸ τοῦ ἡλίου ἀνώνυμον· ἀλλ' ὁμοίως ἔχει
τοῦτο πρὸς τὸν ἥλιον καὶ τὸ σπείρειν πρὸς τὸν καρπόν,
διὸ εἴρηται "σπείρων θεοκτίσταν φλόγα." ἔστι δὲ τῷ 8
τρόπῳ τούτῳ τῆς μεταφορᾶς χρῆσθαι καὶ ἄλλως, προσ-
35 αγορεύσαντα τὸ ἀλλότριον ἀποφῆσαι τῶν οἰκείων τι,

---

10. τό om. apogr.   14. τί add. Twining.   27. ἡμέρας . . .
δυσμὰς apogr.: ἡμέρας ἢ ὥσπερ 'Εμπεδοκλῆς καὶ τὸ γῆρας ἑσπέραν βίου ἢ
δυσμὰς βίου Aᶜ, Vahlen.   29. τῶν Aᶜ: τὸ apogr., Bekker.   32.
<τὸν ἀφιέντα> τὸν καρπόν Castelvetro.

to genus, or from species to species, or by analogy, that is,
proportion. Thus from genus to species, as: 'There lies 5
my ship'; for lying at anchor is a species of lying.
From species to genus, as: 'Verily ten thousand noble
deeds hath Odysseus wrought'; for ten thousand is a
species of large number, and is here used for a large
number generally. From species to species, as: 'With
blade of bronze drew away the life,' and 'Cleft the water
with the vessel of unyielding bronze.' Here ἀρύσαι, 'to
draw away,' is used for ταμεῖν, 'to cleave,' and ταμεῖν
again for ἀρύσαι,—each being a species of taking away.
Analogy or proportion is when the second term is to the 6
first as the fourth to the third. We may then use the
fourth for the second, or the second for the fourth.
Sometimes too we qualify the metaphor by adding the
term to which the proper word is relative. Thus the
cup is to Dionysus as the shield to Ares. The cup may,
therefore, be called 'the shield of Dionysus,' and the
shield 'the cup of Ares.' Or, again, as old age is to life,
so is evening to day. Evening may therefore be called
'the old age of the day,' and old age, 'the evening of
life' or, in the phrase of Empedocles, 'life's setting sun.'
In some cases one of the terms of the proportion has no 7
specific name; still, the metaphor may be used. For
instance, to scatter seed is called sowing: but the action
of the sun in scattering his rays is nameless. Still this
process bears to the sun the same relation as sowing to
the seed. Hence the expression of the poet, 'sowing the
god-created light.' There is another way in which this 8
kind of metaphor may be employed. We may apply an
alien term, and then deny of that term one of its proper

οἷον εἰ τὴν ἀσπίδα εἴποι φιάλην μὴ "Αρεως ἀλλ' ἄοινον.
πεποιημένον δ' ἐστὶν ὃ ὅλως μὴ καλούμενον ὑπὸ τινῶν 9
αὐτὸς τίθεται ὁ ποιητής, δοκεῖ γὰρ ἔνια εἶναι τοιαῦτα,
οἷον τὰ κέρατα ἐρνύγας καὶ τὸν ἱερέα ἀρητῆρα. ἐπεκ- 10
1458 a τεταμένον δέ ἐστιν ἢ ἀφῃρημένον τὸ μὲν ἐὰν φωνήεντι
μακροτέρῳ κεχρημένον ᾖ τοῦ οἰκείου ἢ συλλαβῇ ἐμβε-
βλημένῃ, τὸ δὲ ἂν ἀφῃρημένον τι ᾖ αὐτοῦ, ἐπεκτεταμένον
μὲν οἷον τὸ πόλεως πόληος καὶ τὸ Πηλέος <Πηλῆος καὶ
5 τὸ Πηλείδου> Πηληιάδεω, ἀφῃρημένον δὲ οἷον τὸ κρῖ καὶ
τὸ δῶ καὶ " μία γίνεται ἀμφοτέρων ὄψ." ἐξηλλαγμένον 11
δ' ἐστὶν ὅταν τοῦ ὀνομαζομένου τὸ μὲν καταλείπῃ τὸ δὲ
ποιῇ, οἷον τὸ "δεξιτερὸν κατὰ μαζόν " ἀντὶ τοῦ δεξιόν.
[αὐτῶν δὲ τῶν ὀνομάτων τὰ μὲν ἄρρενα τὰ δὲ θήλεα 12
10 τὰ δὲ μεταξύ, ἄρρενα μὲν ὅσα τελευτᾷ εἰς τὸ Ν καὶ Ρ
καὶ Σ καὶ ὅσα ἐκ τούτου σύγκειται, ταῦτα δ' ἐστὶν δύο,
Ψ καὶ Ξ, θήλεα δὲ ὅσα ἐκ τῶν φωνηέντων εἴς τε τὰ ἀεὶ
μακρά, οἷον εἰς Η καὶ Ω, καὶ τῶν ἐπεκτεινομένων εἰς Α·
ὥστε ἴσα συμβαίνει πλήθει εἰς ὅσα τὰ ἄρρενα καὶ τὰ
15 θήλεα. τὸ γὰρ Ψ καὶ τὸ Ξ ταὐτά ἐστιν. εἰς δὲ ἄφωνον
οὐδὲν ὄνομα τελευτᾷ, οὐδὲ εἰς φωνῆεν βραχύ. εἰς δὲ τὸ
Ι τρία μόνον, μέλι κόμμι πέπερι. εἰς δὲ τὸ Υ πέντε.
τὰ δὲ μεταξὺ εἰς ταῦτα καὶ Ν καὶ Σ.]
XXII λέξεως δὲ ἀρετὴ σαφῆ καὶ μὴ ταπεινὴν εἶναι. σα-
20 φεστάτη μὲν οὖν ἐστιν ἡ ἐκ τῶν κυρίων ὀνομάτων, ἀλλὰ
ταπεινή. παράδειγμα δὲ ἡ Κλεοφῶντος ποίησις καὶ ἡ

---

36. ἀλλ' ἄοινον Vettori: ἄλλα οἴνου codd.   1458 a 2. κεχρημένος
Hermann.   4. Πηλῆος καὶ τὸ Πηλείδου add. M. Schmidt.   6. ὄψ
Vettori: ὄης Ac (h. c. ὄιις vel ὄψις).   11. καὶ Σ apogr., Maggi,
Arabs: om. Ac.   12. ἐκ seclus. Ueberweg.   14. πλήθει apogr.:
πλήθη Ac.   15. ante ταὐτὰ add. τῷ Σ Tyrwhitt.   17. post πέντε
add. apogr. τὸ πῶυ τὸ νᾶπυ τὸ γόνυ τὸ δόρυ τὸ ἄστυ.

attributes; as if we were to call the shield, not 'the cup of Ares,' but 'the wineless cup.'

A newly-coined word is one which has never been 9 even in local use, but is invented by the poet himself. Some such words there appear to be : as ἐρνύγες, 'sprouters,' for κέρατα, 'horns,' and ἀρητήρ, 'supplicator,' for ἱερεύς, 'priest.'

1458 a   A word is lengthened when its own vowel is exchanged 10 for a longer one, or when a syllable is inserted. A word is contracted when some part of it is removed. Instances of lengthening are,—πόληος for πόλεως, Πηλῆος for Πηλέος, and Πηληιάδεω for Πηλείδου: of contraction,—κρῖ, δῶ, and ὄψ, as in μία γίνεται ἀμφοτέρων ὄψ.

An altered word is one in which part of the ordinary 11 form is left unchanged, and part is re-cast; as in δεξιτερὸν κατὰ μαζόν, δεξιτερόν is for δεξιόν.

[Nouns in themselves are either masculine, feminine, 12 or neuter. Masculine are such as end in ν, ρ, ς, or in some letter compounded with ς,—these being two, ψ and ξ. Feminine, such as end in vowels that are always long, as η and ω, and—of vowels that admit of lengthening—those in a. Thus the number of letters in which nouns masculine and feminine end is the same; for ψ and ξ are equivalent to endings in ς. No noun ends in a mute or a vowel short by nature. Three only end in ι, —μέλι, κόμμι, πέπερι : five end in υ. Neuter nouns end in these two latter vowels; also in ν and ς.]

XXII   The perfection of style is to be clear without being mean. The clearest style is that which uses only current or proper words; at the same time it is mean :—witness the poetry of Cleophon and of Sthenelus. That diction,

G

Σθενέλου. σεμνὴ δὲ καὶ ἐξαλλάττουσα τὸ ἰδιωτικὸν ἡ
τοῖς ξενικοῖς κεχρημένη. ξενικὸν δὲ λέγω γλῶτταν καὶ
μεταφορὰν καὶ ἐπέκτασιν καὶ πᾶν τὸ παρὰ τὸ κύριον.
25 ἀλλ' ἄν τις ἅμα ἅπαντα τοιαῦτα ποιήσῃ, ἢ αἴνιγμα ἔσται 2
ἢ βαρβαρισμός· ἂν μὲν οὖν ἐκ μεταφορῶν, αἴνιγμα, ἐὰν
δὲ ἐκ γλωττῶν, βαρβαρισμός· αἰνίγματός τε γὰρ ἰδέα
αὕτη ἐστί, τὸ λέγοντα ὑπάρχοντα ἀδύνατα συνάψαι.
κατὰ μὲν οὖν τὴν τῶν <ἄλλων> ὀνομάτων σύνθεσιν οὐχ
30 οἷόν τε τοῦτο ποιῆσαι, κατὰ δὲ τὴν μεταφορὰν ἐνδέχεται,
οἷον " ἄνδρ' εἶδον πυρὶ χαλκὸν ἐπ' ἀνέρι κολλήσαντα,"
καὶ τὰ τοιαῦτα. ἐκ τῶν γλωττῶν βαρβαρισμός. δεῖ 3
ἄρα κεκρᾶσθαί πως τούτοις· τὸ μὲν γὰρ μὴ ἰδιωτικὸν
ποιήσει μηδὲ ταπεινόν, οἷον ἡ γλῶττα καὶ ἡ μεταφορὰ
35 καὶ ὁ κόσμος καὶ τἆλλα τὰ εἰρημένα εἴδη, τὸ δὲ κύριον
1458 b τὴν σαφήνειαν. οὐκ ἐλάχιστον δὲ μέρος συμβάλλεται 4
εἰς τὸ σαφὲς τῆς λέξεως καὶ μὴ ἰδιωτικὸν αἱ ἐπεκτάσεις
καὶ ἀποκοπαὶ καὶ ἐξαλλαγαὶ τῶν ὀνομάτων· διὰ μὲν γὰρ
τὸ ἄλλως ἔχειν ἢ ὡς τὸ κύριον, παρὰ τὸ εἰωθὸς γιγνό-
5 μενον, τὸ μὴ ἰδιωτικὸν ποιήσει, διὰ δὲ τὸ κοινωνεῖν τοῦ
εἰωθότος τὸ σαφὲς ἔσται. ὥστε οὐκ ὀρθῶς ψέγουσιν οἱ 5
ἐπιτιμῶντες τῷ τοιούτῳ τρόπῳ τῆς διαλέκτου καὶ διακω-
μῳδοῦντες τὸν ποιητήν, οἷον Εὐκλείδης ὁ ἀρχαῖος, ὡς
ῥᾴδιον ποιεῖν, εἴ τις δώσει ἐκτείνειν ἐφ' ὁπόσον βούλεται,
10 ἰαμβοποιήσας ἐν αὐτῇ τῇ λέξει. " Ἐπιχάρην εἶδον

---

25. τις ἅπαντα vel τις ἅμα ἅπαντα apogr.: ἂν ἅπαντα Aᶜ.   ποιήσῃ
apogr.: ποιῆσαι Aᶜ.   29. ἄλλων coni. Margoliouth, collato Arabe
'reliqua nomina': κυρίων Heinsius.   32. ante vel post ἐκ . . .
βαρβαρισμός lacunam statuit Gomperz: ἐκ τ'<ἀμίκτ>ων γλωττῶν Tucker.
33. κεκρᾶσθαι Maggi e cod. Lampridii, habuit iam Σ (cf. Arab. 'si mis-
centur haec'): κεκρίσθαι ceteri codd.   1458 b 1. συμβάλλεται Aᶜ:
συμβάλλονται apogr.   10. ᾔτει χάριν Aᶜ: 'Επιχάρην Bursian praeeunte
Tyrwhitt ('Ηπιχάρην): ἐπὶ χάριν Σ, ut videtur ('appellatum cum favore'
Arabs).   εἶδον apogr.: ἴδον Aᶜ: ἰδὼν Gomperz.

on the other hand, is lofty and raised above the commonplace which employs unusual words. By unusual, I
mean strange (or rare) words, metaphorical, lengthened,—
anything, in short, that differs from the normal idiom.
Yet a style wholly composed of such words is either a 2
riddle or a jargon; a riddle, if it consists of metaphors;
a jargon, if it consists of strange (or rare) words. For the
essence of a riddle is to express true facts under impossible combinations. Now this cannot be done by any
arrangement of ordinary words, but by the use of metaphor it can. Such is the riddle:—'A man I saw who
on another man had glued the bronze by aid of fire,' and
others of the same kind. A diction that is made up of
strange (or rare) terms is a jargon. A certain infusion, 3
therefore, of these elements is necessary to style; for the
strange (or rare) word, the metaphorical, the ornamental,
and the other kinds above mentioned, will raise it above
the commonplace and mean, while the use of proper
words will make it perspicuous. But nothing contributes 4
1458 b more to produce a clearness of diction that is remote
from commonness than the lengthening, contraction, and
alteration of words. For by deviating in exceptional
cases from the normal idiom, the language will gain
distinction; while, at the same time, the partial con-
formity with usage will give perspicuity. The critics, 5
therefore, are in error who censure these licenses of
speech, and hold the author up to ridicule. Thus
Eucleides, the elder, declared that it would be an easy
matter to be a poet if you might lengthen syllables at
will. He caricatured the practice in the very form of
his diction, as in the verse:

Μαραθῶνάδε βαδίζοντα," καὶ "οὐκ ἂν γ' ἐράμενος τὸν
ἐκείνου ἐλλέβορον." τὸ μὲν οὖν φαίνεσθαί πως χρώμενον 6
τούτῳ τῷ τρόπῳ γελοῖον, τὸ δὲ μέτρον κοινὸν ἁπάντων
ἐστὶ τῶν μερῶν· καὶ γὰρ μεταφοραῖς καὶ γλώτταις καὶ
15 τοῖς ἄλλοις εἴδεσι χρώμενος <ἀπρε>πῶς καὶ ἐπίτηδες ἐπὶ
τὰ γελοῖα τὸ αὐτὸ ἂν ἀπεργάσαιτο. τὸ δὲ ἁρμόττον 7
ὅσον διαφέρει ἐπὶ τῶν ἐπῶν θεωρείσθω ἐντιθεμένων τῶν
<κυρίων> ὀνομάτων εἰς τὸ μέτρον. καὶ ἐπὶ τῆς γλώττης
δὲ καὶ ἐπὶ τῶν μεταφορῶν καὶ ἐπὶ τῶν ἄλλων ἰδεῶν
20 μετατιθεὶς ἄν τις τὰ κύρια ὀνόματα κατίδοι ὅτι ἀληθῆ
λέγομεν· οἷον τὸ αὐτὸ ποιήσαντος ἰαμβεῖον Αἰσχύλου
καὶ Εὐριπίδου, ἐν δὲ μόνον ὄνομα μεταθέντος, ἀντὶ
[κυρίου] εἰωθότος γλῶτταν, τὸ μὲν φαίνεται καλὸν τὸ δ'
εὐτελές. Αἰσχύλος μὲν γὰρ ἐν τῷ Φιλοκτήτῃ ἐποίησε
25   φαγέδαινα <δ'> ἥ μου σάρκας ἐσθίει ποδός,
ὁ δὲ ἀντὶ τοῦ ἐσθίει τὸ θοινᾶται μετέθηκεν. καὶ
     νῦν δέ μ' ἐὼν ὀλίγος τε καὶ οὐτιδανὸς καὶ ἀεικής,[1]
εἴ τις λέγοι τὰ κύρια μετατιθεὶς
     νῦν δέ μ' ἐὼν μικρός τε καὶ ἀσθενικὸς καὶ ἀειδής·

---

[1] Odyss. ix. 515, νῦν δέ μ' ἐὼν ὀλίγος τε καὶ οὐτιδανὸς καὶ ἄκικυς.

---

11. ἂν γ' ἐράμενος apogr.: ἂν γεράμενος A°: γευσάμενος Tyrwhitt: πριά-
μενος Gomperz.   12. πως: ἀπρεπῶς Twining: πάντως Hermann:
ἀναισθήτως Tucker.   15. ἐπὶ τὰ γελοῖα seclus. Gomperz.   16.
ἁρμόττον apogr.: ἁρμόττοντος A°.   17. ἐπῶν: ἐπεκτάσεων Tyrwhitt.
18. κυρίων coni. Vahlen.   21. Αἰσχύλῳ Εὐριπίδου Essen.   22.
μεταθέντος Ald.: μετατιθέντος A°.   23. κυρίου vel εἰωθότος secludendum
coni. Vahlen : κυρίου <καὶ> εἰωθότος Heinsius.   25. δ' (vel τ') add.
Ritter: φαγέδαιν' ἀεὶ Nauck.   27. ἀεικής Castelvetro (var. lec. Odyss.
l. c.), Arabs 'ut non conveniat': δειδής codd.: ἄκικυς Odyss. l. c.

or,

'Επιχάρην εἶδον Μαραθῶνάδε βαδίζοντα,

οὐκ ἄν γ' ἐράμενος τὸν ἐκείνου ἐλλέβορον.

To employ such license at all obtrusively is, no doubt, 6 grotesque; but in any mode of poetic diction there must be moderation. Even metaphors, strange (or rare) words, or any similar forms of speech, would produce the like effect if used without propriety, and with the express purpose of being ludicrous. How great a differ- 7 ence is made by the appropriate use of lengthening, may be seen in Epic poetry by the insertion of ordinary forms in the verse. So, again, if we take a strange (or rare) word, a metaphor, or any similar mode of expression, and replace it by the current or proper term, the truth of our observation will be manifest. For example Aeschylus and Euripides each composed the same iambic line. But the alteration of a single word by Euripides, who employed the rarer term instead of the ordinary one, makes one verse appear beautiful and the other trivial. Aeschylus in his Philoctetes says:

φαγέδαινα <δ'> ἥ μου σάρκας ἐσθίει ποδός·

Euripides substitutes θοινᾶται 'feasts on' for ἐσθίει 'feeds on.' Again, in the line,

νῦν δέ μ' ἐὼν ὀλίγος τε καὶ οὐτιδανὸς καὶ ἀεικής,

the difference will be felt if we substitute the common words,

νῦν δέ μ' ἐὼν μικρός τε καὶ ἀσθενικὸς καὶ ἀειδής.

30 καὶ

δίφρον [τ'] ἀεικέλιον καταθεὶς ὀλίγην τε τράπεζαν,[1]
δίφρον μοχθηρὸν καταθεὶς μικράν τε τράπεζαν.
καὶ τὸ "ἠιόνες βοόωσιν"[2] ἠιόνες κράζουσιν. ἔτι δὲ 8
Ἀριφράδης τοὺς τραγῳδοὺς ἐκωμῴδει, ὅτι ἃ οὐδεὶς ἂν
35 εἴποι ἐν τῇ διαλέκτῳ τούτοις χρῶνται, οἷον τὸ δωμάτων
ἄπο ἀλλὰ μὴ ἀπὸ δωμάτων, καὶ τὸ σέθεν καὶ τὸ ἐγὼ
1459 a δέ νιν, καὶ τὸ Ἀχιλλέως πέρι ἀλλὰ μὴ περὶ Ἀχιλλέως,
καὶ ὅσα ἄλλα τοιαῦτα. διὰ γὰρ τὸ μὴ εἶναι ἐν τοῖς
κυρίοις ποιεῖ τὸ μὴ ἰδιωτικὸν ἐν τῇ λέξει ἅπαντα τὰ
τοιαῦτα· ἐκεῖνος δὲ τοῦτο ἠγνόει. ἔστιν δὲ μέγα μὲν 9
5 τὸ ἑκάστῳ τῶν εἰρημένων πρεπόντως χρῆσθαι, καὶ
διπλοῖς ὀνόμασι καὶ γλώτταις, πολὺ δὲ μέγιστον τὸ
μεταφορικὸν εἶναι. μόνον γὰρ τοῦτο οὔτε παρ' ἄλλου
ἔστι λαβεῖν εὐφυΐας τε σημεῖόν ἐστι· τὸ γὰρ εὖ μετα-
φέρειν τὸ τὸ ὅμοιον θεωρεῖν ἐστιν. τῶν δ' ὀνομάτων τὰ 10
10 μὲν διπλᾶ μάλιστα ἁρμόττει τοῖς διθυράμβοις, αἱ δὲ
γλῶτται τοῖς ἡρωικοῖς, αἱ δὲ μεταφοραὶ τοῖς ἰαμβείοις.
καὶ ἐν μὲν τοῖς ἡρωικοῖς ἅπαντα χρήσιμα τὰ εἰρημένα,
ἐν δὲ τοῖς ἰαμβείοις διὰ τὸ ὅτι μάλιστα λέξιν μιμεῖσθαι
ταῦτα ἁρμόττει τῶν ὀνομάτων ὅσοις κἂν ἐν [ὅσοις] λόγοις
15 τις χρήσαιτο· ἔστι δὲ τὰ τοιαῦτα τὸ κύριον καὶ μεταφορὰ καὶ κόσμος.

περὶ μὲν οὖν τραγῳδίας καὶ τῆς ἐν τῷ πράττειν μιμήσεως ἔστω ἡμῖν ἱκανὰ τὰ εἰρημένα.

---

[1] Odyss. xx. 259, δίφρον ἀεικέλιον καταθεὶς ὀλίγην τε τράπεζαν.
[2] Iliad xvii. 265.

---

31. τ' ἀεικέλιον codd.: τ' αἰκέλιον Vahlen: τε seclus. Susemihl ed. 1.
35. εἴποι apogr.: εἴπηι A°.　1459 a 5. τὸ apogr.: τῶι A°.　14.
κἂν Harles: καὶ codd.　ὅσοις del. Ald.: <τοῖς> λόγοις Gomperz:
ὁδοῖς Σ, ut videtur (Ellis), cf. Arab. 'quot usurpant homines in via.'

Or, if for the line,

δίφρον [τ'] ἀεικέλιον καταθεὶς ὀλίγην τε τράπεζαν,

we read,

δίφρον μοχθηρὸν καταθεὶς μικράν τε τράπεζαν.

Or, for ἠιόνες βοόωσιν, ἠιόνες κράζουσιν.

Again, Ariphrades ridiculed the tragedians for using 8 phrases which no one would employ in ordinary speech : for example, δωμάτων ἄπο instead of ἀπὸ δωμάτων, 1459 a σέθεν, ἐγὼ δέ νιν, 'Αχιλλέως πέρι instead of περὶ 'Αχιλλέως, and the like. It is precisely because such phrases are not part of the current idiom that they give distinction to the style. This, however, he failed to see.

It is a great matter to observe propriety in these 9 several modes of expression—compound words, strange (or rare) words, and so forth. But the greatest thing by far is to have a command of metaphor. This alone cannot be imparted by another; it is the mark of genius, —for to make good metaphors implies an eye for resemblances.

Of the various kinds of words, the compound are 10 best adapted to dithyrambs, rare words to heroic poetry, metaphors to iambic. In heroic poetry, indeed, all these varieties are serviceable. But in iambic verse, which reproduces, as far as may be, familiar speech, the most appropriate words are those which are found even in prose. These are,—the current or proper, the metaphorical, the ornamental.

Concerning Tragedy and imitation by means of action, this may suffice.

XXIII   περὶ δὲ τῆς διηγηματικῆς καὶ ἐν<ὶ> μέτρῳ μιμη-
20 τικῆς, ὅτι δεῖ τοὺς μύθους καθάπερ ἐν ταῖς τραγῳδίαις
συνεστάναι δραματικοὺς καὶ περὶ μίαν πρᾶξιν ὅλην καὶ
τελείαν, ἔχουσαν ἀρχὴν καὶ μέσα καὶ τέλος, ἵν᾽ ὥσπερ
ζῷον ἓν ὅλον ποιῇ τὴν οἰκείαν ἡδονήν, δῆλον· καὶ μὴ
ὁμοίας ἱστορίαις τὰς συνθέσεις εἶναι, ἐν αἷς ἀνάγκη οὐχὶ
25 μιᾶς πράξεως ποιεῖσθαι δήλωσιν ἀλλ᾽ ἑνὸς χρόνου, ὅσα
ἐν τούτῳ συνέβη περὶ ἕνα ἢ πλείους, ὧν ἕκαστον ὡς
ἔτυχεν ἔχει πρὸς ἄλληλα. ὥσπερ γὰρ κατὰ τοὺς αὐτοὺς 2
χρόνους ἥ τ᾽ ἐν Σαλαμῖνι ἐγένετο ναυμαχία καὶ ἡ ἐν
Σικελίᾳ Καρχηδονίων μάχη οὐδὲν πρὸς τὸ αὐτὸ συντεί-
30 νουσαι τέλος, οὕτω καὶ ἐν τοῖς ἐφεξῆς χρόνοις ἐνίοτε
γίνεται θάτερον μετὰ θάτερον, ἐξ ὧν ἓν οὐδὲν γίνεται
τέλος. σχεδὸν δὲ οἱ πολλοὶ τῶν ποιητῶν τοῦτο δρῶσι.
διό, ὥσπερ εἴπομεν ἤδη, καὶ ταύτῃ θεσπέσιος ἂν φανείη 3
Ὅμηρος παρὰ τοὺς ἄλλους, τῷ μηδὲ τὸν πόλεμον καίπερ
35 ἔχοντα ἀρχὴν καὶ τέλος ἐπιχειρῆσαι ποιεῖν ὅλον· λίαν
γὰρ ἂν μέγας καὶ οὐκ εὐσύνοπτος ἔμελλεν ἔσεσθαι, ἢ
τῷ μεγέθει μετριάζοντα καταπεπλεγμένον τῇ ποικιλίᾳ.
νῦν δ᾽ ἓν μέρος ἀπολαβὼν ἐπεισοδίοις κέχρηται αὐτῶν
πολλοῖς, οἷον νεῶν καταλόγῳ καὶ ἄλλοις ἐπεισοδίοις, οἷς
40 διαλαμβάνει τὴν ποίησιν. οἱ δ᾽ ἄλλοι περὶ ἕνα ποιοῦσι
1459 b καὶ περὶ ἕνα χρόνον καὶ μίαν πρᾶξιν πολυμερῆ, οἷον ὁ

---

19. ἐνὶ (vel ἐν ἑνὶ) μέτρῳ conieci (cf. 1449 b 11, 1459 b 36): ἐν ἑξαμέτρῳ
Heinsius: ἐν μέτρῳ codd.   21. συνεστάναι coni. Vahlen: συνιστᾶναι
Aᶜ.   24. ἱστορίαις τὰς συνθέσεις Dacier, confirmare videtur Arabs:
ἱστορίας τὰς συνήθεις codd.   28. ναυμαχία apogr.: ναύμαχος Aᶜ.
31. μετὰ θάτερον Castelvetro, Hermann: μετὰ θατέρου codd.   34. τῷ
apogr.: τὸ Aᶜ.   36. μέγα (rec. corr. μέγας) . . . εὐσύνοπτος . . .
μετριάζοντα Aᶜ: μέγα . . . εὐσύνοπτον . . . μετριάζον posito commate
post ἔσεσθαι Bursian.   38. αὐτῶν seclus. Christ: αὐτοῦ Heinsius.
39. οἷς apogr.: δὶς pr. Aᶜ et ceteri codd.

XXIII   As to that poetic imitation which is narrative in form and employs a single metre, the plot manifestly ought, as in a tragedy, to be constructed on dramatic principles. It should have for its subject a single action, whole and complete, with a beginning, a middle, and an end. It will thus resemble a single and coherent picture of a living being, and produce the pleasure proper to it. It will differ in structure from historical compositions, which of necessity present not a single action, but a single period, and all that happened within that period to one person or to many, little connected together as the events may be. For as the sea-fight at 2 Salamis and the battle with the Carthaginians in Sicily took place at the same time, but did not tend to one result, so in the sequence of events, one thing sometimes follows another, and yet the two may not work up to any common end. Such is the practice, we may say, of most poets. Here again, then, as has been already 3 observed, the transcendent excellence of Homer is manifest. He never attempts to make the whole war of Troy the subject of his poem, though that war had a beginning and an end. It would have been too vast a theme, and not easily embraced in a single view. If, again, he had kept it within moderate limits, it must have been over-complicated by the variety of the incidents. As it is, he detaches a single portion, and admits as episodes many events from the general story of the war—such as the Catalogue of the ships and others—thus diversifying the poem. All other poets 1459 b take a single hero, a single period, or an action single indeed, but with a multiplicity of parts. Thus did the

τὰ Κύπρια ποιήσας καὶ τὴν μικρὰν Ἰλιάδα. τοιγαροῦν 4
ἐκ μὲν Ἰλιάδος καὶ Ὀδυσσείας μία τραγῳδία ποιεῖται
ἑκατέρας ἢ δύο μόναι, ἐκ δὲ Κυπρίων πολλαὶ καὶ τῆς
5 μικρᾶς Ἰλιάδος [πλέον] ὀκτώ, οἷον ὅπλων κρίσις,
Φιλοκτήτης, Νεοπτόλεμος, Εὐρύπυλος, πτωχεία, Λά-
καιναι, Ἰλίου πέρσις καὶ ἀπόπλους [καὶ Σίνων καὶ
Τρῳάδες].

XXIV   ἔτι δὲ [ἔτι δὲ] τὰ εἴδη ταὐτὰ δεῖ ἔχειν τὴν ἐποποιίαν
10 τῇ τραγῳδίᾳ, ἢ γὰρ ἁπλῆν ἢ πεπλεγμένην ἢ ἠθικὴν ἢ
παθητικήν· καὶ τὰ μέρη ἔξω μελοποιίας καὶ ὄψεως
ταὐτά· καὶ γὰρ περιπετειῶν δεῖ καὶ ἀναγνωρίσεων καὶ
παθημάτων· ἔτι τὰς διανοίας καὶ τὴν λέξιν ἔχειν καλῶς.
οἷς ἅπασιν Ὅμηρος κέχρηται καὶ πρῶτος καὶ ἱκανῶς. 2
15 καὶ γὰρ καὶ τῶν ποιημάτων ἑκάτερον συνέστηκεν ἡ μὲν
Ἰλιὰς ἁπλοῦν καὶ παθητικόν, ἡ δὲ Ὀδύσσεια πεπλεγ-
μένον (ἀναγνώρισις γὰρ διόλου) καὶ ἠθική. πρὸς δὲ
τούτοις λέξει καὶ διανοίᾳ πάντα ὑπερβέβληκεν. δια- 3
φέρει δὲ κατά τε τῆς συστάσεως τὸ μῆκος ἡ ἐποποιία
20 καὶ τὸ μέτρον. τοῦ μὲν οὖν μήκους ὅρος ἱκανὸς ὁ
εἰρημένος· δύνασθαι γὰρ δεῖ συνορᾶσθαι τὴν ἀρχὴν καὶ
τὸ τέλος. εἴη δ' ἂν τοῦτο, εἰ τῶν μὲν ἀρχαίων ἐλάτ-
τους αἱ συστάσεις εἶεν, πρὸς δὲ τὸ πλῆθος τραγῳδιῶν
τῶν εἰς μίαν ἀκρόασιν τιθεμένων παρήκοιεν. ἔχει δὲ 4
25 πρὸς τὸ ἐπεκτείνεσθαι τὸ μέγεθος πολύ τι ἡ ἐποποιία
ἴδιον διὰ τὸ ἐν μὲν τῇ τραγῳδίᾳ μὴ ἐνδέχεσθαι ἅμα

1459 b 2. Κύπρια Tyrwhitt: κυπρικὰ Aᶜ.   5. πλέον et καὶ Σίνων καὶ
Τρῳάδες seclus. Hermann.   9. δεῖ apogr.: δὴ Aᶜ.   10. ἠθικὴν om.
Arabs.   12. καὶ ἠθῶν post ἀναγνωρίσεων add. Susemihl.   14.
ἱκανῶς apogr.: ἱκανὸς Aᶜ.   17. ἀναγνωρίσεις Christ.   ἠθικὸν rec.
sup. scr. Aᶜ.   δὲ apogr.: γὰρ Aᶜ.   18. πάντας Ald.   24.
Fort. καθιεμένων Richards.

author of the Cypria and of the Little Iliad. For this 4
reason the Iliad and the Odyssey each furnish the
subject of one tragedy, or, at most, of two; while the
Cypria supplies materials for many, and the Little Iliad
eight—the Award of the Arms, the Philoctetes, the
Neoptolemus, Eurypylus, the Mendicant Odysseus, the
Laconian Women, the Fall of Ilium, the Departure of
the Fleet.

XXIV   Again, Epic poetry must have as many kinds as
Tragedy : it must be simple, or complex, or 'ethical,'
or 'pathetic.'   The parts also, with the exception of
song and scenery, are the same; for it requires
Reversals, Recognitions, and Tragic Incidents.   Moreover,
the thoughts and the diction must be artistic.   In all 2
these respects Homer is our earliest and sufficient model.
Indeed each of his poems has a twofold character.   The
Iliad is at once simple and 'pathetic,' and the Odyssey
complex (for Recognition scenes run through it), and
at the same time 'ethical.'   Moreover, in diction and
thought he is supreme.

Epic poetry differs from Tragedy in the scale on 3
which it is constructed, and in its metre.   As regards
scale or length, we have already laid down an adequate
limit :—the beginning and the end must be capable of
being brought within a single view.   This condition
will be satisfied by poems on a smaller scale than the
old epics, and answering in length to the group of
tragedies presented at a single sitting.

Epic poetry has, however, a great — a special— 4
capacity for enlarging its dimensions, and we can see the
reason.   In Tragedy we cannot imitate several actions

πραττόμενα πολλὰ μέρη μιμεῖσθαι ἀλλὰ τὸ ἐπὶ τῆς
σκηνῆς καὶ τῶν ὑποκριτῶν μέρος μόνον· ἐν δὲ τῇ
ἐποποιίᾳ διὰ τὸ διήγησιν εἶναι ἔστι πολλὰ μέρη ἅμα
30 ποιεῖν περαινόμενα, ὑφ' ὧν οἰκείων ὄντων αὔξεται ὁ
τοῦ ποιήματος ὄγκος. ὥστε τοῦτ' ἔχει τὸ ἀγαθὸν εἰς
μεγαλοπρέπειαν καὶ τὸ μεταβάλλειν τὸν ἀκούοντα καὶ
ἐπεισοδιοῦν ἀνομοίοις ἐπεισοδίοις· τὸ γὰρ ὅμοιον ταχὺ
πληροῦν ἐκπίπτειν ποιεῖ τὰς τραγῳδίας. τὸ δὲ μέτρον 5
35 τὸ ἡρωικὸν ἀπὸ τῆς πείρας ἥρμοκεν. εἰ γάρ τις ἐν
ἄλλῳ τινὶ μέτρῳ διηγηματικὴν μίμησιν ποιοῖτο ἢ ἐν
πολλοῖς, ἀπρεπὲς ἂν φαίνοιτο· τὸ γὰρ ἡρωικὸν στασι-
μώτατον καὶ ὀγκωδέστατον τῶν μέτρων ἐστίν (διὸ καὶ
γλώττας καὶ μεταφορὰς δέχεται μάλιστα· περιττὴ γὰρ
40 καὶ <ταύτῃ> ἡ διηγηματικὴ μίμησις τῶν ἄλλων). τὸ
1460 a δὲ ἰαμβεῖον καὶ τετράμετρον κινητικά, τὸ μὲν ὀρχηστικὸν
τὸ δὲ πρακτικόν. ἔτι δὲ ἀτοπώτερον, εἰ μιγνύοι τις 6
αὐτά, ὥσπερ Χαιρήμων. διὸ οὐδεὶς μακρὰν σύστασιν
ἐν ἄλλῳ πεποίηκεν ἢ τῷ ἡρῴῳ, ἀλλ' ὥσπερ εἴπομεν
5 αὐτὴ ἡ φύσις διδάσκει τὸ ἁρμόττον [αὐτῇ] [δι-]
αἱρεῖσθαι. Ὅμηρος δὲ ἄλλα τε πολλὰ ἄξιος ἐπαινεῖ- 7
σθαι καὶ δὴ καὶ ὅτι μόνος τῶν ποιητῶν οὐκ ἀγνοεῖ ὃ
δεῖ ποιεῖν αὐτόν. αὐτὸν γὰρ δεῖ τὸν ποιητὴν
ἐλάχιστα λέγειν· οὐ γάρ ἐστι κατὰ ταῦτα μιμητής.
10 οἱ μὲν οὖν ἄλλοι αὐτοὶ μὲν δι' ὅλου ἀγωνίζονται,

---

40. καὶ codd.: καὶ ταύτῃ Twining: κἂν ταύταις Bywater.   μίμησις
apogr.: κίνησις Aᶜ.   1460 a 1. κινητικαὶ Λᶜ: κινητικά Ald., Bekker:
κινητικὰ καὶ Vahlen: κινητικά, εἰ Gomperz.   2. μιγνύοι Ald.: μιγνύει
apogr.: μηγνύη Aᶜ (fuit μὴ, et η extremum in litura corr.): μὴ γνοίη
Σ, cf. Arab. 'si quis nesciret' (Margoliouth).   5. αὐτῇ apogr.: αὐτὴ
Λᶜ: seclus. Gomperz.   αἱρεῖσθαι Bonitz, confirmare videtur Arabs
(Margoliouth): διαιρεῖσθαι Λᶜ.

carried on at one and the same time ; we must confine
ourselves to the action on the stage and the part taken
by the players.   But in Epic poetry, owing to the
narrative form, many events simultaneously transacted
can be presented ; and these, if relevant to the subject,
add mass and dignity to the poem.   The Epic has here
an advantage, and one that conduces to grandeur of
effect, also diverting the mind of the hearer and relieving
the story with varying episodes.   For sameness of
incident soon produces satiety, and makes tragedies fail
on the stage.

As for the metre, the heroic measure has proved its 5
fitness by the test of experience.   If a narrative poem
in any other metre or in many metres were now composed, it would be found incongruous.   For of all
measures the heroic is the stateliest and the most
massive ; and hence it most readily admits rare words
and metaphors, which is another point in which the
narrative form of imitation stands alone.   On the other
1460 a hand, the iambic and the trochaic tetrameter are stirring
measures, the latter being akin to dancing, the former
expressive of action.   Still more absurd would it be to 6
mix together different metres, as was done by Chaeremon.
Hence no one has ever composed a poem on a great scale
in any other than heroic verse.   Nature herself, as we
have said, teaches the choice of the proper measure.

Homer, admirable in all respects, has the special merit 7
of being the only poet who rightly appreciates the part
he should take himself.   The poet should speak as little
as possible in his own person, for it is not this that makes
him an imitator.   Other poets appear themselves upon

μιμοῦνται δὲ ὀλίγα καὶ ὀλιγάκις· ὁ δὲ ὀλίγα φροιμια-
σάμενος εὐθὺς εἰσάγει ἄνδρα ἢ γυναῖκα ἢ ἄλλο τι
[ἦθος] καὶ οὐδέν· ἀήθη ἀλλ' ἔχοντα ἤθη. δεῖ μὲν 8
οὖν ἐν ταῖς τραγῳδίαις ποιεῖν τὸ θαυμαστόν, μᾶλλον
15 δ' ἐνδέχεται ἐν τῇ ἐποποιίᾳ τὸ ἄλογον, δι' ὃ συμβαίνει μάλιστα τὸ θαυμαστόν, διὰ τὸ μὴ ὁρᾶν εἰς τὸν
πράττοντα· ἐπεὶ τὰ περὶ τὴν Ἕκτορος δίωξιν ἐπὶ
σκηνῆς ὄντα γελοῖα ἂν φανείη, οἱ μὲν ἑστῶτες καὶ οὐ
διώκοντες, ὁ δὲ ἀνανεύων, ἐν δὲ τοῖς ἔπεσιν λανθάνει.
20 τὸ δὲ θαυμαστὸν ἡδύ· σημεῖον δέ· πάντες γὰρ προστι-
θέντες ἀπαγγέλλουσιν ὡς χαριζόμενοι. δεδίδαχεν δὲ 9
μάλιστα Ὅμηρος καὶ τοὺς ἄλλους ψευδῆ λέγειν ὡς δεῖ.
ἔστι δὲ τοῦτο παραλογισμός. οἴονται γὰρ ἄνθρωποι,
ὅταν τουδὶ ὄντος τοδὶ ᾖ ἢ γινομένου γίνηται, εἰ τὸ
25 ὕστερον ἔστιν, καὶ τὸ πρότερον εἶναι ἢ γίνεσθαι· τοῦτο
δέ ἐστι ψεῦδος. διὸ δή, ἂν τὸ πρῶτον ψεῦδος, ἀλλ'
οὐδέ, τούτου ὄντος, ἀνάγκη <κἀκεῖνο> εἶναι ἢ γενέσθαι
[ἢ] προσθεῖναι· διὰ γὰρ τὸ τοῦτο εἰδέναι ἀληθὲς ὄν,
παραλογίζεται ἡμῶν ἡ ψυχὴ καὶ τὸ πρῶτον ὡς ὄν.
30 παράδειγμα δὲ τούτου ἐκ τῶν Νίπτρων. προαιρεῖσθαί 10
τε δεῖ ἀδύνατα εἰκότα μᾶλλον ἢ δυνατὰ ἀπίθανα· τούς
τε λόγους μὴ συνίστασθαι ἐκ μερῶν ἀλόγων, ἀλλὰ

---

13. ἦθος om. Reiz, habuit iam Σ: εἶδος Bursian.   οὐδέν' ἀήθη apogr.:
οὐδένα ἤθη Δᶜ.   ἔχοντα ἦθος coni. Christ.   14. Post οὖν add. < καὶ ἐν
τοῖς ἔπεσιν καὶ> Christ, fort. recte: κἀν ταῖς Gomperz.   15. ἄλογον
Vettori: ἀνάλογον codd., Σ.   δι' ὃ Vettori: διὸ codd.   17. ἐπεὶ τὰ
apogr.: ἔπειτα τὰ Δᶜ, Σ.   24. ᾖ ἢ apogr.: ἢν Aᶜ, rec. corr. ᾖ.
25. γενέσθαι coni. Christ.   26. δή: δεῖ Bonitz, Christ.   ἄλλου δὲ
Aᶜ: ἀλλ' οὐδὲ rec. corr.: ἄλλο δὲ cod. Robortelli, Bonitz: ἄλλο δ' ὃ
Vahlen: ἄλλο, ὃ Christ: κἀκεῖνο add. Tucker.   Cum verbis ἀλλ'
οὐδὲ . . . ἀνάγκη . . . προσθεῖναι contulerim Rhet. i. 2. 13, 1357 a 17,
ἐὰν γὰρ ᾖ τι τούτων γνώριμον, οὐδὲ δεῖ λέγειν· αὐτὸς γὰρ τοῦτο προστίθησιν ὁ ἀκροατής, et 18, τὸ δ' ὅτι στεφανίτης τὰ Ὀλύμπια, οὐδὲ δεῖ προσθεῖναι.
28. ἢ seclus. Bonitz, Christ: ᾖ Vahlen.   30. τούτου codex Robortelli:
τοῦτο Δᶜ: τούτων apogr.

the scene throughout, and imitate but little and rarely. Homer, after a few prefatory words, at once brings in a man, or woman, or other personage; none of them wanting in characteristic qualities, but each with a character of his own.

The element of the wonderful is admitted in Tragedy. 8 The irrational, on which the wonderful depends for its chief effects, has wider scope in Epic poetry, because there the person acting is not seen. Thus, the pursuit of Hector would be ludicrous if placed upon the stage—the Greeks standing still and not joining in the pursuit, and Achilles waving them back. But in the Epic poem the absurdity passes unnoticed. Now the wonderful is pleasing: as may be inferred from the fact that, in telling a story, every one adds something startling of his own, knowing that his hearers like it. It is Homer who 9 has chiefly taught other poets the art of telling lies skilfully. The secret of it lies in a fallacy. For, assuming that if one thing is or becomes, a second is or becomes, men imagine that, if the second is, the first likewise is or becomes. But this is a false inference. Hence, where the first thing is untrue, it is quite unnecessary, provided the second be true, to add that the first is or has become. For the mind, knowing the second to be true, falsely infers the truth of the first. There is an example of this in the Bath Scene of the Odyssey.

Accordingly, the poet should prefer probable im- 10 possibilities to improbable possibilities. The tragic plot must not be composed of irrational parts. Everything

μάλιστα μὲν μηδὲν ἔχειν ἄλογον, εἰ δὲ μή, ἔξω τοῦ
μυθεύματος, ὥσπερ Οἰδίπους τὸ μὴ εἰδέναι πῶς ὁ Λάιος
35 ἀπέθανεν, ἀλλὰ μὴ ἐν τῷ δράματι, ὥσπερ ἐν 'Ηλέκτρᾳ
οἱ τὰ Πύθια ἀπαγγέλλοντες, ἢ ἐν Μυσοῖς ὁ ἄφωνος
ἐκ Τεγέας εἰς τὴν Μυσίαν ἥκων. ὥστε τὸ λέγειν ὅτι
ἀνῄρητο ἂν ὁ μῦθος γελοῖον· ἐξ ἀρχῆς γὰρ οὐ δεῖ
συνίστασθαι τοιούτους· ἂν δὲ θῇ καὶ φαίνηται εὐλογω-
40 τέρως, ἐνδέχεσθαι καὶ ἄτοπον <ὄν>· ἐπεὶ καὶ τὰ ἐν
'Οδυσσείᾳ ἄλογα τὰ περὶ τὴν ἔκθεσιν ὡς οὐκ ἂν ἦν
1460 b ἀνεκτὰ δῆλον ἂν γένοιτο, εἰ αὐτὰ φαῦλος ποιητὴς
ποιήσειε· νῦν δὲ τοῖς ἄλλοις ἀγαθοῖς ὁ ποιητὴς ἀφανίζει
ἡδύνων τὸ ἄτοπον. τῇ δὲ λέξει δεῖ διαπονεῖν ἐν τοῖς 11
ἀργοῖς μέρεσιν καὶ μήτε ἠθικοῖς μήτε διανοητικοῖς·
5 ἀποκρύπτει γὰρ πάλιν ἡ λίαν λαμπρὰ λέξις τά τε
ἤθη καὶ τὰς διανοίας.

XXV   περὶ δὲ προβλημάτων καὶ λύσεων, ἐκ πόσων τε καὶ
ποίων εἰδῶν ἐστιν, ὧδ' ἂν θεωροῦσιν γένοιτ' ἂν φανερόν.
ἐπεὶ γάρ ἐστι μιμητὴς ὁ ποιητὴς ὡσπερανεὶ ζωγράφος
10 ἤ τις ἄλλος εἰκονοποιός, ἀνάγκη μιμεῖσθαι τριῶν ὄντων
τὸν ἀριθμὸν ἕν τι ἀεί, ἢ γὰρ οἷα ἦν ἢ ἔστιν, ἢ οἷά
φασιν καὶ δοκεῖ, ἢ οἷα εἶναι δεῖ. ταῦτα δ' ἐξαγγέλ- 2
λεται λέξει <ἢ κυρίοις ὀνόμασιν> ἢ καὶ γλώτταις καὶ
μεταφοραῖς· καὶ πολλὰ πάθη τῆς λέξεως ἐστί, δίδομεν

---

34. <ὁ> Οἰδίπους Bywater.   40. ἀποδέχεσθαι apogr.   ὄν addidi.
1460 b 2. ποιήσειε Heinsius: ποιήσει codd.: ἐποίησεν Spengel.   5. τε
apogr.: δὲ Λᵒ.   8. ποίων εἰδῶν apogr.: ποίων ἂν εἰδῶν Aᶜ.   11. τὸν
ἀριθμὸν vel τῷ ἀριθμῷ apogr.: τῶν ἀριθμῶν Λᵒ.   12. ἢ οἷα apogr.:
οἷα Λᵒ.   13. <ἢ κυρίοις ὀνόμασιν> coni. Vahlen: <ἢ κυρίᾳ>
Gomperz sec. Vahlen.   14. καὶ ὅσ' ἄλλα πάθη coni. Vahlen.

irrational should, if possible, be excluded; or, at all
events, it should lie outside the action of the play (as,
in the Oedipus, the hero's ignorance as to the manner
of Laius' death); not within the drama,—as in the
Electra, the messenger's account of the Pythian games;
or, as in the Mysians, the man who comes from Tegea to
Mysia without speaking. The plea that otherwise the
plot would have been ruined, is ridiculous. Such a plot
should not in the first instance be constructed. But
once it has been framed and an air of likelihood imparted to it, the absurdity itself should be tolerated.
Take the irrational incidents in the Odyssey, where
Odysseus is left upon the shore of Ithaca. How in-
tolerable even these might have been would be apparent
1460 b if an inferior poet were to treat the subject. As it is,
the absurdity is veiled by the poetic charm with which
the poet invests it.

The diction should be elaborated in the pauses of 11
the action, where there is no expression of character
or thought. For, conversely, character and thought are
merely obscured by a diction that is over brilliant.

XXV   With respect to critical difficulties and their solutions,
the number and nature of the sources from which they
may be drawn may be thus exhibited.

The poet being an imitator, like a painter or any
other artist, must of necessity imitate one of three
objects,—things as they were or are, things as they are
said or thought to be, or things as they ought to be.
The vehicle of expression is language,—either current 2
terms or, it may be, rare words or metaphors. There
are also many modifications of language, which we

II

15 γὰρ ταῦτα τοῖς ποιηταῖς. πρὸς δὲ τούτοις οὐχ ἡ αὐτὴ 3
ὀρθότης ἐστὶν τῆς πολιτικῆς καὶ τῆς ποιητικῆς οὐδὲ
ἄλλης τέχνης καὶ ποιητικῆς. αὐτῆς δὲ τῆς ποιητικῆς
διττὴ ἁμαρτία, ἡ μὲν γὰρ καθ' αὑτήν, ἡ δὲ κατὰ συμβεβηκός. εἰ μὲν γάρ <τι> προείλετο μιμήσασθαι <μὴ 4
20 ὀρθῶς δὲ ἐμιμήσατο δι'> ἀδυναμίαν, αὐτῆς ἡ ἁμαρτία·
εἰ δὲ <διὰ> τὸ προελέσθαι μὴ ὀρθῶς, ἀλλὰ τὸν ἵππον
<ἅμ'> ἄμφω τὰ δεξιὰ προβεβληκότα ἢ τὸ καθ' ἑκάστην
τέχνην ἁμάρτημα οἷον τὸ κατ' ἰατρικὴν ἢ ἄλλην τέχνην
[ἢ ἀδύνατα πεποίηται] ὁποιανοῦν, οὐ καθ' ἑαυτήν. ὥστε
25 δεῖ τὰ ἐπιτιμήματα ἐν τοῖς προβλήμασιν ἐκ τούτων
ἐπισκοποῦντα λύειν. πρῶτον μὲν εἰ πρὸς αὐτὴν τὴν 5
τέχνην ἀδύνατα πεποίηται, ἡμάρτηται, ἀλλ' ὀρθῶς ἔχει,
εἰ τυγχάνει τοῦ τέλους τοῦ αὐτῆς (τὸ γὰρ τέλος εἴρηται),
εἰ οὕτως ἐκπληκτικώτερον ἢ αὐτὸ ἢ ἄλλο ποιεῖ μέρος.
30 παράδειγμα ἡ τοῦ Ἕκτορος δίωξις. εἰ μέντοι τὸ τέλος
ἢ μᾶλλον ἢ <μὴ> ἧττον ἐνεδέχετο ὑπάρχειν καὶ κατὰ
τὴν περὶ τούτων τέχνην, [ἡμαρτῆσθαι] οὐκ ὀρθῶς· δεῖ
γὰρ εἰ ἐνδέχεται ὅλως μηδαμῇ ἡμαρτῆσθαι. ἔτι ποτέρων
ἐστὶ τὸ ἁμάρτημα, τῶν κατὰ τὴν τέχνην ἢ κατ' ἄλλο
35 συμβεβηκός; ἔλαττον γὰρ εἰ μὴ ᾔδει ὅτι ἔλαφος θήλεια
κέρατα οὐκ ἔχει ἢ εἰ ἀμιμήτως ἔγραψεν. πρὸς δὲ 6
τούτοις ἐὰν ἐπιτιμᾶται ὅτι οὐκ ἀληθῆ, ἀλλ' ἴσως <ὡς>

19. τι addidi.   μὴ ὀρθῶς . . . δι' addidi : post μιμήσασθαι coni.
Vahlen ὀρθῶς, ἥμαρτε δ' ἐν τῷ μιμήσασθαι δι'.   21. εἰ apogr. : ἢ Aᶜ.
διὰ add. Ueberweg.   22. ἅμ' add. Vahlen.   24. ἢ ἀδύνατα
πεποίηται seclus. Düntzer : τέχνην ὁποιανοῦν [ἢ] ἀδύνατα πεποίηται Christ.
26. εἰ : τὰ Aᶜ, εἰ sup. scr.   τὰ πρὸς αὐτὴν τὴν τέχνην· plerique edd.
27. εἰ add. Vahlen ante ἀδύνατα.   28. εἴρηται : εὕρηται Heinsius :
τηρεῖται M. Schmidt.   31. ἢ μὴ ἧττον Ueberweg, ἧττον Aᶜ: ἢ ἧττον
rec. Aᶜ, Vahlen.   32. ἡμαρτῆσθαι seclus. Bywater, Ussing : ἡμάρτηται
Ald., Bekker : τὴν περὶ τούτων τέχνην <μὴ> ἡμαρτῆσθαι, Tucker.   37.
ὡς coni. Vahlen.

concede to the poets.   Add to this, that the standard of 3
correctness is not the same in poetry and politics, any
more than in poetry and any other art.   Within the art
of poetry itself there are two kinds of faults,—those
which touch its essence, and those which are accidental.
If a poet has proposed to himself to imitate something, 4
< but has imitated it incorrectly > through want of capacity,
the error is inherent in the poetry.   But if the failure
is due to the thing he has proposed to do—if he has
represented a horse as throwing out both his off legs at
once, or introduced technical inaccuracies in medicine, for
example, or in any other art—the error is not essential to
the poetry.   These are the points of view from which
we should consider and answer the objections raised by
the critics.

First we will suppose the poet has represented things 5
impossible according to the laws of his own art.   It is
an error; but the error may be justified, if the end of
the art be thereby attained (the end being that already
mentioned),—if, that is, the effect of this or any other
part of the poem is thus rendered more striking.   A
case in point is the pursuit of Hector.   If, however, the
end might have been as well, or better, attained without
violating the special rules of the poetic art, the error is
not justified: for every kind of error should, if possible,
be avoided.

Again, does the error touch the essentials of the
poetic art, or some accident of it ?   For example,—not
to know that a hind has no horns is a less serious matter
than to paint it inartistically.

Further, if it be objected that the description is not 6

δεῖ—οἷον καὶ Σοφοκλῆς ἔφη αὐτὸς μὲν οἵους δεῖ ποιεῖν,
Εὐριπίδην δὲ οἷοι εἰσίν—ταύτῃ λυτέον. εἰ δὲ μηδετέρως, 7
40 ὅτι οὕτω φασίν· οἷον τὰ περὶ θεῶν, ἴσως γὰρ οὔτε
βέλτιον οὕτω λέγειν οὔτ᾽ ἀληθῆ, ἀλλ᾽ <εἰ> ἔτυχεν
1461 a ὥσπερ Ξενοφάνει· ἀλλ᾽ οὖν φασι. τὰ δὲ ἴσως οὐ
βέλτιον μέν, ἀλλ᾽ οὕτως εἶχεν, οἷον τὰ περὶ τῶν ὅπλων,
"ἔγχεα δέ σφιν Ὀρθ᾽ ἐπὶ σαυρωτῆρος·"[1] οὕτω γὰρ
τότ᾽ ἐνόμιζον, ὥσπερ καὶ νῦν Ἰλλυριοί. περὶ δὲ τοῦ 8
5 καλῶς ἢ μὴ καλῶς ἢ εἴρηταί τινι ἢ πέπρακται, οὐ μόνον
σκεπτέον εἰς αὐτὸ τὸ πεπραγμένον ἢ εἰρημένον βλέποντα,
εἰ σπουδαῖον ἢ φαῦλον, ἀλλὰ καὶ εἰς τὸν πράττοντα ἢ
λέγοντα, πρὸς ὃν ἢ ὅτε ἢ ὅτῳ ἢ οὗ ἕνεκεν, οἷον ἢ μείζονος
ἀγαθοῦ, ἵνα γένηται, ἢ μείζονος κακοῦ, ἵνα ἀπογένηται.
10 τὰ δὲ πρὸς τὴν λέξιν ὁρῶντα δεῖ διαλύειν, οἷον γλώττῃ 9
"οὐρῆας μὲν πρῶτον·"[2] ἴσως γὰρ οὐ τοὺς ἡμιόνους λέγει
ἀλλὰ τοὺς φύλακας, καὶ τὸν Δόλωνα "ὅς ῥ᾽ ἦ τοι εἶδος
μὲν ἔην κακός"[3] οὐ τὸ σῶμα ἀσύμμετρον ἀλλὰ τὸ
πρόσωπον αἰσχρόν, τὸ γὰρ εὐειδὲς οἱ Κρῆτες εὐπρόσ-
15 ωπον καλοῦσι· καὶ τὸ "ζωρότερον δὲ κέραιε"[4] οὐ τὸ
ἄκρατον ὡς οἰνόφλυξιν ἀλλὰ τὸ θᾶττον. τὸ δὲ κατὰ 10

---

[1] Iliad x. 152.
[2] Ib. xxiii. 111, 115 (Verrall), potius quam i. 50.
[3] Ib. x. 316.   [4] Ib. ix. 203.

39. Εὐριπίδην Heinsius: εὐριπίδης codd., tuetur Gomperz, cf. 1448 a 37
(ἀθηναῖοι codd.).   40. οὕτω apogr.: οὔτε Aᶜ.   41. εἰ coni. Vahlen.
1461 a 1. ξενοφάνει vel ξενοφάνης apogr.: ξενοφάνη Aᶜ: παρὰ Ξενοφάνει
Ritter.   οὖν Tyrwhitt: οὐ Aᶜ, οὖν rec. Aᶜ: οὕτω Spengel.   7. εἰ
apogr.: ἢ Aᶜ.   8. Commate distinxi post λέγοντα: <ἢ> πρὸς ὃν
Carroll.   οἷον ἢ Aᶜ: οἷον εἰ apogr.   9. ἢ rec. Aᶜ add.   16.
τὸ δὲ Aᶜ: τὰ δὲ Spengel.

true to fact, the poet may perhaps reply,—'But the objects are as they ought to be': just as Sophocles said that he drew men as they ought to be; Euripides, as they are. In this way the objection may be met. If, 7 however, the representation be of neither kind, the poet may answer,—'This is how men say the thing is.' This applies to tales about the gods. It may well be that these stories are not higher than fact nor yet true to 1461 a fact: they are, very possibly, what Xenophanes says of them. But anyhow, 'this is what is said.' Again, a description may be no better than the fact: 'still, it was the fact'; as in the passage about the arms: 'Upright upon their butt-ends stood the spears.' This was the custom then, as it now is among the Illyrians.

Again, in examining whether what has been said or 8 done by some one is poetically right or not, we must not look merely to the particular act or saying, and ask whether it is poetically good or bad. We must also consider by whom it is said or done, to whom, when, in whose interest, or for what end; whether, for instance, it be to secure a greater good, or avert a greater evil.

Other difficulties may be resolved by due regard to the 9 diction. We may note a rare word, as in οὐρῆας μὲν πρῶτον, where the poet perhaps employs οὐρῆας not in the sense of mules, but of sentinels. So, again, of Dolon: 'ill-favoured indeed he was to look upon.' It is not meant that his body was ill-shaped, but that his face was ugly; for the Cretans use the word εὐειδές, 'well-favoured,' to denote a fair face. Again, ζωρότερον δὲ κέραιε, 'mix the drink livelier,' does not mean 'mix it stronger' as for hard drinkers, but 'mix it quicker.'

μεταφορὰν εἴρηται, οἷον "πάντες μέν ῥα θεοί τε καὶ
ἀνέρες Εὗδον παννύχιοι·"¹ ἅμα δέ φησιν "ἦ τοι ὅτ'
ἐς πεδίον τὸ Τρωικὸν ἀθρήσειεν, Αὐλῶν συρίγγων θ'
20 ὅμαδον·"² τὸ γὰρ πάντες ἀντὶ τοῦ πολλοὶ κατὰ μεταφορὰν εἴρηται, τὸ γὰρ πᾶν πολύ τι· καὶ τὸ "οἴη δ'
ἄμμορος"³ κατὰ μεταφοράν, τὸ γὰρ γνωριμώτατον μόνον.
κατὰ δὲ προσῳδίαν, ὥσπερ Ἱππίας ἔλυεν ὁ Θάσιος τὸ 11
"δίδομεν δέ οἱ"⁴ καὶ "τὸ μὲν οὐ καταπύθεται ὄμβρῳ."⁵
25 τὰ δὲ διαιρέσει, οἷον Ἐμπεδοκλῆς "αἶψα δὲ θνήτ' 12
ἐφύοντο, τὰ πρὶν μάθον ἀθάνατ' <εἶναι> Ζωρά τε πρὶν
κέκρητο." τὰ δὲ ἀμφιβολίᾳ, "παρῴχηκεν δὲ πλέω 13
νύξ·"⁶ τὸ γὰρ πλείω ἀμφίβολόν ἐστιν. τὰ δὲ κατὰ 14
τὸ ἔθος τῆς λέξεως· τῶν κεκραμένων <οἰονοῦν> οἰνόν

---

¹ *Iliad* ii. 1, ἄλλοι μέν ῥα θεοί τε καὶ ἀνέρες ἱπποκορυσταὶ
εὗδον παννύχιοι.
Ib. x. 1, ἄλλοι μὲν παρὰ νηυσὶν ἀριστῆες Παναχαιῶν
εὗδον παννύχιοι.
² *Ib.* x. 11, ἦ τοι ὅτ' ἐς πεδίον τὸ Τρωικὸν ἀθρήσειεν,
θαύμαζεν πυρὰ πολλὰ τὰ καίετο Ἰλιόθι πρό,
αὐλῶν συρίγγων τ' ἐνοπὴν ὅμαδόν τ' ἀνθρώπων.
³ *Ib.* xviii. 489, οἴη δ' ἄμμορός ἐστι λοετρῶν Ὠκεανοῖο.
⁴ *Ib.* xxi. 297, δίδομεν δέ οἱ εὖχος ἀρέσθαι. Sed in *Iliade* ii. 15 (do
quo hic agitur) Τρώεσσι δὲ κῆδε' ἐφῆπται.
⁵ *Ib.* xxiii. 328, τὸ μὲν οὐ καταπύθεται ὄμβρῳ.
⁶ *Ib.* x. 251,   μάλα γὰρ νὺξ ἄνεται, ἐγγύθι δ' ἠώς,
ἄστρα δὲ δὴ προβέβηκε, παρῴχηκεν δὲ πλέων νὺξ
τῶν δύο μοιράων, τριτάτη δ' ἔτι μοῖρα λέλειπται.

---

17. πάντες Gräfenhan: ἄλλοι Aᶜ.   18. ἱπποκορυσταὶ post ἀνέρες add.
Christ, habuit iam Σ, cf. Arab. 'ceteri quidem homines et dei qui equis
armati insident.'   20. τοῦ apogr.: om. Aᶜ.   26. εἶναι add. Vettori
collato Athenaeo, x. 423.   ζωρά Athenaeus: ζῶά codd.   τε <ἃ> πρὶν
Gomperz sec. Bergk.   27. κέκρητο Aᶜ, ι rec. sup. scr.: κέκριτο apogr. :
ἄκρητα Karsten ed. Empedoclis.   πλέω Aᶜ: πλέον apogr.: πλέων
Ald.   ʔ 28. πλείω: πλεῖον vel πλέον apogr.   29. οἰονοῦν add. Tucker.
<ὅσα> τῶν κεκραμένων Vahlen: <ὅσα πο>τῶν κεκραμένων Ueberweg:
πᾶν κεκραμένον Bursian: <ἔνια> olim conieci auto οἰνόν. ʔ

Sometimes an expression is metaphorical, as 'Now all 10 gods and men were sleeping through the night,'—while at the same time the poet says : 'Often indeed as he turned his gaze to the Trojan plain, he marvelled at the sound of flutes and pipes.' 'All' is here used metaphorically for 'many,' all being a species of many.   So in the verse,—'alone she hath no part . . ,' οἴη, 'alone,' is metaphorical ; for the best known may be called the only one.

Again, the solution may depend upon accent or 11 breathing.   Thus Hippias of Thasos solved the difficulties in the lines,—δίδομεν (διδόμεν) δέ οἱ, and τὸ μὲν οὗ (οὐ) καταπύθεται ὄμβρῳ.

Or again, the question may be solved by punctuation, 12 as in Empedocles,—'Of a sudden things became mortal that before had learnt to be immortal, and things unmixed before mixed.'

Or again, by ambiguity of construction,—as in 13 παρῴχηκεν δὲ πλέω νύξ, where the word πλέω is ambiguous.

Or by the usage of language.   Thus any mixed 14 drink is called οἶνος, 'wine.'   Hence Ganymede is said

30 φασιν εἶναι, [ὅθεν πεποίηται " κνημὶς νεοτεύκτου κασσιτέροιο,"]¹ ὅθεν εἴρηται ὁ Γανυμήδης " Διὶ οἰνοχοεύει,"²
οὐ πινόντων οἶνον, καὶ χαλκέας τοὺς τὸν σίδηρον ἐργα-
ζομένους. εἴη δ' ἂν τοῦτό γε <καὶ> κατὰ μεταφοράν. 15
δεῖ δὲ καὶ ὅταν ὄνομά τι ὑπεναντίωμά τι δοκῇ σημαίνειν,
35 ἐπισκοπεῖν ποσαχῶς ἂν σημαίνοι τοῦτο ἐν τῷ εἰρημένῳ,
οἷον τὸ " τῇ ῥ' ἔσχετο χάλκεον ἔγχος,"³ τὸ ταύτῃ κωλυ- 16
θῆναι ποσαχῶς ἐνδέχεται. ὡδὶ <δὲ> [ἢ ὡς] μάλιστ'
1461 b ἄν τις ὑπολάβοι, κατὰ τὴν καταντικρὺ ἢ ὡς Γλαύκων
λέγει, ὅτι ἔνια ἀλόγως προυπολαμβάνουσιν καὶ αὐτοὶ
καταψηφισάμενοι συλλογίζονται καὶ ὡς εἰρηκότος ὅ τι
δοκεῖ ἐπιτιμῶσιν, ἂν ὑπεναντίον ᾖ τῇ αὐτῶν οἰήσει.
5 τοῦτο δὲ πέπονθε τὰ περὶ Ἰκάριον. οἴονται γὰρ αὐτὸν
Λάκωνα εἶναι· ἄτοπον οὖν τὸ μὴ ἐντυχεῖν τὸν Τηλέ-
μαχον αὐτῷ εἰς Λακεδαίμονα ἐλθόντα. τὸ δ' ἴσως ἔχει
ὥσπερ οἱ Κεφαλῆνές φασι· παρ' αὐτῶν γὰρ γῆμαι
λέγουσι τὸν Ὀδυσσέα καὶ εἶναι Ἰκάδιον ἀλλ' οὐκ Ἰκά-
10 ριον. δι' ἁμάρτημα δὴ τὸ πρόβλημα εἰκός ἐστιν. ὅλως 17
δὲ τὸ ἀδύνατον μὲν πρὸς τὴν ποίησιν ἢ πρὸς τὸ βέλτιον

---

¹ *Iliad* xxi. 592.   ² *Ib.* xx. 234.
³ *Ib.* xx. 272, τῇ ῥ' ἔσχετο μείλινον ἔγχος.

---

30. ὅθεν πεποίηται . . . κασσιτέροιο seclus. M. Schmidt.   31. ὅθεν
εἴρηται . . . οἶνον in codd. post ἐργαζομένοις, huc revocavit Maggi sec.
cod. Lampridii.   33. καὶ add. Heinsius.   35. σημαίνοι olim
Vahlen: σημαίνοιε Aᶜ: σημήνειεν vel σημαίνειε apogr.: σημήνειε Vahlen
ed. 3.   36-38. οἷον τὸ <ἐν τῷ> . . . τὸ ταύτῃ κωλυθῆναι [ποσαχῶς]
ἐνδέχεται διπλῶς, ἢ πῶς μάλιστ' ἄν τις κ.τ.λ. M. Schmidt.   37. δὲ
addidi: ἢ ὡς seclus. Bywater.   ὡδὶ ἢ <ὡδί>, ὡς coni. Vahlen:
ἐνδέχεται· ὡδὶ ἢ ὡς μάλιστ' ἄν τις ὑπολάβοι, Ueberweg. Interpunxerunt
post ὡδὶ et ὑπολάβοι plerique edd.   1461 b 2. ἔνια: ἔνιοι Vettori.
3. εἰρηκότος ὅ τι Castelvetro: εἰρηρότες ὅτι Aᶜ.   4. αὐτῶν Heinsius:
αὑτῶν codd.   8. αὐτῶν Bekker: αὑτῶν codd.   10. δι' ἁμάρτημα
Maggi: διαμάρτημα codd., Bekker.   δὴ Gomperz: δὲ codd.   <εἶναι>
εἰκός ἐστιν Hermann, fort. recte: (cf. εἰκός ἐστι <γενέσθαι> Gomperz).
11. <ἢ> πρὸς Ald., Bekker, fort. recte.

'to pour the wine to Zeus,' though the gods do not drink wine. So too workers in iron are called χαλκέας, or workers in bronze. This, however, may also be taken as a metaphor.

Again, when a word seems to involve some incon- 15 sistency of meaning, we should consider how many senses it may bear in the particular passage. For 16 example: 'there was stayed the spear of bronze'—we should ask in how many ways we may take 'being checked there.' The true mode of interpretation is the 1461 b precise opposite of what Glaucus mentions. Critics, he · says, jump at certain groundless conclusions; they pass adverse judgment and then proceed to reason on it; and, assuming that the poet has said whatever they·happen to think, find fault if a thing is inconsistent with their own fancy. The question about Icarius has been treated in this fashion. The critics imagine he was a Lacedae-monian. They think it strange, therefore, that Tele-machus should not have met him when he went to Lacedaemon. But the Cephallenian story may perhaps be the true one. They allege that Odysseus took a wife from among themselves, and that her father was Icadius not Icarius. It is merely a mistake, then, that gives plausibility to the objection.

In general, the impossible must be justified by 17 reference to artistic requirements, or to the higher

ἢ πρὸς τὴν δόξαν δεῖ ἀάνγειν. πρός τε γὰρ τὴν ποίησιν
αἱρετώτερον πιθανὸν ἀδύνατον ἢ ἀπίθανον καὶ δυνατόν.
<καὶ ἴσως ἀδύνατον> τοιούτους εἶναι, οἵους Ζεῦξις
15 ἔγραφεν, ἀλλὰ βέλτιον· τὸ γὰρ παράδειγμα δεῖ ὑπερ-
έχειν. πρὸς <δ'> ἅ φασιν, τἄλογα· οὕτω τε καὶ ὅτι
ποτὲ οὐκ ἄλογόν ἐστιν· εἰκὸς γὰρ καὶ παρὰ τὸ εἰκὸς
γίνεσθαι. τὰ δ' ὑπεναντίως εἰρημένα οὕτω σκοπεῖν, 18
ὥσπερ οἱ ἐν τοῖς λόγοις ἔλεγχοι, εἰ τὸ αὐτὸ καὶ πρὸς τὸ
20 αὐτὸ καὶ ὡσαύτως, ὥστε καὶ λυτέον ἢ πρὸς ἃ αὐτὸς
λέγει ἢ ὃ ἂν φρόνιμος ὑποθῆται. ὀρθὴ δ' ἐπιτίμησις 19
καὶ ἀλογίᾳ καὶ μοχθηρίᾳ, ὅταν μὴ ἀνάγκης οὔσης μηθὲν
χρήσηται τῷ ἀλόγῳ, ὥσπερ Εὐριπίδης τῷ Αἰγεῖ, ἢ τῇ
πονηρίᾳ, ὥσπερ ἐν Ὀρέστῃ τοῦ Μενελάου. τὰ μὲν οὖν 20
25 ἐπιτιμήματα ἐκ πέντε εἰδῶν φέρουσιν, ἢ γὰρ ὡς ἀδύνατα
ἢ ὡς ἄλογα ἢ ὡς βλαβερὰ ἢ ὡς ὑπεναντία ἢ ὡς παρὰ
τὴν ὀρθότητα τὴν κατὰ τέχνην. αἱ δὲ λύσεις ἐκ τῶν
εἰρημένων ἀριθμῶν σκεπτέαι, εἰσὶν δὲ δώδεκα.

XXVI   πότερον δὲ βελτίων ἡ ἐποποιικὴ μίμησις ἢ ἡ τραγική,
30 διαπορήσειεν ἄν τις. εἰ γὰρ ἡ ἧττον φορτικὴ βελτίων,
τοιαύτη δ' ἡ πρὸς βελτίους θεατάς ἐστιν ἀεί, λίαν δῆλον

14. <καὶ ἴσως ἀδύνατον> Gomperz, sec. Margoliouth, collato Arabe
('fortasse enim impossibile est . . .'): καὶ εἰ ἀδύνατον iam coni.
Vahlen.   οἵους Ald., Bekker: οἷον codd.   16. δ' add. Ueberweg
(coni. Vahlen).   18. ὑπεναντίως Twining, cf. Arab. 'quae dicta
sunt in modum contrarii': ὡς ὑπεναντία Heinsius: ὑπεναντία ὡς codd.
20. ὥστε καὶ αὐτὸν codd.: ὥστε καὶ λυτέον M. Schmidt: οὕτως τε καὶ εἰ
καθ' αὐτὸν coni. Christ.   21. φρόνιμος apogr.: φρόνημον Λᶜ, φρόνιμον
rec. Λᵃ.   22. ἀλογίᾳ καὶ μοχθηρίᾳ Vahlen: ἀλογίᾳ καὶ μοχθηρία
codd., serv. Christ, del. Spengel.   Fort. <πρὸς> μηδὲν Gomperz.
23. τῷ Αἰγεῖ ἢ τῇ apogr. (margo): τῶ αἰγειήτη Λᶜ.   29. βελτίων
apogr.: βέλτιον Λᵉ.   31. δ' ἡ apogr.: δὴ Λᶜ.   ἀεί, λίαν Vahlen:
δειλίαν codd.

reality, or to received opinion. With respect to the requirements of art, a probable impossibility is to be preferred to a thing improbable and yet possible. Again, it may be impossible that there should be men such as Zeuxis painted. 'Yes,' we say, 'but the impossible is the higher thing; for the ideal type must surpass the reality.' To justify the irrational, we appeal to what is commonly said to be. In addition to which, we urge that the irrational sometimes does not violate reason; just as 'it is probable that a thing may happen contrary to probability.'

Things that sound contradictory should be examined 18 by the same rules as in dialectical refutation—whether the same thing is meant, in the same relation, and in the same sense. We should therefore solve the question by reference to what the poet says himself, or to what is tacitly assumed by a person of intelligence.

The element of the irrational, and, similarly, depravity 19 of character, are justly censured when there is no inner necessity for introducing them. Such is the irrational element in the Aegeus of Euripides, and the badness of Menelaus in the Orestes.

Thus, there are five sources from which critical 20 objections are drawn. Things are censured either as impossible, or irrational, or morally hurtful, or contradictory, or contrary to artistic correctness. The answers should be sought under the twelve heads above mentioned.

XXVI   The question may be raised whether the Epic or Tragic mode of imitation is the higher. If the more refined art is the higher, and the more refined in every case is that which appeals to the better sort of audience,

ὅτι ἡ ἅπαντα μιμουμένη φορτική· ὡς γὰρ οὐκ αἰσθανο-
μένων ἂν μὴ αὐτὸς προσθῇ, πολλὴν κίνησιν κινοῦνται,
οἷον οἱ φαῦλοι αὐληταὶ κυλιόμενοι ἂν δίσκον δέῃ μιμεῖ-
35 σθαι, καὶ ἕλκοντες τὸν κορυφαῖον ἂν Σκύλλαν αὐλῶσιν·
ἡ μὲν οὖν τραγῳδία τοιαύτη ἐστίν, ὡς καὶ οἱ πρότερον 2
τοὺς ὑστέρους αὐτῶν ᾤοντο ὑποκριτάς· ὡς λίαν γὰρ
ὑπερβάλλοντα πίθηκον ὁ Μυννίσκος τὸν Καλλιππίδην
1462 a ἐκάλει, τοιαύτη δὲ δόξα καὶ περὶ Πινδάρου ἦν· ὡς δ’
οὗτοι ἔχουσι πρὸς αὑτούς, ἡ ὅλη τέχνη πρὸς τὴν
ἐποποιίαν ἔχει· τὴν μὲν οὖν πρὸς θεατὰς ἐπιεικεῖς φασιν
εἶναι <οἳ> οὐδὲν δέονται τῶν σχημάτων, τὴν δὲ τραγι-
5 κὴν πρὸς φαύλους· εἰ οὖν φορτική, χείρων δῆλον ὅτι ἂν 3
εἴη. πρῶτον μὲν <οὖν> οὐ τῆς ποιητικῆς ἡ κατηγορία
ἀλλὰ τῆς ὑποκριτικῆς, ἐπεὶ ἔστι περιεργάζεσθαι τοῖς
σημείοις καὶ ῥαψῳδοῦντα, ὅπερ [ἐστὶ] Σωσίστρατος, καὶ
διᾴδοντα, ὅπερ ἐποίει Μνασίθεος ὁ Ὀπούντιος. εἶτα
10 οὐδὲ κίνησις ἅπασα ἀποδοκιμαστέα, εἴπερ μηδ’ ὄρχησις,
ἀλλ’ ἡ φαύλων, ὅπερ καὶ Καλλιππίδῃ ἐπετιμᾶτο καὶ
νῦν ἄλλοις ὡς οὐκ ἐλευθέρας γυναῖκας μιμουμένων. ἔτι
ἡ τραγῳδία καὶ ἄνευ κινήσεως ποιεῖ τὸ αὑτῆς, ὥσπερ ἡ
ἐποποιία· διὰ γὰρ τοῦ ἀναγινώσκειν φανερὰ ὁποία τίς
15 ἐστιν· εἰ οὖν ἐστι τά γ’ ἄλλα κρείττων, τοῦτό γε οὐκ
ἀναγκαῖον αὐτῇ ὑπάρχειν. ἔστι δ’ ἐπεὶ τὰ πάντ’ ἔχει 4
ὅσαπερ ἡ ἐποποιία, καὶ γὰρ τῷ μέτρῳ ἔξεστι χρῆσθαι,

---

33. κινοῦνται apogr.: κινοῦντα Aᶜ.   1462 a 2. ἔχουσι apogr.: δ’
ἔχουσι Aᶜ.   αὐτοὺς Hermann : αὐτοὺς codd.   4. οἳ add. Vettori :
ἐπεὶ Christ.   5. εἰ apogr.: ἡ Aᶜ.   6. οὖν add. Bywater, Ussing.
8. ἐστὶ seclus. Spengel.   9. διᾴδοντα apogr.: διαδόντα Aᶜ.   13.
αὑτῆς apogr.: αὑτῆς Aᶜ.   16. αὐτῇ apogr.: αὐτῇ Aᶜ.   ἔστι δ’
ἐπεὶ τὰ Gomperz: ἔστι δ’, ὅτι Usener : ἔπειτα διότι codd.

the art which imitates anything and everything is manifestly most unrefined. The audience is supposed to be too dull to comprehend unless something of their own is thrown in by the performers, who therefore indulge in restless movements. Bad flute-players twist and twirl, if they have to represent 'the quoit-throw,' or hustle the coryphaeus when they perform the 'Scylla.' Tragedy, 2 it is said, has this same defect. We may compare the opinion that the older actors entertained of their successors. Mynniscus used to call Callippides 'ape' on account of the extravagance of his action, and the same 1462 a view was held of Pindarus. Tragic art, then, as a whole, stands to Epic in the same relation as the younger to the elder actors. So we are told that Epic poetry is addressed to a cultivated audience, who do not need gesture; Tragedy, to an inferior public. Being then 3 unrefined, it is evidently the lower of the two.

Now, in the first place, this censure attaches not to the poetic but to the histrionic art; for gesticulation may be equally overdone in epic recitation, as by Sosistratus, or in lyrical competition, as by Mnasitheus the Opuntian. Next, all action is not to be condemned—any more than all dancing—but only that of bad performers. Such was the fault found in Callippides, as also in others of our own day, who are censured for representing degraded women. Again, Tragedy like Epic poetry produces its effect even without action; it reveals its power by mere reading. If, then, in all other respects it is superior, this fault, we say, is not inherent in it.

And superior it is, because it has all the epic 4 elements—it may even use the epic metre—with the

καὶ ἔτι οὐ μικρὸν μέρος τὴν μουσικὴν καὶ τὰς ὄψεις, δι'
ἃς αἱ ἡδοναὶ συνίστανται ἐναργέστατα. εἶτα καὶ τὸ
20 ἐναργὲς ἔχει καὶ ἐν τῇ ἀναγνώσει καὶ ἐπὶ τῶν ἔργων.
1462 b ἔτι τῷ ἐν ἐλάττονι μήκει τὸ τέλος τῆς μιμήσεως εἶναι· 5
τὸ γὰρ ἀθροώτερον ἥδιον ἢ πολλῷ κεκραμένον τῷ χρόνῳ·
λέγω δ' οἶον εἴ τις τὸν Οἰδίπουν θείη τὸν Σοφοκλέους
ἐν ἔπεσιν ὅσοις ἡ Ἰλιάς. ἔτι ἧττον [ἡ] μία μίμησις ἡ 6
5 τῶν ἐποποιῶν· σημεῖον δέ· ἐκ γὰρ ὁποιασοῦν [μιμήσεως]
πλείους τραγῳδίαι γίνονται· ὥστε ἐὰν μὲν ἕνα μῦθον
ποιῶσιν, ἢ βραχέως δεικνύμενον μύουρον φαίνεσθαι, ἢ
ἀκολουθοῦντα τῷ συμμέτρῳ μήκει ὑδαρῆ. * * λέγω δὲ
οἶον ἐὰν ἐκ πλειόνων πράξεων ᾖ συγκειμένη, ὥσπερ ἡ
10 Ἰλιὰς ἔχει πολλὰ τοιαῦτα μέρη καὶ ἡ Ὀδύσσεια ἃ καὶ
καθ' ἑαυτὰ ἔχει μέγεθος· καίτοι ταῦτα τὰ ποιήματα
συνέστηκεν ὡς ἐνδέχεται ἄριστα καὶ ὅτι μάλιστα μιᾶς
πράξεως μίμησις. εἰ οὖν τούτοις τε διαφέρει πᾶσιν καὶ 7
ἔτι τῷ τῆς τέχνης ἔργῳ (δεῖ γὰρ οὐ τὴν τυχοῦσαν ἡδονὴν
15 ποιεῖν αὐτὰς ἀλλὰ τὴν εἰρημένην), φανερὸν ὅτι κρείττων
ἂν εἴη μᾶλλον τοῦ τέλους τυγχάνουσα τῆς ἐποποιίας.

περὶ μὲν οὖν τραγῳδίας καὶ ἐποποιίας, καὶ αὐτῶν 8
καὶ τῶν εἰδῶν καὶ τῶν μερῶν, καὶ πόσα καὶ τί διαφέρει,
καὶ τοῦ εὖ ἢ μὴ τίνες αἰτίαι, καὶ περὶ ἐπιτιμήσεων καὶ
20 λύσεων, εἰρήσθω τοσαῦτα. * * *

---

18. καὶ τὰς ὄψεις seclus. Spengel: collocavit post ἐναργέστατα Gomperz, qui
δι' ἧς legit: καὶ τὴν ὄψιν Ald., Bekker.   δι' ἃς vel αἶς coni. Vahlen:
δι' ἧς codd.   20. ἀναγνώσει Maggi: ἀναγνωρίσει Aᶜ.   21. τῷ:
τὸ Winstanley, Gomperz.   1462 b 2. ἥδιον ἢ Maggi: ἡδεῖον ἢ apogr.:
ἡδονὴ Aᶜ.   3. θείη θείη Aᶜ.   4. Alt. ἢ om. Ald.   5. μιμήσεως seclus.
Gomperz.   7. μείουρον Gomperz praeeunte Tyrwhitt, fort. recte.   8.
συμμέτρῳ Bernays: τοῦ μέτρου codd.   Post ὑδαρῆ, < ἐὰν δὲ πλείους > Ald.,
Bekker: < λέγω δὲ οἶον * * ἂν δὲ μή, οὐ μία ἡ μίμησις > supplendum
coni. Vahlen: < ἐὰν δὲ πλείους, οὐ μία ἡ μίμησις > Teichmüller: < ἄλλως
δὲ ποικίλον > Gomperz.   10. ἃ add. apogr.   11. καίτοι ταῦτα τὰ
Ald.: καὶ τοιαῦτ' ἄττα Aᶜ et plerique codd.   19. ἢ apogr.: εἰ Aᶜ.

music and scenic effects as important accessories; and these produce the most vivid of pleasures. Further, it has vividness of impression in reading as well as in representation. Moreover, the art attains its end within 5 1462 b narrower limits; for the concentrated effect is more pleasurable than one which is spread over a long time and so diluted. What, for example, would be the effect of the Oedipus of Sophocles, if it were cast into a form as long as the Iliad? Once more, the Epic imitation 6 has less unity; as is shown by this,—that any Epic poem will furnish subjects for several tragedies. Now if the story be worked into a unity, it will, if concisely told, appear truncated; or, if it conform to the Epic canon of length, it will seem weak and watery. *   *   * What I mean by a story composed of several actions may be illustrated from the Iliad and Odyssey, which have many parts, each with a certain magnitude of its own. Yet these poems are as perfect as possible in structure; each is, in the highest degree attainable, an imitation of a single action.

If, then, Tragedy is superior to Epic poetry in all these 7 respects, and, moreover, fulfils its specific function better as an art—for each art ought to produce, not any chance pleasure, but the pleasure proper to it, as already stated —it plainly follows that Tragedy is the higher art, as attaining its end more perfectly.

Thus much may suffice concerning Tragic and Epic 8 poetry in general; their several kinds and parts, with the number of each and their differences; the causes that make a poem good or bad; the objections of the critics and the answers to these objections. *   *   *

www.ingramcontent.com/pod-product-compliance
Lightning Source LLC
Chambersburg PA
CBHW032009010726
47493CB00007B/2328